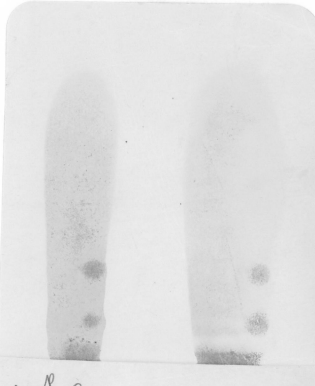

Rutland Place

m
PER

Rutland Place

Anne Perry

ST. MARTIN'S PRESS/NEW YORK

Library of Congress Cataloging in Publication Data

Perry, Anne.
    Rutland Place.
    I. Title.   235p.
PR6066.E693R8 1983   823'.914   83–2984
ISBN 0-312-69621-3

First Edition

10 9 8 7 6 5 4 3 2 1

M
PER

Dedicated

with love to my father,
with friendship to Judy,
with gratitude to the city of Toronto

Rutland Place

Chapter One

Charlotte Pitt took the letter and looked at the errand boy in some surprise. He gazed back with round, intelligent eyes. Was he waiting for a financial reward? She hoped not. She and Thomas had only recently moved from their previous house into this larger, airier one, with its extra bedroom and tiny garden, and it had taken all their resources.

"Will there be a reply, ma'am?" the boy said cheerfully, a trifle amused by her slowness. He was generally employed in a wealthier part of the city; people in these streets ran their own errands. But this was the sort of place he aspired to one day in the dim, adult future: a terraced house of his own with a clean step, curtains at the windows, a flower box or two, and a handsome woman to open the door and welcome him in at the end of the day.

"Oh," Charlotte breathed out in relief. "Just a moment." She tore the envelope, pulled out the single sheet of paper, and read:

12 Rutland Place, London.
23rd March, 1886.

My dear Charlotte,
A curious and most disturbing thing has happened here lately, and I would value your advice upon it. In fact, knowing your past skill and experience with things of tragic or criminal nature, perhaps even your help? Of course this is nothing like the unspeakable affairs you have unfortunately been drawn into before, in Paragon Walk, or that appalling business near Resurrection Row, thank heavens—simply a small theft.

But since the article I have lost is of great sentimental value to me, I am more than a little distressed over it, and most anxious to have it returned.

My dear, would you help me in this, at least with your advice? I know you have a maid now who can look after Jemima for you in your absence. If I send the carriage for you tomorrow about eleven o'clock, will you come and take luncheon with me, and we can talk over this wretched business? I do so look forward to seeing you.

Your loving mother,
Caroline Ellison.

Charlotte folded the letter and looked back at the boy.

"If you wait just a moment I shall write a reply," she said with a little smile, and then, after a small interval, returned to hand him her acceptance.

"Thank you, ma'am." The boy nodded and scampered off. Apparently he had not expected more; his reward no doubt customarily came from the sender. Anyway, he was far too worldly wise not to know precisely who was worth how much, and who would or would not part with it.

Charlotte closed the door and went back along the corridor to the kitchen where her eighteen-month-old daughter Jemima was sitting in her crib chewing a pencil. Charlotte took it from her absentmindedly and handed her a colored brick instead.

"I've asked you not to give her pencils, Gracie," she

said to the little maid, who was peeling potatoes. "She doesn't know what they're for. She only eats them."

"Didn't know she had it, ma'am. She can reach ever so far between those bars. Leastways, it keeps her from getting into the coal scuttle or the stove."

There was an abacus of bright wooden beads set into the railings of the crib, and Charlotte knelt down and rattled them lightly. Jemima was immediately attracted and stood up. Charlotte began to count them out for her, and Jemima repeated the words, concentrating hard, her eyes going from the beads to Charlotte's face, waiting after each word for approval.

Charlotte was only half alert to Jemima. Most of her concentration was on her mother. Her parents had accepted it extremely well when she had told them she was going to marry, of all things, a policeman! Edward had prevaricated a little and asked her very soberly if she was perfectly sure she knew what she was doing. But right from the start Caroline had understood that her most awkward daughter had found someone whom she loved, and the trials of such a radical drop in both social and financial status would be far less difficult for her than a politely arranged marriage to someone she did not love and who could not hold her interest or respect.

But in spite of their continued affection, it was most unlike Caroline to send for Charlotte over something as trivial as a petty theft. After all, such things did occur every so often. If it was a trinket, it was probably one of the servant girls borrowing it to wear for an evening out. It might well turn up again, if a few judicious hints were dropped. Caroline had had servants all her life; she ought to be able to cope with such a matter without recourse to advice from anyone.

Still, Charlotte would go; it would be a pleasant day, and she had been through a time of hard work getting the house into the order she wished.

"I'm going out tomorrow, Gracie," she said casually. "My mother has invited me to take luncheon with her. We can leave doing the landing curtains until the day after. You can look after Jemima and scrub this floor and the wooden cupboard in the corner. Get some good soap into it. It still smells odd to me."

"Yes, ma'am, and there'll be some laundry. And shall I take Miss Jemima for a walk if it's fine?"

"Yes, please, that would be excellent." Charlotte stood up. If she was going to be out for most of tomorrow, then she had better get on with the bread this afternoon, and see what her best day dress looked like after hanging up in a wardrobe over the winter. Gracie was only fifteen, but she was a competent little thing and liked nothing better than caring for Jemima. Charlotte had already told her that in six months' time there would be another baby to care for. And it was part of the terms of Gracie's employment that she should do the heavy laundry that another child would entail as well as the usual kitchen and household chores. Far from being daunted by the prospect, Gracie appeared to be positively excited. She came from a large family herself, and she missed the constant demanding and noisy companionship of children.

Pitt was tired when he came in from work a little before six. He had spent most of the day in the profitless pursuit of a couple of dragsmen, thieves who stole especially from carriages, and had ended up with nothing more for his exercise than half a dozen descriptions that did not match. An inspector of his experience would not have been called to deal with the affair at all had not one of the victims been a gentleman of title who was loath to have anything to do with the police. The man had lost a gold pocket watch inherited from his father-in-law, and did not care to have to explain its absence.

Charlotte welcomed him with the same strange mixture of excitement and comfort she always felt at the sight of his untidy, skew-collared, rumple-coated figure. She hugged him for several long, close minutes, then presented him with hot soup and his dinner. She did not disturb him with so trivial a matter as her mother's mislaid item.

The following morning she stood in front of the cheval glass in her bedroom and adjusted the lace fichu at her neck to hide the place where she had taken off last year's collar. Then she put on her best cameo brooch. The effect was entirely satisfactory; she was three months with child, but there was not yet any observable change in her figure, and with the customary whalebone corseting that laced even the most recalcitrant waist into elegant curves—uncomfortable though it was for the more generously made and almost crippling for the plump—she looked as slender as ever. The dark green wool was becoming to the warmth of her complexion and the richness of her hair, and the fichu took away from the severeness of the dress, making it a little more feminine. She did not wish Caroline, of all people, to think she had become dowdy.

The carriage came at eleven, and before half past it had crossed the city, trotted along the sedate length of Lincolnshire Road, and turned into the quiet, tree-lined elegance of Rutland Place. It stopped in front of the white portico of number 12, and the footman opened the door and handed Charlotte out onto the damp pavement.

"Thank you," she said without looking around, as if she were perfectly accustomed to it, as indeed she had been until only a few years ago.

The door opened before she reached it, and the butler appeared.

"Good morning, Miss Charlotte," he said, inclining his head a little.

"Good morning, Maddock." She smiled at him. She had known him since she was sixteen and he had first come as butler when her family lived in Cater Street, before the murders there during which she had met and married Pitt.

"Mrs. Ellison is in the withdrawing room, Miss Charlotte." Maddock moved easily just before her to push the door.

Inside, Caroline was standing in the middle of the room, a bright fire burning behind her against the chill spring, a bowl of daffodils spilling gold reflections all over the polished table. She was wearing a gown of pink peach, as soft as an evening sky, which must have cost her a month's dress allowance. There were not more than a dozen threads of gray in her dark hair. She stepped forward immediately.

"My dear, I'm so glad to see you. You look extremely well. Do come in and warm yourself. I don't know why spring is so cold. Everything looks marvelous, bursting with life, but the wind is like a blade. Thank you, Maddock. We'll take luncheon in about an hour."

"Yes, ma'am." He closed the door behind him, and Caroline put her arms round Charlotte and hugged her hard.

"You should come more often, Charlotte. I really do miss you. Emily is so busy these days with all her social circle, I hardly see her."

Charlotte tightened her arms round her for a moment, then stood back. Her younger sister Emily had married into the aristocracy and was enjoying every opportunity it afforded. Neither of them spoke of her other sister, Sarah, who had died so dreadfully in Cater Street.

"Well, sit down, my dear." Caroline arranged herself elegantly on the sofa and Charlotte sat opposite in the big chair.

"How is Thomas?" Caroline asked.

"Very well, thank you. And Jemima." Charlotte dealt with all the expected questions. "And the house is very comfortable and my new maid is working out most satisfactorily."

Caroline sighed with faint amusement.

"You don't change, do you, Charlotte? You still speak your mind the minute you think it. You are about as subtle as a railway engine! I don't know what I would have done with you if you had not married Thomas Pitt!"

Charlotte smiled broadly.

"You would still be shuffling me round endless polite and disgusting parties hoping to persuade some unfortunate young man's mother that I am really better than I sound!"

"Charlotte! Please!"

"What have you had stolen, Mama?"

"Oh dear! I simply can't imagine how you ever detect anything. You couldn't trick a policeman into telling you the time!"

"I shouldn't need to, Mama. Policemen are always perfectly willing to tell you the time, in the unlikely event they know it. I can be devious if I wish."

"Then you have changed since I ever knew you!"

"What did you lose, Mama?"

Caroline's face changed, the laughter dying out of it. She hesitated as if trying to choose exactly the right words for something that was surely simple enough.

"A piece of jewelry," she began. "A small locket on a gold bow. It is not of especial value, of course. It's not very large, and I don't imagine it is solid gold for a moment! But it was very pretty. It had a little pearl set in the front, and of course it opened."

Charlotte voiced her first thoughts. "Do you not think one of the maids could have borrowed it, meaning to return it immediately, and forgotten?"

"My dear, don't you imagine I've thought of that?" Caroline's tone was more anxious than irritated. "But none of them had an evening off between the time I last saw it and when I missed it. And quite apart from that, I really don't believe any of them would. The kitchenmaid would have no opportunity—and she's only fourteen. I really don't think it would occur to her. The parlormaid"—she smiled a little bleakly—"is as handsome as most parlormaids are. I did not realize Maddock had such excellent taste in employing our staff! Nature has endowed her quite well enough not to need the assistance of stolen jewelry, with all its risks. And my own maid I trust absolutely. I've had Mary since we moved here, and she came from Lady Buxton, who'd known her since she was a child. She's the daughter of their cook. No." Her face creased in distress again. "I'm afraid it is someone outside this house."

Charlotte tried the next avenue. "Are any of your maids courting? Do they have followers?"

Caroline's eyebrows rose. "Not so far as I know. Maddock is very strict. And certainly not inside the house, with access to my dressing room!"

"I suppose you've asked Maddock?"

"Of course I have! Charlotte, I'm perfectly capable of

doing the obvious myself! If it were so simple, I should not have troubled you." She took a deep breath and let it out slowly, shaking her head a little. "I'm sorry. It's just—the whole affair is so wretched! I can't bear to think one of my friends could have taken it, or someone in their households, and yet what else is there to think?"

Charlotte looked at her unhappy mother, her fingers knotted together in her lap, twisting her handkerchief until the lace threatened to tear. She understood the dilemma now. To institute inquiries, even to allow the loss to be known, would sow doubt among all her acquaintances. The whole of Rutland Place would imagine Caroline suspected them of theft. Old friendships would be ruined. Perhaps perfectly innocent servants would lose their jobs, or even their reputations. The rebounding unpleasantness would be like ripples in a pool, troubling and distorting everything.

"I would forget it, Mama," she said quickly, reaching to touch Caroline's hand. "The regaining of a locket would be far less valuable than avoiding all the pain inquiry would cause. If anyone asks, say the pin was loose and it must have fallen out. What did you wear it on?"

"The coat to my plum-colored outfit."

"Then that's easy. It could have fallen anywhere—even in the street."

Caroline shook her head.

"The pin was excellent, and it had a chain with a small extra safety catch, which I always fastened as well!"

"For goodness' sake, you don't need to mention that—if anyone should ask, which they probably won't. Who gave it to you? Papa?"

Caroline's eyes moved slightly to look over Charlotte's shoulder out the window at the spring sun dappling the laurel bush.

"No, I would explain it to him easily enough. It was your grandmama, for last Christmas, and you know what a precise memory she has when she chooses to!"

Charlotte had a peculiar feeling that some essence had

eluded her, that she had heard something important and had failed to understand it.

"But Grandmama must have lost things herself," she said reasonably. "Explain to her before she misses it. She'll probably be a bit self-righteous, but that's not unbearable. She'll be that sometime or another anyway." She smiled. "This will only give her an excuse."

"Yes," Caroline said, blinking, but a certain tone in her voice belied any conviction.

Charlotte looked around the room, at the pale green curtains and soft carpet, the warm bowl of daffodils, the pictures on the walls, the piano in the corner that Sarah used to play, with the family photographs on it. Caroline was sitting on the edge of the sofa, as if she were in a strange place and were keeping herself ready to leave.

"What is it, Mama?" Charlotte asked a little sharply. "Why does this locket matter so much?"

Caroline looked down at her hands, avoiding Charlotte's eyes.

"I had a memento in it—of—of a quite personal nature. I should feel most—embarrassed if it should fall into anyone else's hands. A sentimental thing. I'm sure you can understand. It is not knowing who has it! Like having someone else read your letters."

Charlotte breathed out in relief. She did not know now what she had been afraid of, but suddenly her muscles relaxed and she felt a wave of warmth ripple through her. It was all so easy, now that she understood.

"For goodness' sake, why didn't you say so to begin with?" There was no point in suggesting the thief might not open it. The first thing any woman would do on finding a locket would be to look inside. "Perhaps that day you forgot to do up the safety clasp, and it really did fall off? I suppose you've looked thoroughly in the carriage?"

"Oh yes, I did that immediately."

"When do you last remember it?"

"I went to an afternoon party at Ambrosine's—Ambrosine Charrington. She lives at number eighteen, a most charming person." Caroline smiled fleetingly. "You would like her. She is quite markedly eccentric."

Charlotte ignored the implication. At the moment the locket was more important.

"Indeed!" she said dryly. "In what way?"

Caroline looked up in surprise.

"Oh, she's perfectly respectable—in fact, more than respectable. Her grandfather was an earl, and her husband, Lovell Charrington, is a most notable man. Ambrosine herself was presented at Court when she came out. Of course, that was a long time ago, but she still has many connections."

"That doesn't sound very eccentric," Charlotte said skeptically, thinking that Caroline's view of eccentricity was probably quite different from her own.

"She likes to sing," Caroline explained. "And some of the oddest songs. I cannot imagine where she learned them. And she is extremely forgetful, even of things one would have thought any woman in Society would remember—such as who called in the last week or so, and who is related to whom. She sometimes makes quite startling mistakes."

Charlotte warmed to her immediately.

"Good for her. That must be most entertaining." She remembered endless afternoons before she was married when Caroline had taken her three daughters to meet the mothers of suitable young men, and they had all sat in over-stuffed chairs drinking lukewarm tea, sizing each other up with regard to income, dress sense, complexion, and agree-ability, while the girls wondered which callow young man they would be introduced to next, and which iron-eyed prospec-tive mother-in-law would inspect them. She shivered at the recollection and thought of Pitt in his linoleum-floor office with its brown desk and files of papers; Pitt stalking in and out of alleys and tenements after forgers and dealers in stolen goods, and just occasionally walking the smarter streets after a safebreaker, or embezzler, or even a killer.

"Charlotte?" Caroline's voice recalled her to Rutland Place and the warm withdrawing room.

"Yes, Mama. Perhaps it would be better if you said nothing at all. After all, if it was stolen, the thief is hardly going to admit it, and anyone decent enough to return it to you would not have looked at what they would know is personal. And even if they did, they would not find it remarkable. After all, we all have private matters."

Caroline forced a smile, overlooking the fact that the thief would not even know it was hers without some natural investigation, which would be bound to include opening it to see the inscription.

"No, of course not." She stood up. "Now I'm sure it must be nearly time to eat. You look very well, my dear, but you mustn't neglect your health. Remember, you are eating not only for yourself!"

The meal was delicious and far more delicate than Charlotte would have had at home, where she tended to skimp on midday meals. She ate with enjoyment. Afterward they repaired to the garden for a short breath of air, and in the shelter of the walls it was very pleasant. A little before three o'clock they went back to the withdrawing room, and within half an hour received the first caller of the afternoon.

"Mrs. Spencer-Brown, ma'am," the parlormaid said formally. "Shall I tell her you are at home?"

"Yes, by all means," Caroline agreed quickly, then waited a moment until the girl left before she turned to Charlotte. "She lives opposite, at number eleven. Her husband is a terrible bore, but she is very lively. Pretty creature, in her own way—"

The door opened again and the parlormaid ushered in the visitor. She was perhaps thirty-three or thirty-four, very slender with fine features, the longest, most graceful neck Charlotte had ever seen, and fair hair that was swept to the back of her head and piled in the latest fashion. She was dressed in ecru-colored lace.

"My dear Mina, how delightful to see you," Caroline said as easily as if no thought had troubled her all day. "How opportune you should call."

Mina turned immediately to Charlotte, her eyes bright.

"I don't believe you have met my daughter Mrs. Thomas Pitt." Caroline performed the awaited introductions. "Charlotte, my dear, this is my most excellent neighbor, Mrs. Spencer-Brown."

"How do you do, Mrs. Spencer-Brown." Charlotte inclined her head a little in something like half a curtsy, and Mina made the same gesture of recognition.

"I have been so interested to meet you," she said, looking Charlotte up and down, mentally taking note of everything she wore, from her slightly scuffed boots to the sleek styling of her hair, in order to assess the skill or otherwise of her maid, and thus the standard of her whole household. Charlotte was used to such judgments, and she met this one with unflickering coolness.

"How kind of you," she said, her eyes amused and frank. "I'm sure had I known of you a little more, I should have looked forward to our meeting just as much." She knew Caroline was regarding her anxiously, trying to get close enough to kick her under her skirts without being observed. Charlotte smiled even more candidly. "How fortunate Mama is to have such an agreeable neighbor. I hope you will stay and take tea with us?"

Mina had had every intention of staying, but was momentarily disconcerted to have the subject mentioned when she was hardly through the door.

"Why—why, thank you, that would be delightful, Mrs. Pitt." They all sat down, Mina opposite Charlotte where she could face her without appearing to stare. "I haven't seen you in Rutland Place before. Do you live far away?"

Charlotte was careful not to make Jemima an excuse. People in Mina's position were not obliged to care for their children themselves; there would be first a wet-nurse, then a child's nurse, then at five or six a nanny, and finally a governess or a tutor, and thus every possible need would be tended to.

"A little distance," she said composedly. "But one gets involved with one's own circle, you know?"

Caroline shut her eyes, and Charlotte heard her give the faintest of sighs.

Mina was temporarily at a loss. The reply had not elicited the information she had expected, nor yet led to another avenue of exploration.

"Yes," she said. "Naturally." She took a deep breath, smoothed her skirts, and began again. "Of course we have had the pleasure of meeting your sister Lady Ashworth—a most charming person."

The implication was being made, very delicately, that if someone of Emily's social distinction could find the time, then Charlotte certainly ought to.

"I'm sure she must have enjoyed it." Charlotte knew quite well that Emily would have been bored to tears, but Emily had always been skilled at hiding her feelings; in fact, she seemed to have the entire family's share of tactfulness.

"I do hope so," Mina replied. "Does Mr. Pitt have interests in the city?"

"Yes," Charlotte said quite truthfully. "I imagine he is there at this moment."

Caroline slid a little down in her chair, as if she were pretending she was absent.

Mina brightened. "Indeed! How sensible. An idle man can so quickly fall into unfortunate company, and end up wasting both his time and his substance, don't you think?"

"I have no doubt of it," Charlotte said, wondering what had prompted the remark.

"Although naturally the city has its pitfalls as well," Mina continued. "Indeed, some of our own neighbors here in the Place have the oddest of habits, with comings and goings in the city! But then, of course, young men are prone to do such things, and I suppose one must expect it of a certain sort. Family background always tells, you know—sooner or later!"

Charlotte had no idea what she was talking about.

Caroline sat up. "If you mean Inigo Charrington," she said with only the barest edge to her voice, although Charlotte noticed her ankles cross and her knees tighten as she deliberately kept her face smooth, "I believe he has friends in the city, and no doubt he cares to dine with them on occasion, or possibly go to the theater, or a concert."

Mina's eyebrows went up.

"Of course! One only hopes he has chosen wisely, and his friends are worthy of him. You didn't know poor Ottilie, did you?"

"No." Caroline shook her head.

Mina made a little face of sympathy. "The poor creature died the summer before you arrived, as I recall. She was so young, not more than twenty-two or twenty-three."

Charlotte looked from one to the other of them, waiting for an explanation.

"Oh, you wouldn't know her," Mina said, seizing the chance. "She was Ambrosine Charrington's daughter—Inigo's sister. Really a most tragic affair altogether. They were away for a few weeks during the summer. Ottilie was in perfect health when they left—at least she seemed so. And then within a mere fortnight she was dead! Quite dreadful! We were all completely at a loss!"

"I'm so sorry." Charlotte meant it; the story of life cut short was suddenly sobering in the midst of all the silly chatter and games of social superiority. "How very painful—for her family, I mean."

Mina's slender fingers roamed over her skirt again, laying it even more smoothly over her knees.

"Actually, they have borne it with the greatest fortitude." Her fine eyebrows rose as if she were still surprised by it. "One cannot but admire them, most especially Ambrosine herself—that is, Mrs. Charrington—she has risen above it so magnificently. If one did not know of it for oneself, one would almost believe it had not happened at all. They never speak of her, you know!"

"No doubt the wound is still there," Charlotte answered. "One never forgets, no matter how brave one's face."

"Oh dear!" Mina crumpled. "I do hope I have not inadvertently said something distressing, my dear Mrs. Pitt?

Nothing was further from my mind than to cause you some painful memory."

Charlotte smiled at her, pushing Sarah from her thoughts and hoping Caroline could do so too.

"I would never imagine that you might," she said quietly. "I expect everyone has suffered some loss or another. There cannot be a family in the land that has never had death rob them of someone."

Before Mina could search for a courteous acceptance of this, the withdrawing-room door opened and a very elderly lady came in, her face creased with irritation, a fine lace shawl drawn round her shoulders, and her black boots polished like glass.

"Good afternoon, Mrs. Spencer-Brown," she said curtly. "Didn't know you were entertaining this afternoon, Caroline. Cook said nothing at luncheon!" She looked at Charlotte, then took a step closer. "Good gracious! It's Charlotte!" She snorted slightly. "Decided to come back into decent Society, have you?"

"Good afternoon, Grandmama." Charlotte stood up and offered her the most comfortable chair, which she herself had been occupying until that moment.

The old lady accepted it after rearranging the cushions and dusting the seat. She sat down, and Charlotte found herself a hard-backed chair.

"Better for you anyway." The old lady nodded. "Get a round back sitting in one of these at your age. Girls always sat up properly when I was young. Knew how to conduct ourselves then. None of this gadding about without chaperones, going to the theater, and the like! And electricity all over the place! It must be unhealthy. Goodness only knows what's in the air! Gas lamps are quite bad enough. If the good Lord had intended it to be light all night, He would have made the moon as bright as the sun."

Mina ignored her and turned to Charlotte with excitement.

"Do you go to the theater alone, Mrs. Pitt? How thrilling! Do tell us, do you have adventures?"

Grandmama pulled out a handkerchief and blew her nose loudly.

Charlotte hovered on the edge of pretending that she did do such a thing, to annoy her grandmother, then decided the embarrassment it would cause Caroline was too great to balance the pleasure.

"No, no, I never have," she said with a touch of regret. "Is it adventurous?"

"Good gracious!" Mina looked startled. "I have no idea! One hears stories, of course, but—" Suddenly she giggled. "I should ask Mrs. Denbigh! She is just the sort of person who would have the courage to do it, if she wished."

"I daresay," Grandmama glowered at her. "But I have often thought that for all that she is a widow and ought to know her place better, Amaryllis Denbigh is no better than she should be! Caroline! Are we going to have tea this afternoon or sit here till dusk chattering dry?"

Caroline reached out and rang the bell.

"Of course we are, Mama. We were merely waiting until you joined us." Over the years she had grown accustomed to calling the woman "Mama," although she was in fact Edward's mother.

"Indeed," Grandmama said skeptically. "I hope there is some cake. I can't bear all that bread cook sends up. The woman has a mania for bread. They used to know how to make a decent cake when I kept servants. Trained them properly—that's what it all comes down to. Don't let them get away with so much—then you'll get cake when you want it!"

"I do get cake when I want it, Mama!" Caroline's temper was wearing thin. "And keeping a good staff these days is a lot harder than it used to be. Times change!"

"Not for the better!" Grandmama glared at Charlotte. She refrained from saying anything about respectable women who married into the police, of all things! But only because there was an outsider present, who, please God, knew nothing about it. If she did, next thing it would be all over the neighborhood! And then heaven knew what people would say, let alone what they would think!

"Not for the better," she said again. "Women working in offices like clerks when they ought to be in good domestic service. Whoever heard of such a thing? Who looks after their morals, I should like to know? There aren't any butlers in offices. Not that there are many women, thank heaven! Women's place is in a house—either their own or, if they haven't one, somebody else's!"

Charlotte thought of several answers and held her tongue on all of them. The conversation degenerated into pleasantries about fashion and the weather, with only occasional references to other residents of Rutland Place, and Grandmama's dour comments upon them. They were almost finished when Edward came in, rubbing his hands a little from the cold.

"Why, Charlotte, my dear!" His face lit up with pleasure and surprise. "I had no idea you were calling or I would have come home sooner." She stood up and he gave her a quick kiss on the cheek. "You look extremely well."

"I am, thank you, Papa." She stepped back and he noticed Mina for the first time, her pale lace almost blending into the brocade of the sofa and its cushions.

"Mrs. Spencer-Brown, how pleasant to see you." He bowed.

"Good afternoon, Mr. Ellison," she answered brightly, her eyes moving from Edward back to Charlotte, interested that he had not been expecting her. "You seem cold," she observed. "Do you care to sit next to the fire?" She moved her skirt to allow him more room on the sofa beside her.

He could not decline without discourtesy, and anyway he considered the spot nearest the fire to be his right. He sat down gingerly.

"Thank you. It does appear that the weather has changed. In fact, I fear it might rain."

"We can hardly expect better at this time of the year," Mina replied.

Caroline met Charlotte's eyes over the low table in a glance of helplessness, then reached for the bell to send for a fresh pot of tea for Edward, and some more cakes.

Edward received them with obvious appetite, and they all engaged in only the barest conversation for several minutes.

"Did you find that brooch you lost, my dear?" he said presently, head toward Caroline but his attention still on the cake.

Caroline colored very slightly. "Not yet, but I daresay it will turn up."

"Didn't know you'd lost anything!" Grandmama exclaimed. "You didn't tell me!"

"No reason why I should, Mama," Caroline replied, avoiding her eyes. "I'm quite sure if you had found it you would have mentioned it to me without my asking."

"What was it?" Grandmama was not going to let go so easily.

"How unfortunate!" Mina joined in. "I hope it was not valuable?"

"I've no doubt it will turn up!" Caroline replied with a note of increasing sharpness in her voice. Charlotte, glancing down, saw her hands twined in the handkerchief again, white where the tightness of the linen bit into her flesh.

"I expect you have mislaid it," she said with a smile she hoped did not look as artificial as it was. "It may be pinned to some garment you had forgotten you had worn."

"I do hope so," Mina said, shaking her head. Her dark blue eyes were enormous in her fragile face. "It is most distressing to have to say so, but, my dear, there have been a number of things—taken—in the Place recently!" She stopped and looked from one to another of them.

"Taken?" Edward said incredulously. "What on earth do you mean?"

"Taken," Mina repeated. "I hate to use a worse word."

"You mean stolen?" Grandmama demanded. "I told you! If you don't train your servants properly and run a house as it ought to be run, then this is the sort of thing you can expect! Sow a wind, and reap a whirlwind! I've always said so."

"It wasn't you who said that, Grandmama," Charlotte said tartly. "It's from the Book of Hosea, in the Bible."

"Don't be impertinent!" Grandmama snapped.

Edward seemed quite unaware of Caroline's distress or of Charlotte's attempt to close the subject.

"Did you say there have been other thefts?" he asked Mina.

"I'm afraid so. It's perfectly dreadful! Poor Ambrosine lost a most excellent gold chain, from her very own dressing table."

"Servants!" Grandmama snorted. "Whole class of servants is going down. I've said so for years! Nothing's been the same since Prince Albert died in '61. He was a man with standards! No wonder the poor Queen is in perpetual mourning—so should I be if my son behaved like the Prince of Wales." She snorted in outrage. "The whole country's heard of his goings-on!"

"And my husband lost an ornamental snuffbox with a crystal lid from our mantelshelf," Mina continued, ignoring her completely. "And poor Eloise Lagarde lost a silver buttonhook from her reticule, unfortunate child." She looked at the old lady candidly. "I cannot imagine any servant who had opportunity to take all those articles. I mean, how would someone else's servant be in my house?"

Grandmama's eyebrows went up and her nostrils flared. "Then obviously we must have more than one dishonest servant in Rutland Place! The whole world is degenerating at a disastrous speed. Heaven only knows where it will all end."

"It will probably end with everyone finding what they have misplaced!" Charlotte said, standing up. "It has been most delightful meeting you, Mrs. Spencer-Brown. I do hope we shall have the opportunity to speak again, but since the afternoon is turning somewhat unpleasant, and it does indeed look like rain, I'm sure you will excuse me if I seek to return to my home before I am drenched." Without waiting for a reply, she bent and gave her grandmother a peck on the cheek, her father a swift touch, and extended her arm to Caroline as if inviting her to accompany her at least as far as the door.

After rather startled murmurs of goodbye, Caroline took advantage of the opportunity. She was almost on Charlotte's heels as they came into the hall, and she shut the withdrawing room door behind them.

"Maddock!" Caroline called sharply. "Maddock!"

He appeared. "Yes, ma'am. Shall I call the carriage for Miss Charlotte?"

"Yes, please. And, Maddock, have Polly close the curtains, please."

"It is still two hours at least until dark, ma'am," he said with slight surprise.

"Don't argue with me, Maddock!" Caroline took a breath and steadied herself. "The wind is rising and it will rain quite shortly. I prefer not to watch it. Please do as you are asked!"

"Yes, ma'am." He withdrew obediently, stiff-shouldered in correct and spotless black.

Charlotte turned to her. "Mama, why does this locket matter so much? And why do you want the curtains drawn at four o'clock in the afternoon?"

Caroline stared at her as if frozen.

Charlotte put out her hands and touched her mother gently. Caroline's body was stiff under the fine material of her dress.

She let out her breath slowly and stared past Charlotte toward the light coming through the hall windows.

"I'm not really sure—it sounds so hysterical—but I feel as if there were someone watching me—and—waiting!"

Charlotte did not know what to say. Caroline was right; it did sound hysterical.

"I know it's foolish," Caroline went on, hunching her shoulders and shivering a little although the hall was perfectly warm, "but I can't get rid of the sensation. I've told myself not to be so fanciful, that everyone else has far too much to do to be interested in my comings and goings. But it's still there—the feeling that there are eyes, and a mind—a mind that knows—and waits!"

The idea was horrible.

"Waits for what?" Charlotte asked, trying to bring some rationality into it.

"I don't know! A mistake? Waits for me to make a mistake."

Charlotte felt a chill of real fear. This was unhealthy, even morbid. It carried a faint whiff of madness. If her mother was as overwrought as this, why on earth had Edward not noticed and called both her and Emily to do something? Even called a doctor! Certainly Grandmama was always watching and criticizing, but then she had done that for as long as Charlotte could remember, and no one had ever really minded before. She did it to everyone; to know better than anybody else was part of her satisfaction in living on when so many of her friends were dead.

Caroline shook herself. "I believe you'll get home before the rain. In fact, I don't think it's going to rain after all."

It was of total indifference to Charlotte whether it rained or even snowed.

"Do you know who took the locket and the other things, Mama?"

"No, of course not! What on earth makes you ask such a thing? I should hardly have asked you to help me in the matter if I already knew!"

"Why not? You might have wished to get it back without bringing in the police if it were a friend, or even a good servant of someone else."

"Well, I told you, Charlotte, I have no idea!"

Suddenly Charlotte had a glimpse of the obvious, and wondered why she had been so blind as not to have seen it before.

"What is in the locket, Mama?"

"In"—Caroline swallowed—"in the locket?"

"Yes, Mama, what is in it?" She almost wished she had not asked. Caroline's face was white, and she stood perfectly still for several seconds. Outside, the carriage wheels rattled on the road and a horse snorted.

"A photograph," Caroline said at last.

Charlotte looked at her. She heard her own voice almost against her will, sounding disembodied and remote.

"Of whom?"

"A—friend. Just a friend. But I would rather it was not found by anyone else. They might misunderstand my feelings and cause me embarrassment, and even—" She stopped, and her eyes came up to meet Charlotte's at last.

"Even what, Mama?" Charlotte asked very softly. Maddock was back in the hall, standing with her cloak, and the footman was at the door.

"Even perhaps—a little pressure," Caroline whispered.

Charlotte was used to ugly words, and ugly thoughts. Crime was part of Pitt's life, and she was too close to him not to share much of his pain, confusion, or pity.

"You mean blackmail?" she said.

Caroline winced. "I suppose I do."

Charlotte put her arms around her and held her tightly for a moment. To Maddock and the footman it must have looked like an affectionate goodbye.

"Then we must find out where it is," she said almost under her breath. "And see that it does no harm. Don't worry! We'll manage." Then she raised her tone to normal and stepped back. "Thank you for a most pleasant afternoon, Mama. I hope I shall come again sooner next time."

Caroline blinked and sniffed in a manner she would have abhorred, had she been aware of it.

"Thank you, my dear," she said. "Thank you so much."

Chapter Two

It was three days after this that Charlotte received another letter from Caroline touching on the same subject. This time she did speak of it to Pitt. They were sitting in front of the fire after Jemima had been put to sleep; Charlotte was sewing, and Pitt was gazing into the flames and sinking gently lower and lower into his chair.

"Thomas." Charlotte looked up from her work and held the needle in the air.

He turned his head and hitched himself a little higher before his feet slipped over the fender. The light flickered and jumped warmly in its glowing brass.

"Yes?"

"I had a letter from Mama today," she remarked casually. "She is distressed about the recent loss of a piece of jewelry."

His eyes narrowed. He knew Charlotte a great deal better than she suspected.

"When you say 'loss,' I take it you do not mean that she misplaced it?" he inquired.

Charlotte hesitated. "I'm really not quite sure. She

may have." She picked up her work again to give herself time to arrange her words. She had not expected him to perceive quite so quickly. Actually, she had thought he was very nearly asleep.

After a moment or two she looked across at him and found his eyes bright and waiting, watching her through his lashes. She took a long breath and abandoned the idea of subtlety.

"It was a locket and there was a picture of somebody inside it," she went on. "She would not say who, but I gathered it was someone whose presence she would prefer not to explain." She smiled a little self-consciously. "Perhaps it was an old love, someone she knew before Papa?"

He straightened up and took his legs off the fender; his feet were getting hot and he would scorch his slippers if he was not careful.

"And she thinks someone has taken it?" he asked the obvious.

"Yes," Charlotte said. "I think she does."

"Any idea who?"

She shook her head. "If she has, she won't say so. And of course if she were to report the loss, it would cause far more unpleasantness than even having it returned would be worth."

Pitt needed no further explanation. He was perfectly familiar with Society's feelings about having police in the house, with the attendant vulgarity. One reported a break-in, of course, and that was regrettable enough, but at least a break-in was an outside affair, a misfortune that could happen to anyone with goods worth the taking. Domestic crime was different; it was something that might involve the questioning, and resultant embarrassment, of one's friends, and therefore resorting to the police was unthinkable.

"Does she expect you to play discreet detective?" he asked with a broad smile.

"I'm not a bad detective," she said defensively. "In Paragon Walk I knew the truth before you did!" As soon as she had spoken, memory came back and brought with it ugliness and pain, and self-congratulation became ridiculous, almost indecent.

"That was murder," he pointed out soberly. "And you nearly got yourself killed for your cleverness. You can hardly go around asking your mother's friends, 'Do you happen to have stolen Mama's locket, and if so, would you please give it back unopened, because it contains some indiscretion, or a picture that might be interpreted as such.'"

"You're not being very helpful!" Charlotte said crossly. "If I could have done it as easily as that, I wouldn't have needed to ask you about it!"

He sat up straight and leaned forward to take her hand. "My darling, if it really does contain something private, then the less said about it the better. Leave it alone!"

She frowned. "It's more than that, Thomas. She feels someone is watching her, and waiting!"

He screwed up his face. "You mean someone has already opened it and is waiting for an opportunity to apply a little blackmail?"

"Yes, I suppose I do." Her fingers grasped around his. "It's horrid, and I think she's really quite frightened."

"If I come in, it will only make it worse," he said softly. "And I can't officially anyway, unless she calls me."

"I know." Her fingers tightened.

"Charlotte, be careful. I know you mean well, but, my dear, you have a transparent face and a tongue about as subtle as an avalanche."

"Oh, that's unfair!" she protested, although at least half of her knew it was not. "I shall be very careful!"

"I still think it would be better if you left it alone—unless someone actually does try blackmail. There may be nothing to it—no more than your mother's own fears painting shadows on the wall. Perhaps a little conscience?"

"I can't do *nothing*," she said unhappily. "She has asked me to come see her, and I can't leave her so distressed without doing all I am able to."

"I suppose not," he conceded. "But for goodness' sake, do as little as you can. Questions will only arouse curiosity and are more likely than anything else to bring about the very speculations she is afraid of!"

Charlotte knew he was right and she nodded, but at the same time she was already making plans to call at Rutland Place the following day.

She found Caroline in and awaiting her anxiously.

"My dear, I'm so glad you were able to come," she said, kissing Charlotte on the cheek. "I have planned for us to make a few calls this afternoon, so you can meet some of the other people in the Place—particularly those I am best acquainted with myself, and to whose houses I have been, or who have come here."

Charlotte's heart sank. Obviously, Caroline intended to pursue the pendant.

"Do you not think it would be better to be quite casual about it, Mama?" she asked as lightly as she could. "You do not wish anyone to realize how important it is to you, or their curiosity will be aroused. Whereas if you say nothing, it may pass almost without remark."

Caroline's lips tightened. "I wish I could believe that, but I feel terribly sure that whoever it is already knows—" She stopped.

"Knows what?" Charlotte asked.

"Knows that it is mine, and that it is important to me," Caroline finished awkwardly. "I told you—I can feel them, feel their eyes on me. And don't say it's foolish! I know it is, but I'm as sure as I have ever been of anything that there is some—person—here who is watching, watching and laughing!" She shivered. "And hating! I—I have even felt once or twice as if they were following me, in the dusk." The red color burned uncomfortably in her cheeks.

"That person sounds like somebody mad," Charlotte said as levelly as she could. "Very unpleasant, but more to be pitied than feared."

Caroline shook her head sharply. "I would prefer to be sorry for madness at a much greater distance."

Charlotte was shaken. Her voice came far more

roughly, more critically than she had intended.

"So would most people," she said. "I think that is what is called 'passing by on the other side.'" Then she stopped, aware of how unjust she was being. She was confused; she was afraid Caroline was hysterical, and she did not know how to treat it.

A look of amazement crossed Caroline's face, followed swiftly by anger.

"Are you suggesting I owe some Christian duty to this creature who stole my pendant, and now is peeping at me and following me?" she said incredulously.

Charlotte was ashamed and angry with herself. She should not have spoken her thoughts so bluntly, especially since they had nothing to do with the problem, and would hardly be of comfort in what was now obviously a far deeper matter than she had appreciated.

"No," she said gravely. "I am trying to make you see that it is not as serious as you believe. If whoever stole or found the pendant is really watching you, and sniggering behind the curtains, then they are not quite right in their minds, and need not be feared so much as viewed with revulsion, and some sense of pity as well. It is not like a personal enemy who wished you harm and had the ability to bring it about."

"You don't understand!" Caroline shut her eyes in exasperation, and the muscles in her face were tight. "They would not need to have any brains to cause me harm! Merely to open the locket and see the picture would be enough! One can be as mad as a bedlamite, and still be able to open a locket and see that the picture inside it is not of your father."

Charlotte sat silent a moment, trying to collect her thoughts. There must be a great deal more to it that Caroline had not said. The picture must be more than some dim, romantic memory. Either the dream was still sharp, the event still capable of causing pain, or else the picture was of some man she knew now, here in Rutland Place!

"Who is it in the picture, Mama?" she asked.

"A friend." Caroline was not looking at her. "A gentleman of my acquaintance. There is no more to it than a— regard, but it could easily be misunderstood."

A flirtation. Charlotte was only momentarily surprised. She had learned a lot since her total innocence at the beginning of the Cater Street murders. Few people are immune to flattery, a little romance to flesh out the ordinariness of every day. Edward had not been, so why should Caroline?

And she had kept a picture in a locket. Foolish, but very human. People kept pressed flowers, theater or dance programs, old letters. A wise husband or wife allowed a little privacy for such things, and did not inquire or dig up old dreams to look for answers.

She smiled, trying to be gentler.

"Don't worry about it, Mama. Everyone has something private." She deliberately phrased it evasively. "I daresay that if you do not make much of it, other people won't. In fact, I don't suppose they will wish to. Quite apart from liking you, they probably have lockets themselves, or letters they would prefer not to lose."

Caroline smiled bleakly. "You have a charitable view, my dear. You have been out of Society too long. You see it from a distance, and lose the detail."

Charlotte took her arm and squeezed it for a moment.

"Above all things, Society is practical, Mama. It knows what it can afford. Now who is it you wish us to visit? Tell me something about them, so I don't say anything tactless and embarrass you."

"Good gracious! What a hope!" Caroline put her hand over Charlotte's in a little gesture of thanks. "First we are going to the Charringtons', to see Ambrosine. I told you about her before. Then I think on to Eloise Lagarde. I don't think I said anything about her."

"No, but was that not a name Mrs. Spencer-Brown mentioned?"

"I don't recall. Anyway, Eloise is a charming person, but quite retiring. She has led a very sheltered life, so please, Charlotte, do give some thought to what you say."

From Charlotte's now wider viewpoint, everyone in

Rutland Place had led a very sheltered life, including Caroline herself, but she forbore saying so. Pitt's broader, teeming world, with its vigor and squalor, farce and tragedy, would only be confusing and frightening to Caroline. In Pitt's world, realities were not softened by evasion and genteel words. Its raw life and death would horrify the inhabitants of Rutland Place, just as the myriad icebound rules of Society would appall a stranger to it.

"Is Eloise in delicate health, Mama?" Charlotte asked.

"I have never heard of any actual illness, but there are many things a person of taste does not discuss. It has occurred to me that she might be consumptive. She seems a little delicate, and I have noticed her faint once or twice. But it is so hard to tell with these fashions whether a girl is robust or not. I confess that when Mary does her best with my whalebone and laces to give me back the twenty-inch waist I used to have, I sometimes feel like fainting myself!" She smiled ruefully, and Charlotte felt another twinge of anxiety. Fashion was all very well, but at Caroline's age she should not care so much.

"I have not seen a great deal of Eloise lately," Caroline continued. "I think perhaps this inclement weather does not agree with her. That would not be hard to understand. It has been distressingly cold. She is quite lovely—she has the whitest skin and the darkest eyes you ever saw, and she moves marvelously. She reminds me of Lord Byron's poem—'She walks in beauty like the night.' " She smiled. "As fragile and as tender as the moon."

"Did he say that, about the moon?"

"No, I did. Anyway, you will meet her and judge for yourself. Her parents both died when she was very young—no more than eight or nine—and she and her brother were cared for by an aunt. Now that the aunt is dead also, the two of them live here most of the time, and only go back to the country house for a few weeks at a time, or perhaps a month."

"Mrs. Spencer-Brown described her as a child," Charlotte said.

Caroline dismissed it. "Oh, that's just Mina's turn of phrase. Eloise must be twenty-two or more, and Tormod, her brother, is three or four years older at least." She reached for the bell and rang it for the maid to bring her coat. "I think it's about time we should leave. I would like you to meet Ambrosine before there are a number of callers."

Charlotte was afraid the matter of the locket was going to be raised again, but she did not argue. She pulled her own coat closed and followed obediently.

It was a very short walk, and Ambrosine Charrington welcomed them with an enthusiasm that startled Charlotte. She was a striking woman, with fine features under a smooth skin only faintly wrinkled around the corners of the mouth and eyes. Her cheekbones were high and swept wide to wings of dark hair. She surveyed Charlotte with interest and gradual approval as her instinct recognized another highly individual woman.

"How do you do, Mrs. Pitt," she said with a charming smile. "I'm delighted you have come at last. Your mother has spoken of you so often."

Charlotte was surprised; she had not realized Caroline would be willing to talk about her socially at all, let alone often! It gave her an unexpected feeling of pleasure, even pride, and she found herself smiling more than the occasion called for.

The room was large and the furnishings a little austere compared to the ornate and bulging interiors that were currently popular. There were none of the usual stuffed animals in glass cases or arrangements of dried flowers, no embroidered samplers, or elaborate antimacassars across the backs of chairs. By comparison with most withdrawing rooms it seemed airy, almost bare. Charlotte found it rather pleasing, except for the phalanxes of photographs on the farthest wall, covering the top of the grand piano, and spread along the mantelshelf. They all appeared to include rather elderly people, and had been taken years before, to judge from the fashions. Obviously they were not of Ambrosine and her children, but rather of a generation earlier. Charlotte presumed the man who appeared in them so frequently was her husband— a vain man, she decided from the number of his pictures.

There were some half-dozen highly exotic weapons displayed above the fireplace.

Ambrosine caught Charlotte's glance. "Horrible, aren't they?" she said. "But my husband insists. His younger brother was killed in the first Afghan War, forty-five years ago, and he's set them up there as a sort of memorial. The maids are always complaining that they are the perfect devil to clean. Collect dust like mad, above the fire."

Charlotte looked up at the knives in their ornamental sheaths and scabbards, and had nothing but sympathy for the maids.

"Quite!" Ambrosine said fervently, observing her expression. "And they are in excellent condition. Bronwen swears someone will wind up with their throat cut one of these days. Although of course it is not her task to clean them. Heathen weapons, she calls them, and I suppose they are."

"Bronwen?" Caroline was at a loss.

"My maid." Ambrosine invited them all to be seated with a gesture of her arm. "The excellent one with the reddish hair."

"I thought her name was Louisa," Caroline said.

"I daresay it is." Ambrosine arranged herself gracefully on the chaise longue. "But the best maid I ever had was called Bronwen, and I don't believe in changing a good thing. I always call my personal maids Bronwen now. Also it saves confusion. There are dozens of Lilies and Roses and Marys."

There was no argument to this, and Charlotte was obliged to turn and look out of the window in order to hide her amusement.

"Finding a really good maid is quite an achievement," Caroline said, pursuing the subject. "So often those who are competent are less than honest, and those whom one can really trust are not as efficient as one would like."

"My dear, you sound most despondent," Ambrosine said with sympathy. "A current misfortune?"

"I'm really not quite sure," Caroline plunged on. "I have missed a small article of jewelry, and I don't know whether it is a theft or merely mischance. It is a wretched feeling. I don't wish to be unjust when the whole affair may be quite accidental."

"Was it of value?" Ambrosine inquired with a little frown.

"Not especially, except that it was a gift from my mother-in-law, and she might be hurt that I had been careless with it."

"Or flattered that of all your pieces someone chose that to take," Ambrosine pointed out.

Caroline laughed without pleasure.

"I hadn't even thought of that. I'm obliged to you. If she makes any observation, I must say that to her."

"I still think you may have mislaid it, Mama," Charlotte said, trying to allow the subject to die. "It may well turn up in a day or two. If you let Grandmama think it has been stolen, she will begin to accuse people, and she will never let the matter rest until someone is blamed."

Caroline caught the sharpness in her voice and perceived the danger she was inviting upon herself.

"You are quite right," she said. "It would be wiser to say nothing."

"People with not enough business of their own to mind will be quick enough to mind yours if you start word of things like theft," Charlotte added for good measure.

"I see your estimate of people's charity matches my own, Mrs. Pitt." Ambrosine reached for the bell cord and pulled it. "I hope you will take tea? As well as a good maid, I also have an excellent cook. I employed her for her ability with cakes and desserts. She makes the most dreadful soups, but then since I don't care for soup, I am perfectly happy to overlook that."

"My husband is extremely fond of soup," Caroline remarked absently.

"So is mine," Ambrosine said. "But one cannot have everything."

The parlormaid came and Ambrosine sent her for the tea.

"You know, Mrs. Pitt," Ambrosine continued, "your

observations about other people's curiosity are peculiarly apposite. I have had the disturbing sensation lately that someone is taking a marked interest in me—not a kindly one, but purely inquisitive. If anything, I have the feeling it is malicious."

Charlotte sat perfectly still. She was conscious of Caroline's body stiffening beside her.

"How distressing," Charlotte said after a moment. "Have you any notion who it may be?"

"No, none at all. That is what makes it so unpleasant. It is merely a repeated impression."

The door opened, and the maid came in with tea and at least a dozen different kinds of cakes and tarts, many of them with whipped cream.

"Thank you," Ambrosine said, eyeing one particular fruit pastry with satisfaction. "Perhaps I am being fanciful," she went on as the maid disappeared again. "I daresay there is no one with as much interest in me as such a thing supposes."

Caroline opened her mouth as if to speak, then said nothing after all.

"You are quite right," Charlotte said, hurrying to fill the silence, her eyes on the tea table. "You have a most accomplished cook. I vow I should grow out of every garment I possess if I were to live with such a woman."

Ambrosine observed Charlotte's still slender figure.

"I hope that does not mean you will not call upon me again?"

Charlotte smiled. "On the contrary, it means that I shall now have two reasons for calling instead of one." She accepted her tea and an enormous cream sponge. No one bothered with the polite fiction of taking bread and butter first.

They had been at tea only a matter of five minutes or so when the door opened again and a gray-haired, middle-aged man came in. Charlotte immediately recognized the short-nosed, rather severe face from the photographs. This man was even wearing the same kind of stiff-winged collar and black tie as the man in the photographs. He had to be Lovell Charrington.

Introductions proved her correct.

"No sandwiches?" He looked at the plates critically.

"Didn't know you would be joining us," Ambrosine replied. "I can always call cook for some if you wish."

"Please! I cannot imagine that all this cream is good for you, my dear. And we should not restrict our visitors to indulging in your somewhat eccentric tastes."

"Oh, we are equally eccentric," Charlotte answered without thinking. Her impulse was to side with Ambrosine; moreover, she had quite enough bread at home. "I am delighted to be able to enjoy them in such happy company."

Ambrosine rewarded her with a smile of satisfaction and surprise.

"If you will not be offended by my saying so, Mrs. Pitt, you remind me of my own daughter, Ottilie. She enjoyed things so much and was not averse to saying so."

Charlotte did not know whether it would be all right to admit knowing of the girl's death, or if it might seem as if she had been talking of the Charringtons' affairs too familiarly. She was saved from her dilemma by Lovell.

"Our daughter has passed on, Mrs. Pitt. I'm sure you will understand if I say that we find it distressing to discuss."

Since Charlotte had not spoken, she thought his manner less than courteous, but for Ambrosine's sake she restrained herself.

"Of course," she said. "I myself seldom speak of those I have lost, for the same reason."

To her satisfaction, he looked a little taken aback. Obviously he had not considered the possibility that she might have feelings on the subject.

"Quite," he said hastily. "Quite!"

Charlotte deliberately took another cream cake, and was forced to spend the next few moments concentrating on eating it without dropping the cream down her bosom.

Conversation became polite and stilted. They discussed the weather, what the newspapers were reporting in the Society columns, and the possibility—or, in Lovell's opinion, the impossibility—of there being any lost treasures in Africa, such as those that were portrayed in Mr. Rider Haggard's novel *King Solomon's Mines,* published the previous year.

"Nonsense," he said firmly. "Dangerous imagination. Fellow ought to employ his time to better purpose. Ridiculous way for a grown man to earn his living, spinning fantasies to beguile foolish women and girls who are susceptible enough to take him seriously. Overstimulating the minds of such persons is bad for their health . . . and their morals!"

"I think it is an excellent way to employ oneself," said a young man of perhaps twenty-nine or thirty, coming into the room with a wave of his arm. He helped himself to the last cake, ate it almost in one gulp, and flashed a dazzling smile at Charlotte, then at Caroline. He picked up the teapot to test if there was anything still in it. "Harms no one and entertains thousands. Brings a little color into lives that might ordinarily never have a dream worth indulging. Without dreams their lives might be unbearable."

"Never heard such nonsense!" Lovell replied. "Panders to overheated imaginations, and to greed. If you wish for tea, Inigo, please ring for the maid and request it instead of swinging the pot around like that. That is what servants are for. I don't think you have been introduced to Mrs. Pitt?"

Inigo looked at Charlotte. "Of course not. If I had, I would most certainly have remembered. How do you do, Mrs. Pitt. I will not ask how you are. You are obviously in excellent health—and spirits."

"Indeed I am." Charlotte tried to keep up the front of dignity she knew Caroline would wish, if not expect. "And if you said less for yourself, I should find it hard to believe," she added.

"Oh!" His eyebrows went up with evident pleasure. "A woman of opinions. You would have liked my sister Tillie. She always had opinions. A few rather odd ones, mind, but she always knew what she thought, and usually said so."

"Inigo!" Lovell's face was deeply flushed. "Your sister

has passed away. Kindly remember that, and do not speak of her in that flippant and overfamiliar manner!" He swung round. "I apologize, Mrs. Pitt. Such indelicacy must be embarrassing to you." His tone lacked conviction. In his mind, Charlotte was already hardly better than his son.

"On the contrary." Charlotte settled more comfortably into her seat. "I find it very easy to understand how one still thinks with great vividness and affection of those whom one has loved. We all bear our losses in different ways—however is easiest for us—and afford others the same comfort."

Lovell's face paled, but before he could reply Caroline stood up, setting her cup and saucer on the table.

"It has been most charming," she said to no one in particular. "But we have other calls it would be only civil to make. I trust you will excuse us? My dear Ambrosine, I do hope I shall see you again soon. Good afternoon, Mr. Charrington, Inigo."

Lovell rose from his chair and bowed. "Good afternoon, Mrs. Ellison, Mrs. Pitt. So delightful to have made your acquaintance."

Inigo opened the door for them and followed them out into the hall.

"I'm so sorry if I caused you distress, Mrs. Pitt," he said with a little frown. "It was not my intention in the least."

"Of course not," Charlotte answered him. "And I think from what I have heard of her that I should have liked your sister very much indeed. I certainly find your mother the most comfortable person I have met for a long time."

"Comfortable!" he said in amazement. "Most people find her quite the opposite."

"I suppose it must be a matter of taste, but I assure you, I like her a great deal."

Inigo smiled broadly, all the anxiety slipping out of his face. He shook her hand warmly.

The footman was helping Caroline with her coat. She fastened it and Charlotte accepted hers. A moment later they were outside in the sharp March wind.

An open carriage rattled by, and the man inside raised his hat to them. Charlotte had a brief impression of a dark, elegant head, with thick hair curving close to the nape of his neck, sleek and beautiful, and of dark, level eyes. She caught only a glimpse, and then the carriage had passed, but it woke a memory in her so sharp it left her tingling. The man in the carriage was Paul Alaric, the Frenchman who had lived in Paragon Walk, only a hundred yards from Emily, and who had stirred so many passions that summer of the murders. Poor Selena had been so obsessed with him it had almost deranged her.

Against all her common sense, Charlotte herself had felt attracted by his cool wit, the charm that seemed almost unconscious, and the very fact that they all knew so little about him—no family, no past, no social category in which to fit him. Even Emily, with all her grace and élan, had not been entirely impervious.

Could it really have been he just now?

She turned and found Caroline standing very straight, her head high, the wind whipping color into her cheeks.

"Do you know him?" Charlotte asked incredulously.

Caroline began to walk again, her steps sharp on the pavement.

"Slightly," she replied. "He is Monsieur Paul Alaric."

Charlotte felt the heat flood through her—so it was he. . . .

"He is acquainted with quite a few residents in the Place," Caroline continued.

Charlotte was about to add that it seemed beyond question that Caroline was one of them; then, without being sure why, she changed her mind.

"He seems to be a person of leisure," she said instead. It was a pointless remark, but suddenly sensible words had left her.

"He has business in the city." Caroline walked more rapidly, and further conversation was whipped away from them by the wind. Twenty or thirty yards on, they were at the Lagardes' front entrance.

"Are they French?" Charlotte whispered under her breath as the door opened and they were conducted into the hall.

"No," Caroline whispered as the parlormaid went to announce them. "Great-grandfather, or something. Came over at the time of the Revolution."

"The Revolution? That was nearly a hundred years ago!" Charlotte whispered back, then fixed her face in an appropriately expectant expression as they were ushered into the withdrawing room.

"All right, then it was further back. I have heard so much history from your grandmother I am tired of it," Caroline snapped. "Good afternoon, Eloise. May I present my daughter Mrs. Pitt," she continued with a total change of voice and expression, without drawing breath.

The girl who faced Charlotte was indeed, as Caroline had said, darkly lovely, with the translucence of moonlight on water. Her hair was soft and full, without sheen, quite unlike Charlotte's, which gleamed like polished wood and was hard to keep pinned because of its weight.

"How delightful of you to call." Eloise stepped back, smiling and by implication inviting them to sit down. "Will you take tea?"

It was a little late, and perhaps it was merely a courtesy that she asked.

"Thank you, but we would not wish to be of inconvenience," Caroline said, declining in an accepted formula. It would be less than flattering to say that they had already taken tea elsewhere. She turned to the mantelshelf. "What a delightful picture! I don't believe I have noticed it before."

Personally, Charlotte would not have given it houseroom, but tastes varied.

"Do you like it?" Eloise looked up, a flicker of amusement in her face. "I always think it makes the house look rather dark, and it isn't really like that at all. But Tormod is fond of it, so I let it hang there."

"That is your country house?" Charlotte asked the obvious question because there was nothing else she could think of to say, and she knew that the reply would provide material for several minutes' polite discussion. They were still on the subject of town and country differences when the door opened and a young man came in who Charlotte knew immediately must be Eloise's brother. He had the same mass of dark hair and the same wide eyes and pale skin. The resemblance in features was not so great, however; he had a higher brow, with the hair sweeping away from it in a broad wave, and his nose was rather aquiline. His mouth was wide, quick to laugh, and, Charlotte judged, quick to sulk. Now he came forward with easy, quite natural grace.

"Mrs. Ellison, what a pleasure to see you." He slipped his arm around Eloise. "I don't believe I have met your companion?"

"My daughter Mrs. Pitt." Caroline smiled back. "Mr. Tormod Lagarde."

He bowed very slightly.

"Welcome to Rutland Place, Mrs. Pitt. I hope we shall see you often."

"That is most kind of you," Charlotte replied.

Tormod sat next to Eloise on a broad sofa.

"I expect I shall call upon my mother more often as the spring approaches," Charlotte added.

"I'm afraid the winter is very grim," he answered. "One feels far more like remaining close to the fire than venturing out to go visiting. In fact, we quite often retreat altogether to our house in the country and simply close the doors all January and February."

Eloise's face warmed as if at some sweet and lingering memory. She said nothing, but Charlotte imagined she could see reflected in her eyes the light of Christmases with trees and lanterns, pinecone fires and hot toast, and long, happy companionship too easy to need the communication of words.

Tormod fished in his pocket and brought out a small package.

"Here." He held it out to Eloise. "To replace the one you lost."

She took it, looking up at him, then down at the little parcel in her hands.

"Open it!" he commanded. "It's not so very special."

Slowly she obeyed, anticipation and pleasure in her face.

Inside the parcel was a small, silver-handled buttonhook.

"Thank you, dear," she said gently. "That really was most thoughtful of you. Especially since it might so easily have been my own fault. I shall feel dreadfully guilty now if the other one turns up and I had merely been careless all the time." She looked over at Charlotte, apology and a touch of embarrassment in her face. "I lost my old one that I had for years. I think it went from my reticule, but I suppose I might have put it somewhere else and forgotten."

Charlotte's desire to know was stronger than her good judgment to keep silent on the subject. "You mean you think it could have been stolen?" she asked, feigning surprise.

Tormod dismissed it. "These things happen sometimes. It's an unpleasant thought, but one must face reality—servants do steal from time to time. But since it appears to have happened in someone else's house, it is far better to say nothing. It would be in very poor taste to embarrass a friend by letting it be known. Besides, as Eloise says, it may turn up—although I doubt it now."

Caroline cleared her throat nervously. "But should theft be condoned?" she said a little hesitantly. "I mean—is that right?"

Tormod was still casual, his voice light. He smiled at her with a little twist of regret.

"I suppose not, if one knew for sure who it was and had proof that it had occurred," he said. "But we haven't. All we would do is rouse suspicion, and perhaps quite unjustly. Better to let the matter lie. Once one begins an inquiry into evil, one can start a train of events that is very difficult to stop. A silver-plated buttonhook is hardly worth all the anger and fear, and the doubts, that inquiry would raise."

"I think you are quite right," Charlotte said quickly.

"After all, a case of something missing—one has no idea where—is very different from actually knowing beyond question that a particular person has stolen it."

"How wise of you." Tormod flashed her a rapid smile. "Justice is not always best served by shouting 'thief.'"

Before Caroline could defend her view, the maid announced another caller.

"Mrs. Denbigh, ma'am," she said to Eloise. "Shall I say that you will receive her?"

Eloise's face tightened almost imperceptibly. In another light, farther from the window, the change in her expression might not have been visible at all.

"Yes, of course, Beryl, please do."

Amaryllis Denbigh was the sort of woman Charlotte felt quite uncomfortable with. She came into the room with assurance, carrying with her an air of always having been successful, always valued. She was not beautiful, but there was an appeal in her face of wide eyes and slightly too round, curved lips, the innocence of an adolescent who does not yet understand her own potential for excitement and hunger. She had an abundance of fair, wavy hair that was dressed just casually enough not to look unnatural. It required a very skilled maid to achieve such an effect. Her dress was undeniably expensive—not in the least ostentatious, but Charlotte knew how much it cost to have a dressmaker cut it so cleverly that the bust looked just that much fuller, the waist those few inches smaller.

Introductions were formal and very complete. Amaryllis weighed Charlotte to an exactness, and dismissed her. She turned to Tormod.

"Shall you be coming to Mrs. Wallace's soirée on Thursday? I do so hope so. I have heard the pianist she has invited is quite excellent. I'm sure you would enjoy it. And Eloise too, of course," she added as an afterthought, a politeness without conviction.

Charlotte noted the tone in her voice and drew conclusions of her own.

"I think we will," Tormod replied. He turned to Eloise.

"You have nothing else prepared, have you, dear?"

"No, not at all. If this pianist is good, it will be a great pleasure. I only hope they do not all make such a noise we cannot hear him."

"My dear, you cannot expect conversation to cease just to listen to a pianist—not at a soirée," Amaryllis said gently. "After all, it is primarily a social event, and the music is merely a diversion, a pleasantness. And of course it gives people something to talk about without having to think too hard for a suitable subject. Some people are so awkward, you know." She smiled at Charlotte. "Do you not think so, Mrs. Pitt?"

"Indeed, I am sure of it," Charlotte agreed frankly. "Some cannot think of anything suitable to say at all, while others speak far too much and at all the wrong times. I greatly like a person who knows how to be silent comfortably, especially when there is good music playing."

Amaryllis' face tightened. She ignored the implication. "Do you play, Mrs. Pitt?" she asked.

"No," Charlotte answered blandly. "I regret I do not. Do you?"

Amaryllis regarded her chillingly.

"I paint," she replied. "I prefer it. So much less intrusive, I think. One can look or not, as one chooses. Oh"—she widened her eyes and bit her lip—"I'm so sorry, Eloise. I had forgotten that you play. I did not mean you, of course! You have never played at anyone's soirée!"

"No, I think I should be very nervous," Eloise said. "Although it would be an honor to be asked. But I rather think I should be irritated if everyone talked so much that no one else could listen." She spoke with some feeling. "Music should be respected, not treated like street sounds, or wallpaper, no more than a sort of background. Then one becomes bored with it, without ever having appreciated its beauty."

Amaryllis laughed, a high, pretty sound that irked Charlotte unreasonably—perhaps because she would have liked to have such a laugh, and knew she did not.

"How philosophical you are!" Amaryllis said brightly. "I warn you, my dear, if you start saying things like that at a soirée, you will become most unpopular. People will not know what to make of you!"

Charlotte gave her mother a sharp nudge on the ankle, and as Caroline bent to touch the place, thinking something had fallen on her, Charlotte pretended to assume she was preparing to leave.

"May I help you, Mama?" she offered, then rose and gave Caroline her arm.

Caroline glanced at her. "I am not yet in need of assistance, Charlotte," she said crisply. But although the idea of sitting down again, out of contrariness, lingered quite clearly in her eyes, after a moment she excused herself politely, and a few minutes later they were both outside in the street again.

"I dislike Mrs. Denbigh," Charlotte said with feeling. "Very much!"

"That was obvious." Caroline pulled her collar up. Then she smiled. "Actually, so do I. It is completely unfair, because I have no idea why, but I find her most irritating."

"She has set her cap at Tormod Lagarde," Charlotte remarked by way of partial explanation. "And she is being very bold about it."

"Do you think so?"

"Of course she is! Don't tell me you had not noticed!"

"Of course I have noticed!" Caroline shivered. "But I have seen a great many more women set their caps at men than you have, my dear, and I had not thought Amaryllis was particularly clumsy. In fact, I think she is really quite patient."

"I still do not care for her!"

"That is because you like Eloise and you cannot think what will happen to her if Tormod marries, since Amaryllis obviously is not fond of her. Perhaps Eloise herself will marry, and that will solve the problem."

"Then it would be a great deal cleverer of Amaryllis to find a suitable young man for Eloise than to sit there disparaging her, wouldn't it! It should not be hard—she is perfectly charming. What is the matter, Mama? You keep hunching your shoulders as if you were in a draft, but it is quite sheltered here."

"Is there anyone behind us?"

Charlotte turned. "No. Why? Were you expecting someone?"

"No! No—I—I just have the feeling that someone is watching us. For goodness' sake, don't stare like that, Charlotte. You will have people think we are watching them, trying to see in through their curtains!"

"What people?" Charlotte forced herself to smile in an effort to hide her anxiety for Caroline. "There isn't anyone," she said reasonably.

"Don't be silly!" Caroline snapped. "There is always someone—a butler or a maid drawing curtains, or a footman at a door."

"Then it is hardly anything to matter." Charlotte dismissed it with words, but in her mind she did not find it so easy. The sensation of being watched—not casually observed by someone about another duty, but deliberately and systematically watched—was extremely unpleasant. Surely Caroline was imagining it? Why should anyone do such a thing? What possible reason would there be?

Caroline had quickened her pace, and now she did so again. They were walking so rapidly Charlotte's skirts whipped round her ankles, and she was afraid that if she did not look where she was going she would trip over one of the paving stones and fall headlong.

Caroline whirled around the gatepost and up the steps to her own front door. She was there before the footman had seen them to open it, and was obliged to wait. She shifted from foot to foot, and once actually turned to stare back into the road.

"Mama, has someone accosted you in the street?" Charlotte asked, touching her arm.

"No, of course not! It's just—" She shook herself angrily. "I have the feeling that I am not alone, even when it would appear in every way that I am. There is someone I cannot see but who I am perfectly sure can see me."

The door opened and Caroline swept in, with Charlotte behind her.

"Close the curtains please, Martin," she said to the footman.

"All of them, ma'am?" His voice rose in surprise. It was still daylight for another two hours, and perfectly pleasant.

"Yes, please! In all the rooms that we shall occupy." Caroline removed her coat and hat and gave them to him; Charlotte did the same.

In the withdrawing room Grandmama was sitting in front of the fire.

"Well?" She surveyed them up and down. "Is there any news?"

"Of what, Mama?" Caroline asked, turning toward the table.

"Of anything, girl! How can I ask for news of something if I do not know what it is? If I already knew it, it would not be news to me, would it?"

It was a fallacious argument, but Charlotte had long ago discovered the futility of pointing that out to her.

"We called upon Mrs. Charrington and Miss Lagarde," she said. "I found them both quite delightful."

"Mrs. Charrington is eccentric." Grandmama's voice was tart, as if she had bitten into a green plum.

"That pleased me." Charlotte was not going to be bested. "She was very civil, and after all that is the important thing."

"And Miss Lagarde—was she civil too? She is far too shy for her own good. The girl seems incapable of flirting with any skill at all!" Grandmama snapped. "She'll never find herself a husband by wandering around looking fey, however pretty her face. Men don't marry just a face, you know!"

"Which is as well for most of us." Charlotte was equally acerbic, looking at Grandmama's slightly hooked nose and heavy-lidded eyes.

The old woman affected not to have understood her. She turned toward Caroline icily. "You had a caller while you were out."

"Indeed?" Caroline was not particularly interested. It was quite usual for at least one person to visit during the afternoon, just as she and Charlotte had visited others; it was part of the ritual. "I expect they left a card and Maddock will bring it in presently."

"Don't you even wish to know who it was?" Grandmama sniffed, staring at Caroline's back.

"Not especially."

"It was that Frenchman with his foreign manners. I forget his name." She chose not to remember because it was not English. "But he has the best tailor I have seen in thirty years."

Caroline stiffened. There was absolute silence in the room, so thick one imagined one could hear carriage wheels two streets away.

"Indeed?" Caroline said again, her voice unnaturally casual. There was a catch in it as if she were bursting to say more and forcing herself to wait so her words would not fall over each other. "Did he say anything?"

"Of course he said something! Do you think he stood there like a fool?"

Caroline kept her back to them. She took one of the daffodils out of the bowl, shortened its stalk, and replaced it.

"Anything of interest?"

"Who ever says anything of interest these days?" Grandmama answered miserably. "There aren't any heroes anymore. General Gordon has been murdered by those savages in Khartoum. Even Mr. Disraeli is dead—not that he was a hero, of course! Or a gentleman either, for that matter. But he was clever. Everyone with any breeding is gone."

"Was Monsieur Alaric discourteous?" Charlotte asked in surprise. He had been so perfectly at ease in Paragon Walk, good manners innate in his nature, even if she had frequently seen humor disconcertingly close beneath.

"No," Grandmama admitted grudgingly. "He was civil enough, but he is a foreigner. He cannot afford not to be civil. If he'd been born forty years earlier, I daresay he would have made something of himself in spite of that. There isn't even a decent war now where a man could go and prove his worth. At least there was the Crimea in Edward's time—not that he went!"

"Crimea is in the Black Sea," Charlotte pointed out. "I don't see what it has to do with us."

"You have no patriotism," Grandmama accused. "No sense of Empire! That's what is wrong with the young. You are not great!"

"Did Monsieur Alaric leave any message?" Caroline turned around at last. Her face was flushed, but her voice was perfectly steady now.

"Were you expecting one?" Grandmama squinted at her.

Caroline breathed in and out again before replying.

"Since I do not know why he called," she said, walking over to the door, "I wondered if he left some word. I think I'll go and ask Maddock." And she slipped out, leaving Charlotte and the old lady alone.

Charlotte hesitated. Should she ask the questions that were teeming in her head? The old woman's sight was poor; she had not seen Caroline's body, the rigid muscles, the slow, controlled turn of her head. Still her hearing was excellent when she chose to listen, and her mind was still as sharp and as worldly as it had ever been. But Charlotte realized that there was not anything Grandmama could tell her she had not already guessed for herself.

"I think I will go and see if Mama can spare the carriage to take me home," she said after a moment or two. "Before dark."

"As you please." Grandmama sniffed. "I don't really know what you came for—just to go calling, I suppose."

"To see Mama," Charlotte answered.

"Twice in one week?"

Charlotte was not disposed to argue. "Goodbye, Grandmama. It has been very nice to see you looking in such good health."

The old lady snorted. "Full of yourself," she said dryly.

"Never did know how to behave. Just as well you married beneath you. You'd never have done in Society."

All the way home, rolling smoothly through the streets in her father's carriage, Charlotte was too consumed by her thoughts to take proper pleasure in how much more comfortable the carriage was than the omnibus.

It was painfully apparent that Caroline's interest in Paul Alaric was not in the least casual. Charlotte could recall too many of the idiotic details of her own infatuation with her brother-in-law Dominic, before she had met Thomas, to be deceived by this. She knew just that affectation of indifference, the clenching of the stomach in spite of all one could do, the heart in the throat when his name was mentioned, when he smiled at her, when people spoke of them in the same breath. It was all incredibly silly now, and she burned with embarrassment at the memory.

But she recognized the same feeling in others when she saw it; she had seen it before for Paul Alaric, more than once. She understood Caroline's stiff back, the overly casual voice, the pretense of disinterest that was not strong enough to stop her from almost running to Maddock to find out if Alaric had left a message.

It had to be Paul Alaric's picture in the locket. No wonder Caroline wanted it back! It was not some anonymous admirer from the past, but a face that might be recognized by any resident of Rutland Place, even the bootboys and the scullery maids.

And there was no possible way she could explain it! There could be no reason but one why she should carry a locket with his picture.

By the time Charlotte reached home, she had made up her mind to tell Pitt something about it and to ask his advice, simply because she could not bear the burden alone. She did not tell him whose picture was in the locket.

"Do nothing," he said gravely. "With any luck, it has been lost in the street and has fallen down a gutter somewhere, or else it has been stolen by someone who has sold it or passed it on, and it will never be seen again in Rutland Place, or by anyone who has the faintest idea who it belonged to, or whose picture it is."

"But what about Mama?" she said urgently. "She is obviously flattered and attracted by this man, and she doesn't intend to send him away."

Pitt weighed his words carefully, watching her face. "Not for a little while, perhaps. But she will be discreet." He saw Charlotte draw breath to argue, and he closed his hand over hers. "My dear, there is nothing you can do about it, and even if there were you have no right to interfere."

"She's my mother!"

"That makes you care—but it does not give you the right to step into her affairs, which you are only guessing at."

"I saw her! Thomas, I'm perfectly capable of putting together what I saw this afternoon, the locket, and what will happen if Papa finds out!"

"Then do what you can to make sure that he doesn't. Warn her to be careful, by all means, and to forget the locket, but don't do anything more. You will only make it worse."

She stared back at him, into his light, clever eyes. This time he was wrong. He knew a lot about people in general, but she knew more about women. Caroline needed more than a warning. She needed help. And whatever Pitt said, Charlotte would have to give it.

She lowered her eyes. "I'll warn her—about pursuing the locket," she agreed.

He understood her better than she knew. He would not press her into a position where she was obliged to lie. He sat back, resigned but unhappy.

Chapter Three

Pitt was too busy with his own duties to harass his mind with anxieties over Caroline. Previous cases had led him into association with people of similar positions in Society, but the circumstances in which he had seen them had necessarily been unusual, and he was aware that these past associations gave him little real understanding of their beliefs or their values. He understood even less of what might be acceptable to them in their relationships, and what would cause irreparable harm.

Pitt felt it was dangerous for Charlotte to get mixed up in the Rutland Place thefts, but he knew that most of his reaction sprang from his emotions rather than his reason: he was afraid she would be hurt. Now that she had moved from Cater Street and left her parents' home, she had absorbed new beliefs, albeit some of them unconsciously, and she had forgotten many assumptions that used to be as natural to her as they still were to her parents. She had changed, and he was afraid that she had not realized how much—or that she had expected them to have changed also. Her loyal, fiercely compassionate, but blind interference could so easily bring pain to them all.

But he did not know how to persuade her from it. She was too close to see.

He was sitting at his brown wood desk at the police station looking at an unpromising list of stolen articles, his mind on Charlotte, when a sharp-nosed constable came in, his face pinched, eyes bright.

"Death," he said simply.

Pitt raised his head. "Indeed. Not an uncommon occurrence, unfortunately. Why does this one interest us?" His mind pictured the alleys and creaking piles of rotting timber of the rookeries, the slums that backed onto the solid and spacious houses of the respectable. People died in them every day, every hour: some died from cold, some from disease or starvation, a few from murder. Pitt could afford to concern himself only with the last, and not always with them.

"Whose?" he asked.

"Woman." The constable was as sparing with words as with his money. "Wealthy woman, good address. Married."

Pitt's interest quickened. "Murder?" he said, half hopeful, and ashamed of it. Murder was a double tragedy—not only for the victim and those who cared for her, but for the murderer also, and whoever loved or needed or pitied the tormented soul. But it was less gray, less inherently part of a problem too vast to begin, than death from street violence, or poverty, which was innate in the very pattern of the rookeries.

"Don't know." The constable's eyes never moved from Pitt's face. "Need to find out. Could be."

Pitt fixed him with a cold stare.

"Who is dead?" he demanded. "And where?"

"A Mrs. Wilhelmina Spencer-Brown," the constable answered levelly, a faint ring of anticipation in his voice at last. "Of number eleven Rutland Place."

Pitt sat up. "Did you say Rutland Place, Harris?"

"Yes, sir. Know it, do you, sir?" He added the "sir" only to keep from being impertinent; usually he did without such extra niceties, but Pitt was his superior and he wanted to work on this job. Even if it was not murder, and it probably was not, a death in Society was still a great deal more interesting than the run-of-the-mill crimes he would otherwise employ himself with. All too seldom did he find a genuine mystery.

"No," Pitt answered him dourly. "I don't." He stood up and pushed his chair back, scraping it along the floor. "But I imagine we are about to. What do you know about Mrs. Wilhelmina Spencer-Brown?"

"Not a lot." Harris fell in behind him as they collected hats, coats, and mufflers, and strode down the police station steps into the March wind.

"Well?" Pitt demanded, keeping his eye on the thoroughfare in hope of seeing an empty cab.

Harris doubled his step to keep up.

"Early thirties, very respectable, nothing said against her. Still," he said hopefully, "there wouldn't be, in that sort of address. Plenty of servants, plenty of money, by the looks. Although looks don't always mean much. Known those as had three servants, bombazine curtains, and nothing but bread and gravy on the table. All appearance."

"Did Mrs. Spencer-Brown have bombazine curtains?" Pitt inquired, moving sideways sharply as a carriage sped by him, splattering a mixture of mud and manure onto the pavement. He swore under his breath, and then yelled "Cabbie!" furiously at the top of his lungs.

Harris winced. "Don't know, sir. Only just got the report. Haven't been there myself. Do you want a cab, sir?"

"Of course I do!" Pitt glared at him. "Fool!" he muttered under his breath, then was obliged to take it back the next moment when Harris leapt into the street with alacrity and stopped a hansom almost in its tracks.

A moment later they were sitting in the warmth of the cab, moving at a sharp trot toward Rutland Place.

"How did she die?" Pitt continued.

"Poison," Harris replied.

Pitt was surprised. "How do you know?"

"Doctor said so. Doctor called us. Got one of them new machines."

"What new machines? What are you talking about?"

"Telephones, sir. Machine what hangs on the wall and—"

"I know what a telephone is!" Pitt said sharply. "So the doctor called on a telephone. Who did he call? We haven't got one!"

"Friend of his who lives just round the corner from us—a Mr. Wardley. This Mr. Wardley sent his man with the message."

"I see. And the doctor said she was poisoned?"

"Yes, sir, that was his opinion."

"Anything else?"

"Not yet, sir. Poisoned this afternoon. Parlormaid found her."

Pitt pulled out his watch. It was quarter past three o'clock.

"What time?" he asked.

"About quarter past two, or just after."

That would be when the maid went to inquire whether they would be expecting callers for tea, or if Mrs. Spencer-Brown was going out herself, Pitt thought. He knew enough about the habits of Society to be familiar with the afternoon routine.

A few moments later they were in Rutland Place, and Pitt looked with interest at the quiet, gracious façades of the houses, set back a little from the pavement, areaways immaculate, some shaded by trees, windows catching the light. A carriage was drawn up outside one, and a footman was handing a lady down, closing the door behind her. Farther along another was leaving, harness glinting in the sun. One of those houses was Caroline's. Pitt had never been there; it was a tacit understanding that such a call would be comfortable for neither the occupants nor Pitt. They met occasionally, but on neutral territory where no comparisons could be made, even though it would be the last thing either had intended.

The hansom stopped, and they climbed out and paid the fare.

"Eleven," Harris said as they mounted the step.

The door opened even before they reached it and a footman hastened them in as forcefully as was consistent with his dignity. One did not desire police to wait on the doorstep so the whole neighborhood was aware one had been obliged to call them in! It was more than his promotion was worth to be clumsy in the handling of such a matter.

"Inspector Pitt," Pitt announced himself quietly, conscious of the presence of tragedy, whatever its nature turned out to be. He was used to death, but it never failed to move him, and he still did not know what to say in the face of loss. No words could make any difference. He hated to sound trite or unfeeling, yet feared he often did, simply because he felt it from the outside. He was an intruder, a reminder of the darkest possibilities, the ugliest explanation.

"Yes, sir," the footman said formally. "You'll be wanting to speak to Dr. Mulgrew, no doubt. A carriage has been sent for Mr. Spencer-Brown, but he is not home yet."

"Do you know where he is?" Pitt asked merely as a matter of course.

"Yes, sir. He went to the city as usual. He has several interests, I believe. He is on the board of directors of a number of important business houses, and a newspaper. If you will come this way, sir, I will show you to the morning room where Dr. Mulgrew is waiting."

Pitt and Harris followed him along the hall toward the back of the house. Pitt eyed the furnishings and noted that a great deal of money had been invested in them, whether purely for appearance's sake or not. If the Spencer-Browns had any financial worries, a few of the pictures on the staircase and hall would have given them an income the like of which Pitt could have lived on for several years. He had come to be a fair judge of the price of a painting in the course of his professional connections with the art world.

The morning-room fire was banked high, and Mulgrew

stood so close to it Pitt fancied he could smell his trousers singeing in the heat. He was a stocky man with white, heavy hair and a fine white mustache. At present his eyes were watery and his nose distinctly red. He sneezed loudly as they came in, and withdrew a large handkerchief from his pocket.

"Cold," he said in completely unnecessary explanation. "Filthy thing. No cure for it. Never has been. Name's Mulgrew. I suppose you are the police?"

"Yes, sir. Inspector Pitt and Constable Harris."

"How do you do. Hate a spring cold—nothing worse, except a summer one."

"I understand the parlormaid found Mrs. Spencer-Brown dead when she came to inquire about the afternoon's arrangements?" Pitt asked. "Did the maid call you?"

"Not precisely." Mulgrew put his handkerchief away. "She told the butler, which is natural, I suppose. Butler came to look for himself, then sent the footman round for me. Only live round the corner. I came straightaway. Wasn't a thing I could do. Poor creature was stone dead. I used the telephone to call a friend of mine, William Wardley. He sent a message to you." He sneezed again and whipped out his handkerchief.

"You ought to take something for that," Pitt said, moving a step back. "Hot drink and a mustard poultice."

"No cure for it." Mulgrew shook his head and waved his hands. "No cure at all. Poison, but I can't say what yet—not for certain."

"You are quite sure?" Pitt did not want to insult him by questioning his competence too obviously. "Couldn't be any form of illness?"

Mulgrew narrowed his eyes and looked at Pitt closely.

"Couldn't take my oath on it, but don't want to wait until I can before I tell you! Too late for you to see the scene if I do! Not a fool, you know?"

Pitt found himself wanting to smile and had to force his mouth into a more appropriate expression.

"Thank you!" It seemed the most civil thing to say. "I take it you are Mrs. Spencer-Brown's regular physician?"

"Yes, naturally. That's why they called me. Perfectly

healthy woman. Usual small ailments from time to time, but then haven't we all?"

"Had she any medicine that you know of which she might have taken in excess, by accident?"

"Nothing I've given her. Only ever had the occasional cold or fit of the vapors. No cure for them, you know? Just part of life—best to put up with it gracefully. A little sympathy, if you can get it, and a good sleep."

Pitt again controlled his desire to smile at the man.

"What about anyone else in the house?" he asked.

"What? Oh. Doubt she'd be stupid enough to take anyone else's medicine. Not a silly woman, as women go! But then I suppose she could have, at that. Not a lot of sense when it comes to medicine, most people." He sneezed again, fiercely. "Gave Mr. Spencer-Brown some stuff for pain in the stomach. Though I think he brings it on himself for the most part. Tried to tell him that and got a flea in my ear for my trouble."

"Pain in his stomach?" Pitt inquired.

"Diet, mostly." Mulgrew shook his head and blew his nose. "Eats all the wrong things, no wonder it gives him a pain. He's an odd fellow—no use for that either!" He looked at Pitt out of the corner of his eye, as if waiting to be argued with.

"Quite," Pitt said. "Anything in this stuff of Mr. Spencer-Brown's that could have killed anyone if taken in excess?"

Mulgrew pulled a face. "I suppose so—if you mixed the whole lot and drank it."

"No possibility of an overdose by accident? If Mrs. Spencer-Brown had a stomach pain, for example, and thought she would relieve it by borrowing some of her husband's medicine?"

"Told him to keep it locked in his cabinet, but I suppose if he didn't, she could have taken it. Still, don't think she could take enough to kill herself by mistake."

"Instructions on the bottle?"

"Box. It's a powder. And yes, of course there are. Don't go handing out poisons willy-nilly, you know."

"Poisons?"

"Has belladonna in it."

"I see. But we don't know what she died of yet. Or at least if we do, you haven't said so?" He watched hopefully.

Mulgrew looked at him over the top of his handkerchief and blew his nose solemnly. He fished in his pocket for another and failed to find one. Pitt pulled out his own spare and soberly handed it over.

"Thank you." Mulgrew took it. "You're a gentleman. That's what makes me unhappy. Can't swear to it yet, but I've a strong suspicion it was belladonna that killed her. Looks like it. Apparently she didn't complain of feeling unwell. She had just come in from making an early call somewhere close by, and she was dead within fifteen or twenty minutes of going into the withdrawing room. All pretty sudden. No vomiting, no blood. Not much in the way of convulsions. You can see the dilated pupils, dry mouth—just what you'd expect from belladonna. Heart stops."

Suddenly the reality hit. Pitt could almost feel it himself: a woman dying alone, the tightness of breath, the pain, the world receding, leaving her to face the darkness, the paralysis, and the terror.

"Poor creature," Pitt said aloud, surprising himself.

Harris coughed in embarrassment.

Mulgrew's face softened, and a flicker of appreciation showed in his eyes as he looked at Pitt.

"Could have been suicide," he said slowly. "At least in theory. Don't know of any reason, but then one usually doesn't. God only understands what private agonies go on behind the polite faces people show. So help me, *I* don't!"

There was nothing for Pitt to say; silence was the only decent answer. He must remember to send Harris to find Mr. Spencer-Brown's medicine box and see precisely how much was gone.

"Do you want to see her?" Mulgrew asked after a moment.

"I suppose I had better," Pitt said.

Mulgrew walked slowly to the door, and Pitt and Harris

followed him out into the hall, past the footman standing gravely to attention, and into the withdrawing room, curtains drawn in acknowledgment of death.

It was a large room, with elegant, pale-covered chairs and sofas in a French style, bowed legs and lots of carved wood. There was much petit-point embroidery in evidence, artificial flowers made of silk in profuse arrangements, and some pleasant pastoral watercolors. In other circumstances, it would have been a charming, if rather overcrowded, room.

Wilhelmina Spencer-Brown was on the chaise longue, her head back, eyes wide, mouth open. There was none of the peace of sleep about her.

Pitt walked over and looked, without touching. There was no spirit left, no privacy to invade, no feelings to hurt, but still he regarded the woman as if there were. He knew nothing about her, whether she had been kind or cruel, generous or mean, brave or a coward; but for himself as much as for her, he wished to accord her some dignity.

"Have you seen all you wish?" he asked Mulgrew without turning around.

"Yes," Mulgrew replied.

Pitt eased her forward a little so she appeared to have been relaxing, folded her hands although he could not unclench them, and closed her eyes.

"She was here only fifteen or twenty minutes before the maid found her like this?" he asked.

"So she says."

"So whatever it was, it acted quickly." He turned and looked around; there was no glass or cup to be seen. "What did she eat or drink?" He frowned. "It doesn't seem to be here now. Did the maid remove anything?"

"Asked her." Mulgrew shook his head. "She says not. Doesn't seem like a flighty girl. Don't see why she should lie. Too shocked when she found her mistress dead to think of tidying up, I would imagine."

"So she didn't take it here," Pitt concluded. "Pity. That would have made it easier. Well, you'll have to do a postmortem and tell me what it was, and if possible how much, and when."

"Naturally."

Pitt looked at the body once more. There was nothing else to learn from it. There were no signs of force, but then since she had been alone he would not have expected any. She had taken the poison willingly; whether or not she had known what it was remained to be discovered.

"Let's go back to the morning room," he suggested. "I can't see anything here to help us."

Gratefully, they returned to the fire. The house was not cold, but there was a chill in the mind that communicated itself to the flesh.

"What sort of woman was she?" Pitt asked when the door was closed. "And don't hide behind professional confidences. I want to know if this was suicide, accident, or murder, and the sooner I do, with the fewest questions of the family, the easier it will be for them. And they'll have enough to bear."

Mulgrew pulled an unhappy face and blew his nose on Pitt's handkerchief.

"I can't imagine an accident," he said, staring at the floor. "Not a silly woman—very capable, in her own way, very quick, noticed things. Least absentminded woman I ever knew."

Pitt did not like the sort of question he had to ask, but there was no way to avoid it, or to make it sound any better.

"Do you know of any reason why she might have taken her own life?"

"No, or I'd have said so."

"She looks as if she was an attractive woman, feminine, delicate. Could she have had a lover?"

"I daresay, if she'd wanted one. But if you mean do I know of one, no, I don't. Never heard any gossip about her whatsoever—even in confidence." He gave Pitt a very direct look.

"What about her husband?" Pitt pressed. "Could he

have had a woman, a mistress? Could she have been driven to suicide over that?"

"Alston?" Mulgrew's eyebrows shot up in surprise at the idea. Obviously it was one he had never considered before. "I should think it highly unlikely. Bloodless sort of creature. Still—you never know—the flesh is full of surprises! Nothing odder about the human animal than his predilections in that area. I'm fifty-two years old, and I've been a doctor for twenty-seven of them. Nothing ought to surprise me—but it does!"

Other, uglier thoughts occurred to Pitt, thoughts about other men—boys, even children. Knowledge of such a thing might drive a wife to feel her life was insupportable. But that was only a wild speculation.

Then again there were other thoughts, perhaps more likely, things that Charlotte had spoken about: thefts, a sense of being watched. Could this woman have been the thief and then, when she realized the watcher knew about it, have killed herself in the face of the overwhelming shame? Society was cruel; it seldom forgave, and it never, ever forgot.

Pitt was touched by a breath of misery as cold as January sleet.

Poor woman.

If he discovered that to be the truth, he would find some way to avoid saying so.

"Don't lay too much on what I say, Inspector." Mulgrew was looking at him soberly. "I don't mean anything by it—just generalizing."

Pitt blinked. "That's all I took it for," he said carefully. "Just that nothing is certain when we come to such things."

There was a commotion out in the hall, a rising and falling of voices, and then the door burst open.

They all turned simultaneously, knowing what it was and dreading it. Only Harris stood straight up, because he knew he would not have to say anything.

Alston Spencer-Brown faced them, bristling with shock and anger.

"Who the devil are you, sir?" He glared at Pitt. "And what are you doing in my house?"

Pitt accepted the anger for what it was, but there was still no way of dealing with it that took away the hurt or the embarrassment afterward.

"Inspector Pitt," he said without pretense. "Dr. Mulgrew called me, as was his duty."

"Duty?" Alston demanded, swinging round to face Mulgrew. "I have the duty in this house, sir. It is my wife who is dead!" He swallowed. "God rest her soul. It is no concern of yours! There is nothing you can do for her now. She must have had a heart attack, poor creature. My butler tells me she had passed away before you even arrived. I cannot think why you are still here. Except perhaps as a courtesy to inform me yourself, for which I thank you. You may feel yourself released from all obligation now, both as physician and as friend. I am obliged to you."

No one moved.

"It was not her heart," Mulgrew said slowly, then sneezed and fished for a handkerchief. "At least it was, but not of itself." He blew his nose. "I'm afraid it was caused by poison."

All the color drained from Alston's face, and for a moment he swayed on his feet. Pitt believed no man could act such a total and paralyzing shock.

"Poison?" Alston spoke with difficulty. "What in heaven's name do you mean?"

"I'm sorry." Mulgrew raised his head slowly to stare at him. "I'm sorry. But she ate or drank something that poisoned her. I think either belladonna or something very like it, but I can't be sure yet. I had to call the police. I had no choice."

"That's preposterous! Mina would never have—" He was lost for words; all reason seemed to have betrayed itself and he abandoned the attempt to understand.

"Come." Mulgrew went toward him and eased him to the big, padded chair.

Pitt went to the door and called the footman for brandy. It came; Pitt poured it and gave it to Alston, who drank without taste or pleasure.

"I don't understand," he repeated. "It's ridiculous. It cannot be true!"

Pitt hated the necessity that drove him to speak.

"I presume you know of no tragedy or fear that could have driven your wife to such a state of distress," he began.

Alston stared at him.

"What are you suggesting, sir? That my wife committed suicide? How—how dare you!" His chin quivered with outrage.

Pitt lowered his voice. He could not look the man in the eyes.

"Can you imagine any circumstance in which your wife would take poison by accident, sir?" he asked.

Alston opened his mouth, then closed it again. The full implication of the question reached him. He let several moments tick by as he fought to see another answer.

"No," he said at length. "I cannot. But then neither can I conceive of any reason whatsoever why she should take it knowingly. She was a perfectly happy woman, she had everything she desired. She was an excellent wife to me, and I was happy to give her everything she wanted—comfort, a place in Society, travel when she desired it, clothes, jewels, whatever she wished. And I am a most moderate man. I have neither ill temper nor any excesses of nature. Wilhelmina was well liked and respected, as indeed she deserved to be."

"Then the answer must be in something we do not yet know." Pitt put the reasoning as gently as he could. "I hope you will understand, sir, that we must persist until we discover what that is."

"No—no, I don't understand! Why can't you let the poor woman rest in peace?" Alston sat more upright and set the brandy glass down on the table. "Nothing any of us can do can help her now. We can at least let her memory rest with dignity. In fact, I demand it!"

Pitt hated this part. He had expected it; it was natural.

It was what most people would feel and do, but that did not make it any easier. It was familiar to him: he had said his part more times than he could count, but it was always the first time for the hearer.

"I'm sorry, Mr. Spencer-Brown, but your wife died in circumstances that have not yet been explained. It may have been an accident, although, on your own word, that seems unlikely. It may have been suicide, but no one knows of a reason why she should do such a thing. It may have been murder." He looked at Alston and met his eyes. "I have to know—the law has to know."

"That is ridiculous," Alston said quietly, too appalled for anger. "Why on earth should anyone wish Mina harm?"

"I have no idea. But if anyone did, then the person must be found."

Alston stared at the empty glass in front of him. All the answers were equally impossible to him, and yet his intelligence told him one of them must be the truth.

"Very well," he said. "But I would be obliged if you would remember that we are a house in mourning, and observe whatever decencies you can. You may be accustomed to sudden death, and she was a stranger to you—but I am not, and she was my wife."

Pitt had not warmed to him instinctively—he was a fussy, deliberate little man, where Pitt was extravagant and impulsive—but there was a dignity about him that commanded respect.

"Yes, sir," Pitt said soberly. "I have seen death many times, but I hope I never find myself accepting it without shock, or a sense of grief for those who cared."

"Thank you." Alston stood up. "I presume you will wish to question the servants?"

"Yes, please."

They were duly brought in one by one, but none of them could furnish anything beyond the simple facts that Mina had arrived home on foot a few minutes after two o'clock, the footman had let her in, she had gone upstairs to her dressing room to prepare herself for the afternoon, and a little after quarter past two the parlormaid had found her dead on the chaise longue in the withdrawing room where Pitt and Mulgrew had seen her. No one knew of any reason why she should be distressed in any way, and no one knew of anyone who wished her harm. Certainly no one knew of anything she had eaten or drunk since her breakfast, which had been at midmorning—far too early for her to have ingested the poison.

When they were gone, and Harris had been dispatched to find the box of Alston's stomach medicine and to perform a routine inspection of the kitchen and other premises, Pitt turned to Mulgrew.

"Could she have taken something at whatever house she was visiting between luncheon and her return home?" he asked.

Mulgrew fished for another handkerchief.

"Depends on what it was. If I'm wrong and it wasn't belladonna, then we start all over again. But if it was, then no, I don't think so. Works pretty quickly. Can't see her taking it in another house, walking all the way back here, going upstairs, tidying herself up, coming down here, and then being taken ill. Sorry. For the time being you'd better assume she took it here."

"One of the servants?" Pitt did not believe it. "In that case it should not be hard to find which one brought her something—only why!"

"Glad it's your job, not mine." Mulgrew looked at his handkerchief with disgust, and Pitt gave him his own best one. "Thanks. What are you going to do?"

Pitt tightened his muffler and thrust his hands into his pockets.

"I'm going to pay a few calls," he said. "Harris will make arrangements to have the body removed. The police surgeon will attend the autopsy, of course. I daresay you'll need to help Mr. Spencer-Brown. He looks pretty shaken."

"Yes." Mulgrew held out his hand, and Pitt shook it.

Five minutes later he was outside in the street feeling cold and unhappy. There was only one realistic step to take now, and he could not reason himself out of it. If Charlotte was right, there was something very unpleasant going on in Rutland Place: petty theft, and perhaps some person peeping and staring with a malicious interest in the private lives of others. He could not overlook the likelihood that Mina's death was a tragic result of some part of this.

He knocked on Caroline's door with his hands shaking. There was no pleasant way of asking her the questions he had to. She would regard the questioning as intolerable prying, and the fact that it was he who was doing it would make it worse, not better.

The parlormaid did not know him.

"Yes, sir?" she said in some surprise. Gentlemen did not usually call at this hour, especially strangers, and this loose-boned, untidy creature on the step, with his wind-ruffled hair and coat done up at sixes and sevens, was certainly not expected.

"Will you please tell Mrs. Ellison that Mr. Pitt is here to see her?" He walked in past her before she had time to protest. "It is a matter of some urgency."

The name was familiar to her, but she could not immediately place it. She hesitated, uncertain whether to allow him in any farther or to call one of the menservants for help.

"Well, sir, if you please to wait in the morning room," she said dubiously.

"Certainly." He was herded obediently out of the hallway into the silence of the back room, and within moments Caroline came in, her face flushed.

"Thomas! Is something wrong with Charlotte?" she demanded. "Is she ill?"

"No! No, she is very well." He put out his hands as if to touch her in some form of reassurance, then remembered his place. "I'm afraid it is something quite different," he finished.

All the anxiety slipped away from her. Then suddenly, as if hearing a cry, it returned, and without anything said, he knew she was afraid Charlotte had told him about the locket with its betraying picture. It would have been better police work if he had allowed her to go on thinking so, since she might have made some slip, but the words came to his tongue in spite of reasoning.

"I'm afraid Mrs. Spencer-Brown has died this afternoon, and the cause is not yet apparent."

"Oh dear!" Caroline put her hand to her mouth in horror. "Oh, how dreadful! Does poor Alston—Mr. Spencer-Brown—know?"

"Yes. Are you all right?" Her face was very pale, but she seemed perfectly composed. "Would you like me to call the maid for you?"

"No, thank you." Caroline sat on the sofa. "It was very civil of you to come to tell me, Thomas. Please sit down. I dislike having to stare up at you like that—you make me feel uncomfortable." She took a breath and smoothed her skirts thoughtfully. "I presume from the fact that you are here it was not an entirely natural death? Was it an accident? Involving some kind of negligence, perhaps?"

He sat down opposite her.

"We don't know yet. But it was not a carriage accident or a fall, if that is what you mean. It appears to have been poison."

She was startled; her eyes widened in disbelief.

"Poison! That's horrible—and ridiculous! It must have been a heart attack, or a stroke or something. It's just a hysterical maid with too many penny novels in her bedroom—" She stopped, her hands clenched on her knees. "Are you trying to say it was murder, Thomas?"

"I don't know what it was. It could have been—or an accident—or suicide." He was obliged to go on. The longer he evaded it the more artificial it would seem, the more pointed. "Charlotte told me there have been a number of small thefts in the neighborhood, and that you have had the unpleasant sensation of being watched."

"Did she?" Caroline's body stiffened, and she sat upright. "I would prefer she had kept my confidence, but I suppose that is academic now. Yes, several people have

missed small articles, and if you want to chastise me about not
having called the police—"

"Not at all," he said, more sharply than he intended.
He resented the criticism of Charlotte. "But now that there
is death involved, I would like to ask your opinion as to
whether you believe it possible Mrs. Spencer-Brown could
have been the thief?"

"Mina?" Caroline opened her eyes in surprise at the
thought.

"It might be a reason why she should have killed herself," he reasoned. "If she realized it was a compulsion she
could not control."

Caroline frowned.

"I don't know what you mean—'could not control'?
Stealing is never right. I can understand people who steal
because they are in desperate poverty, but Mina had everything she needed. And anyway none of the things that are
missing are of any great value, just little things, silly things
like a handkerchief, a buttonhook, a snuffbox—why on earth
should Mina take those?"

"People sometimes take things because they cannot
help it." He knew even as he said it that explanation was
useless. Her values had been learned in the nursery where
good and evil are absolute, and although life had taught her
complexity in human relationships, the right to property was
one of the cornerstones of Society and order, the framework
for all morality, and its precepts had never been questioned.
Compulsions belonged to fear and hunger, were even accepted, if deplored, where certain appetites of the flesh were
concerned, at least in men—not in women, of course. But
compulsions of loneliness or inadequacy, frustration, or other
gray pains without names were beyond consideration, outside
the arc of thought.

"I still don't know what you mean," she said quietly.
"Perhaps Mina knew who it was who had been taking things.
She did give certain hints from time to time that she was aware
of rather more than she felt she ought to say. But surely no

one would murder just to hide a few wretched little thefts? I mean, one would certainly dismiss a servant who had stolen, but one might not prosecute because of the embarrassment—not only to oneself but to one's friends. No one wishes to have to make statements and answer questions. But where murder is concerned one has no choice—the person is hanged. The police see to it."

"If we catch them—yes." Pitt did not want to go into the morality of the penal system now. There was no possibility of their agreeing on it. They would not even be talking of the same things; their visions would be of worlds that did not meet at the fringes of the imagination. She had never seen a treadmill or a quarry, never smelled bodies crawling with lice, or sick with jail fever, or seen fingers worked to blood picking oakum—let alone the death cell and the rope.

She sank deeper into the sofa, shivering, thinking of past terrors and Sarah's death.

"I'm sorry," he said quickly, realizing where her memories were. "There is no reason yet to suppose it was murder. We must look first for reasons why she might have taken her own life. It is a delicate question to ask, but suicide is not a respecter of feelings. Do you have any idea if she had a romantic involvement of any nature that could have driven her to such despair?" At the back of his mind was beating Charlotte's conviction of the depth of Caroline's own affairs, and he felt it so loudly he almost expected Caroline to answer these thoughts instead of the rather prim words he actually spoke. He felt guilty, as if he had peeped in through someone's dressing-room window.

If Caroline was surprised, she did not show it. Perhaps she had had sufficient warning to expect such a question.

"If she had," she replied, "I certainly have heard no word of it. She must have been extraordinarily discreet! Unless—"

"What?"

"Unless it was Tormod," she said thoughtfully. "Please, Thomas, you must realize I am giving voice to things that are merely the faintest of ideas, just possibilities—no more."

"I understand that. Who is Tormod?"

"Tormod Lagarde. He lives at number three. She had known him for some years, and was certainly very fond of him."

"Is he married?"

"Oh no. He lives with his younger sister. They are orphans."

"What sort of a person is he?"

She considered for a moment before replying, weighing the kind of facts he would want to know.

"He is very handsome," she said deliberately. "In a romantic way. There is something about him that seems to be unattainable—lonely. He is just the sort of man women do fall in love with, because one can never get close enough to him to spoil the illusion. He remains forever just beyond one's reach. Amaryllis Denbigh is in love with him now, and there have been others in the past."

"And does he—" Pitt did not know how to phrase acceptably what he wanted to say.

She smiled at him, making him feel suddenly clumsy and very young.

"Not so far as I know," she answered. "And I believe if he did, I should have heard. Society is very small, you know, especially in Rutland Place."

"I see." He felt his face grow warm. "So Mrs. Spencer-Brown might have been suffering an unrequited affection?"

"Possibly."

"What do you know about Mr. Spencer-Brown?" he asked, moving on to the other major avenue for exploration. "Is he the sort of man who might have become involved with other women and caused Mrs. Spencer-Brown sufficient grief, if she discovered it, to take her own life?"

"Alston? Good gracious, no! I should find that almost impossible to believe. Of course he's pleasant enough, in his own way, but certainly not possessed of any passion to spare."

She smiled bleakly. "Poor man. I imagine he is very upset by her death—by the manner of it as much as the event. Do clear it up as soon as you can, Thomas. Suspicion and speculation hurt more deeply than I think sometimes you know."

He did not argue. Who could say how much anyone understood the endless ripples of one pain growing out of another?

"I will," he promised. "Can you tell me anything else?" He knew he ought to ask her about being watched, and whether the watcher, whoever it was, could have known about Mina and Tormod Lagarde, if there was anything to know; or if Mina was the thief. Or the other great possibility: if Mina knew who was the thief, and had been killed for it.

Or yet another thought: that Mina was the thief, and in her idle pickings had taken something so potentially dangerous for the owner that she had been killed in order to redeem it silently. Something like a locket with a telltale picture in it, or more damning than that! What else might she have stolen? Had she understood it, and tried her hand at blackmail—not necessarily for money, perhaps, but for the sheer power of it?

He looked at Caroline's smooth face with its peach-bloom cheeks, the high bones and slender throat that reminded him of Charlotte, the long, delicate hands so like hers. He could not bring himself to ask.

"No," she said candidly, unaware of the battle in him. "I'm afraid I can't, at the moment."

Again he let the opportunity go.

"If you recall anything, send a message and I'll come straightaway." He stood up. "As you say, the sooner we know the truth the less painful it will be for everyone." He walked over to the door and turned. "I don't suppose you know where Mrs. Spencer-Brown went early this afternoon? She called upon someone close by, because she walked."

Caroline's face tightened a little and she drew in her breath, knowing the meaning.

"Oh, didn't you know? She went to the Lagardes'. I was at the Charringtons' a little later and someone mentioned it—I don't remember who now."

"Thank you," he said gently. "Perhaps that explains what happened. Poor woman. And poor man. Please don't speak of it to anyone else. It would be a decency to let it pass unknown—if possible."

"Of course." She took a step toward him. "Thank you, Thomas."

Chapter Four

Charlotte was not nearly so gentle with Caroline as Pitt had been, largely because she was afraid, and the feeling was so raw and urgent inside her it overruled the caution with which her mind would otherwise have softened her words. Old memories came flooding back as if the shock and the disillusion had come yesterday. The need to protect was stronger now, though, because she could see everything so much more sharply, and this time she was on the outside, not numbed by her own emotions as she had been then.

"Mama, I think we cannot reasonably place any hope in the idea that Mina took poison by accident," she said frankly as she sat in Caroline's withdrawing room the following day. She had called as soon as she could after hearing the news from Pitt. Gossip would fly very quickly; mistakes might be made at a single encounter.

"It would be very tragic to think the poor woman was wretched enough to take her own life," she went on, "and even worse to believe someone else hated her enough to commit murder, but closing our eyes to it will not remove the truth."

"I have already told Thomas the very little I know," Caroline said unhappily. "I even made some rather wild guesses that I wish now I had not. I have probably been extremely unjust."

"And rather less than honest," Charlotte added harshly. "You told him nothing about Monsieur Alaric's picture being in your stolen locket."

Caroline froze, her fingers locked as if she had a sudden spasm; only her eyes were hot, scalding Charlotte with contempt.

"And did you?" Caroline said slowly.

Charlotte saw the anger in her, but she was too concerned with the danger to spare time for hurt.

"Of course not!" She dismissed the question without bothering to defend herself. "But that does not alter the fact that if you lost such a thing, maybe someone else did too!"

"And if they did, what has that to do with Mina's death?" Caroline was still stiff with chill.

"Oh, don't be so silly!" Charlotte exploded with exasperation. Why was Caroline being so obtuse? "If Mina were the thief, then she might have been murdered to recover the stolen article, whatever it is! And if she were the victim, maybe it was something that mattered to her so much, was so dangerous for her, that she would rather die than face having it known!"

There was silence. A pan was dropped in the scullery, and the dim echo of it penetrated the room. Very slowly the hard anger died out of Caroline's face as she understood. Charlotte watched her without speaking.

"What could there be that was worse than death?" Caroline said at last.

"That is what we need to find out." Charlotte finally relaxed her body enough to sit properly in her chair and lean against the back. "Thomas can find facts, but it may take you or me to understand them. After all, you cannot expect the police to know the feelings of someone like Mina. Something that would seem trivial to them might have been overwhelming to her."

It was not necessary to explain all the differences of class, sex, and the whole framework of customs and values that lay between Pitt and Mina. Both Charlotte and Caroline understood that all the sensitivity or imagination he was capable of would not guide him to see with Mina's eyes or recognize what it was that had accomplished her death.

"I wish I didn't have to know," Caroline said wearily, looking away from Charlotte. "I would so much rather bury her in peace. I have no curiosity. I can abide a mystery perfectly well. I have learned that one is not very often happier for having found all the answers."

Charlotte knew that at least half her mother's feeling sprang from a desire for privacy herself, the need to keep her own secrets. So much of the pleasure of a flirtation was that other people should see your conquest, and this realization added to her fear. Caroline must be very enchanted with Paul Alaric if she was content for the relationship to be unobserved. That meant it was far more than a game; there was something in it that Caroline wanted very much, something more than admiration alone.

"You cannot afford not to know!" Charlotte said sharply, wanting to shock her mother into fear acute enough to bring her to some sense. "If Mina were the thief, then she may still have your locket! When her possessions are sorted out, Alston will find it—or Thomas will!"

This had all the jarring effect she intended. Caroline's face tightened into a mask. She swallowed with difficulty.

"If Thomas finds it—" she began; and then the enormity of it hit her. "Oh, dear heaven! He might think I killed Mina! Charlotte—he couldn't think that—could he?"

The danger was too real for soft words and lies.

"I don't suppose Thomas himself would think so," she answered quietly. "But other police might. There must have been some reason why Mina died, so we had better find it first, before the locket turns up and anyone else has the chance to think anything at all."

"But what?" Caroline shut her eyes in desperation, searching blindly for some explanation in the darkness of her mind. "We don't even know if it was suicide or murder! I did tell Thomas about Tormod Lagarde."

"What about him?" Thomas had not mentioned Tormod or any possible connection.

"That Mina might have been in love with him," Caroline replied. "She definitely had an admiration for him. It could have been more than we thought. And she did go to the Lagardes' house just before she died. Perhaps she had some kind of interview with him and he rejected her in a way that she could not bear?"

The idea of a married woman finding the end of such a relationship cause for suicide disturbed Charlotte. It was frightening and pathetic in a way that repelled her, especially since she could not put Caroline and Paul Alaric from her mind. But then she did not know how disagreeable or empty the Spencer-Browns' marriage might have been. She had no right to judge. So many marriages were "appropriate"—and even those born of love could sour. She reproved herself for making too hasty a judgment, an act she despised in others.

"I suppose Eloise Lagarde might know," Charlotte said thoughtfully. "We shall have to be very tactful in inquiring. No one would wish to believe they might have been the cause, however unintentionally, of someone else's taking her own life. And Eloise is bound to protect her brother."

The hope faded from Caroline's face. "Yes. They are very close. I suppose it comes from having only each other when their parents died so young."

"There are several other possibilities," Charlotte continued. "Someone has been stealing. Perhaps they took from Mina some lover's keepsake from Tormod, and the fear that it might become public was unbearable to her. Perhaps they even went to her and threatened to give it to Alston if she did not give them money—or whatever else they wished." Her imagination went on to thoughts that might drive a person into thinking of death. "Perhaps it was another man who desired her. And that was the price of his silence."

"Charlotte!" Caroline sat bolt upright. "What a truly appalling mind you have, girl! You would never have been capable of such thoughts when you lived in my house!"

Charlotte had on her tongue a few pointed words about Caroline, Paul Alaric, and the question of morality, but she refrained from speaking them.

"Some truly appalling things happen, Mama," she said instead. "And I am a few years older than I was then."

"And you also appear to have forgotten a great deal about the sort of people we are. No man in Rutland Place would stoop to such a thing!"

"Not so openly, perhaps," Charlotte said quietly. She had her own ideas about what was done but would be called by a pleasanter name. "But he doesn't have to be one of you. Why not a footman—or even a bootboy? Can you answer for them so surely?"

"Oh, dear God! You can't be serious!"

"Why not? Might not that have been enough to make Mina, or any other woman, think of suicide? Might you not?"

"I—" Caroline stared at her. She let out her breath very slowly, as if she had given up some fight. "I don't know. I should think it is one of those things that would be so dreadful you could not know how you would feel unless it happened to you." She moved her eyes to look down at the floor. "Poor Mina. She so hated anything in the least unseemly. Something like that would have—shriveled her to the heart!"

"We don't know that that was what happened, Mama." Charlotte leaned forward and touched her. "There are other things it could have been. Perhaps Mina was the thief, and she could not face the shame of being discovered."

"Mina? Oh, surely—" Caroline began, then stopped, suspicion fighting incredulity in her face.

"Someone is," Charlotte pointed out soberly. "And

considering where the articles were stolen from, it doesn't appear that any one servant could have taken them. But some-one like Mina could!"

"But she lost something herself," Caroline argued. "A snuffbox."

"You mean she said she did," Charlotte corrected. "And it was her husband's, not hers. Surely the most intelli-gent way to direct suspicion from oneself would be to take something of your own as well? It does not take a great deal of brains to work that out."

"I suppose not. And you think this person who is watching knew about it?"

"It is a possibility."

Caroline shook her head. "I find it terribly hard to believe."

"Do you find any of it easy? Yesterday Mina was alive."

"I know! It's all so ugly and useless and stupid. Some-times it seems impossible to believe how so much can change irrevocably in a few hours."

Charlotte tried another line of thought. "Do you still have the sensation of being watched?"

Caroline looked startled. "I've no idea! I haven't even considered it. What does a Peeping Tom matter now, com-pared with Mina's death?"

"It might have something to do with it. I'm just trying to think of everything I can."

"Well, none of it seems worth anyone dying over." Caroline stood up. "I think it is time we took luncheon. I asked for it to be ready at quarter to one, and it is past that now."

Charlotte followed her obediently and they repaired to the breakfast room where the small table was set and the parlormaid ready to serve.

After the maid had gone, Charlotte began her soup, at the same time trying to recall some of the conversation that had taken place when she had met Mina a week ago. Mina had made a number of remarks about Ottilie Charrington and her death, possibly even implying that there was something mysterious about it. It was an ugly idea, but once it was in Charlotte's mind it had to be explored.

"Mama, Mina had lived here for some time, had she not?"

"Yes, several years." Caroline was surprised. "Why?"

"Then she probably knew everyone fairly well. Quite well enough that if she were the thief, and took something important, she might well understand its meaning, don't you think?"

"Such as what?"

"I don't know. Ottilie Charrington's death? She said a lot about it when she was here—almost as if she suspected there could be a secret, something the family would rather were not known."

Caroline put her soup spoon back in the bowl. "You mean that it was not natural?"

Charlotte frowned uncertainly. "Not anything quite so awful as that. But perhaps she was not as respectable as Mr. Charrington, at least, would have liked. Mina said she was very high-spirited, and definitely implied she was also indiscreet. Maybe there would have been some sort of scandal if she had not died when she did?"

Caroline started to eat again, breaking a piece of bread.

"What an unpleasant thought, but I suppose you are right," she said. "Mina did drop several hints that there was a lot more to know about Ottilie than most people realized. I never asked her, because I am so fond of Ambrosine I did not wish to encourage talk. But Mina did make me a little curious about Theodora as well, now that I come to remember."

Charlotte was puzzled. "Who is Theodora?"

"Theodora von Schenck, Amaryllis Denbigh's sister. She's a widow with two children. I don't know her very well, but I confess to liking her considerably."

Charlotte found it hard to imagine liking anyone

related to Amaryllis. "Indeed," she said, unaware how skeptical she sounded.

Caroline smiled dryly. "They are not at all alike. For a start, Theodora does not appear to have any desire to marry again, even though she has very little means, as far as anyone knows. And, of course, people do know! In fact, when she came here a few years ago, she had nothing but the house, which she inherited from her parents. Now she has a new coat with a collar and trim right down to the ground I would swear is sable! I remember when she got it that Mina remarked about it. I am ashamed of myself, but I cannot help wondering how she came by it!"

"A lover?" Charlotte suggested the obvious.

"Then she is incredibly discreet!"

"It doesn't seem very discreet to wear a sable collar out of the blue, with no explanation!" Charlotte protested. "She can hardly be naïve enough to imagine it would pass unnoticed! I would wager every woman in Rutland Place could price the garments of every other woman to within a guinea! And probably name the dressmaker who made them and the month in which they were cut!"

"Oh, Charlotte! That's unfair! We are not so—so ill-disposed or so trivial-minded as you seem to think!"

"Not ill-disposed, Mama, but practical, and with an excellent eye to value."

"I suppose so." Caroline finished the last of her soup, and the maid reappeared to serve the next dish. The two women began to eat slowly. It was a delicate fish, and extremely well cooked; at any other occasion Charlotte would have enjoyed it.

"Theodora obviously has more money now than she used to," Caroline went on reluctantly. "Mina once suggested that she did something quite appalling to earn it, but I was sure at the time that she was only being facetious. She had rather poor taste sometimes." She looked up. "Charlotte, do you think perhaps it could have been true and Mina knew something about it?"

"Perhaps." Charlotte weighed the idea. "Or perhaps on the other hand Mina was merely being spiteful—or saying something for the sake of making an effect. The stupidest stories get started that way sometimes."

"But Mina wasn't like that," Caroline argued. "She very seldom talked about other people, except as everybody does. She was much more inclined to listen."

"Then it begins to look as if it was something to do with Tormod," Charlotte reasoned. "Or some other man we don't know of yet. Or perhaps something to do with Alston that we do not know. Or else simply that she was the thief."

"Suicide?" Caroline pushed her plate away. "What a dreadful thing it is that another human being, another woman you thought of as much like yourself, only a few houses away, could be so wretched as to take her own life rather than live another day—and you know nothing about it at all. You go about your own trivial little affairs, thinking of menus and seeing that the linen is repaired, and whom to call upon, exactly as if there were nothing else to do."

Charlotte put her hand across the table to touch Caroline.

"I don't suppose you could have done anything even if you had known," she said quietly. "She gave no clue at all that she was so desperately unhappy—and one cannot intrude into everyone's business to inquire. Grief is sometimes more easily borne for being private, and a humiliation is the last thing one wishes to share. The kindest thing one can do is to affect not to have noticed."

"I suppose you're right. But I still feel guilty. There must have been something I could have done."

"Well, there isn't anything now, except speak well of her."

Caroline sighed. "I sent a letter to Alston, of course, but I feel it is too early to call upon him yet. He is bound to be very shocked. But poor Eloise is unwell also. I thought we might call there this afternoon and express our sympathy. She has taken the whole thing very badly. I think perhaps she is even more delicate than I had realized."

It was not a prospect Charlotte looked forward to, but she could see it was quite plainly a duty. And if the Lagardes had been the last people, apart from Mina's own servants, to see her alive, then perhaps something could be learned.

Charlotte was stunned when she walked behind Caroline into the Lagarde withdrawing room. Eloise looked so different from the woman she had seen the week before that for a moment she almost expected a new introduction. Eloise's face was almost colorless, and she moved so slowly she might have been fumbling in her sleep. She forced herself to smile, but it was a small gesture. Death was in the Place, and the formality of the usual pretended delight was not expected now.

"How kind of you to call," she said quietly, first to Caroline, then to Charlotte. "Please do sit, and make yourselves comfortable. It still seems to be quite cold." She had on a heavy shawl over her dress and kept it closed around her.

Charlotte sat down in a chair across the room, as far as she could get with courtesy from the fire that roared up the chimney as if it had been midwinter. It was a pleasant spring day outside, bright though not yet warm.

Caroline appeared to be at a loss for words. Perhaps her own anxieties were too pressing for her to organize her thoughts into polite remarks. Charlotte rushed in with speech before Eloise should become aware of it.

"I'm afraid summer is always longer in coming than one hopes," she said meaninglessly. "One fancies because the daylight hours are longer that the sun will be warmer, and it so seldom is."

"Yes," Eloise said, looking at the square of blue through the window. "Yes, it is easy to be deceived. It looks so bright, but one doesn't know till one is in it quite how cold it is."

Caroline recollected her manners and the purpose of their visit.

"We will not stay long," she said, "because this is not a time for social visits, but both Charlotte and I were concerned to know how you were and if there was anything we could say or do to be of comfort to you."

For a moment Eloise seemed almost not to understand her; then comprehension flooded her face.

"That is very kind of you." She smiled at them both. "I cannot think that I feel it more deeply than we all do. Poor Mina. How very suddenly the whole world can alter! One minute everything is as usual, and the next enormous and dreadful changes have taken place and are as complete as if years had gone by."

"Some changes are just the results of appalling accidents." Charlotte dared not miss an opportunity to press for knowledge; it was too important. "But others must have been growing all the time. It is just that we did not recognize them for what they were."

Eloise's eyes widened, momentarily confused, seeking to understand Charlotte's curious remark.

"What do you mean?"

"I'm not quite sure," Charlotte hedged. She must avoid seeming to pry. "Only I suppose that if poor Mrs. Spencer-Brown took her own life, then it can only have been a tragedy that had been growing, unknown to us, for some time." She had intended to be far more subtle, but Eloise was so candid herself that Charlotte could not play word games with her as she might have with someone more devious.

Eloise looked down at the folds of her skirt arranged over her knees.

"You think Mina took her own life?" She pronounced the words one by one, very clearly, weighing them. "That seems rather a cowardly thing to do. I always thought of Mina as stronger than that."

Charlotte was surprised. She had expected more pity, and more understanding.

"We don't know what pain she was faced with," she said rather less gently. "At least I don't."

"No." Eloise did not look up, a flash of contrition in her face. "I suppose we seldom even guess at anyone else's pain—how big it is, how sharp, how often it cuts." She shook her head. "But I still think that taking one's life is a kind of surrender."

"Some people grow too tired to fight anymore, or the wound is greater than they can overcome," Charlotte persisted, wondering at the back of her mind why she was defending Mina so hard. She had not especially liked her; indeed she had felt a greater warmth for Eloise.

"We do not know that poor Mina took her own life," Caroline said, intervening at last. "It may have been some sort of horrible accident. I cannot help believing that if there had been something distressing her so dreadfully, we would have been aware of it."

"I cannot agree with you, Mama," Charlotte replied. "Do you think that was what happened, Miss Lagarde? You knew her quite well, did you not?"

Eloise sat without answering for several seconds.

"I don't know. I used to think I knew all the obvious things, and heard most of the gossip one way or another, and imagined I could evaluate its worth. Now . . ." Her voice trailed away and she stood up, turning her back to them, and walked over to the garden window. "Now I realize that I knew almost nothing at all."

Charlotte was about to press her when the door opened and Tormod came in. His glance went immediately to Eloise at the window, then to Charlotte and Caroline. There was anxiety in his face, and his body was stiff.

"Good afternoon," he said politely. "How kind of you to call." His eyes went to Eloise again, dark and troubled. "I'm afraid Eloise has taken this appalling tragedy very hard. It has distressed her till she is quite unwell." There was a warning in his face to be careful, choose their words, or they might add to the burden.

Caroline murmured understandingly.

"It is a very dreadful affair," Charlotte said. "A person of sensibility would be bound to feel for everyone concerned. And I believe you were the last to see the poor woman alive."

Tormod gave her a glance of profound appreciation.

"Of course . . . and it cannot but distress poor Eloise to wonder if perhaps there might have been something we could have done. Naturally, her own servants actually—"

"Oh, servants," Charlotte said, waving them away with a little gesture of her fingers. "But that is not the same as friends, whom one might have confided in."

"Exactly!" Tormod said. "Unfortunately she did not. I really think it must have been some sort of accident, perhaps a wrong dosage of a medicine."

"Perhaps," Charlotte said doubtfully. "Of course I did not know her very well. Was she so absentminded?"

"No." Eloise turned from the window. "She always seemed to know precisely what she was doing. If she did something so fatally foolish, then she must have been very distracted in her mind, or she would have noticed immediately that she had poured from a wrong bottle, or a wrong box, and disposed of it instead of drinking it."

Tormod went to her and put his arm around her gently.

"You really must stop thinking about it, dear," he said. "There is nothing we can do for her now, and you are distressing yourself. You will make yourself ill, and that will help no one, and it will hurt me very much. Tomorrow we shall go into the country, back to Five Elms, and think of other things. The weather is improving all the time. The first daffodils will be out in the wood, and we shall take the carriage and go driving to see them—perhaps even with a picnic basket, if it is warm enough. Wouldn't you like that?"

She smiled at him, her face softening in gentle, melting pleasure, more as if she were comforting him than he supporting her.

"Yes, of course I should." She put her hand over his. "Thank you."

Tormod turned to Caroline. "It was most thoughtful of you to call, Mrs. Ellison, and you, Mrs. Pitt. We appreciate it. Such courtesies of friendship make these things easier to bear. And I am sure you must feel very shocked as well. After all, poor Mina was a friend of yours also."

"Indeed, I am completely at a loss," Caroline said a little ambiguously.

Charlotte was still pondering what she meant by that when the maid opened the door and announced Mrs. Denbigh. Amaryllis came in so close behind her there was no time to say whether the call was acceptable or not.

Eloise looked at her bleakly, almost through her. Tormod remained with his arm still around her and smiled politely.

Amaryllis' face stiffened and her round eyes were glittering sharp.

"Are you ill, Eloise?" she said with surprise, her voice ambivalent between sympathy and impatience. "If you are faint, let me help you upstairs to lie down. I have salts, if you wish?"

"No, thank you, I am not faint, but it is most civil of you to offer."

"Are you sure?" Amaryllis' eyes swept her up and down with chilly condescension. "You do not look at all well, my dear. In fact, you are really very peaked, if you do not mind my saying so. I am the last person in the world to wish my visiting you to cause you to overstrain yourself."

"I am not ill!" Eloise said a little more sharply.

Tormod's arm tightened around her almost as if he were bearing her weight, although to Charlotte she looked quite steady.

"Of course not, dear," he said. "But you have suffered a deep shock—"

"And you are not strong," Amaryllis added. "Perhaps if you send for a tisane? Shall I ring for your maid for you?"

"Thank you," Tormod accepted quickly. "That would be an excellent idea. I'm sure Mrs. Ellison and Mrs. Pitt would care for a cup of tisane as well. It is a most distressing time for all of us. You will take some refreshment, won't you?"

"Thank you," Charlotte said immediately. She was not sure what could be gained from remaining, but since she had learned nothing so far, she must at least try. "I hardly knew poor Mrs. Spencer-Brown, but I still feel most profoundly sad for her death."

"How tenderhearted of you," Amaryllis said skeptically.

Charlotte affected an air of innocence. "Do you not feel the same, Mrs. Denbigh? I am sure I can understand Miss Lagarde's emotions with the greatest of sympathy. To know you were the last person to see a friend and talk with them before such overwhelming despair of mind overtook them that they found life itself insupportable—I'm sure I also should be far from well."

Amaryllis' eyebrows rose. "Are you saying, Mrs. Pitt, that you are of the belief that Mrs. Spencer-Brown took her own life?"

"Oh dear!" Charlotte weighed all the consternation into her voice that she could contrive. "Surely you don't believe someone else—oh dear—how very dreadful!"

For once, Amaryllis was too confused for words. It was obviously the last thing she had intended to imply.

"Well, no! I mean—" she stumbled and retreated into silence, her skin flushed and her eyes cold with awareness of having been outmaneuvered.

"I hardly think that is likely," Tormod said, coming to her rescue—or was it Charlotte's? "Mina was not in the least the kind of woman to rouse such an enmity in anyone. In fact, I cannot believe she would even know a person who would conceive of such an abominable thing."

"Of course!" Amaryllis said gratefully. "I expressed myself less clearly than I should. Such a thing is unthinkable. If you had known better"—she looked meaningfully at Charlotte—"the sort of people who were her friends, then you would not have mistaken me so."

Charlotte forced a smile she did not feel. "I am sure I should not. But I am at a disadvantage, and you will have to forgive me. Did you mean that it was some kind of accident?"

Put baldly like that, the idea of having walked home and calmly taken a fatal dose of poison, by pure mischance, was so ridiculous that there was nothing Amaryllis could say.

Her round eyes looked at Charlotte with cold dislike.

"I simply do not know what happened, Mrs. Pitt. And I really think we should refrain from discussing the subject in front of poor Eloise." She let the condescension drip from her voice. "You must have appreciated that she is most delicate and suffers from a nervous and sensitive disposition. We are causing her distress by pursuing this so tastelessly. Eloise, dear." She swiveled around with a smile so glittering it sent shivers down Charlotte's spine and produced a feeling of revulsion so sharp it almost burst over into words. "Eloise, are you sure you would not care to come upstairs and rest a little? You look quite extraordinarily pale."

"Thank you," Eloise said coolly. "I do not wish to retire. I would greatly prefer to remain down here. We must share this grief together and be what comfort we can to each other."

But Tormod was not satisfied. "Here." He brushed Amaryllis aside, led Eloise to lie on the chaise longue, and lifted her feet for her. Charlotte caught a flicker of anger on Amaryllis' face so hot it would have scorched Eloise to the skin had she known of it. It gave Charlotte an acute satisfaction of which she was not proud, but she did nothing to try to rid herself of it; rather she relished it with peculiar warmth. She savored the turn of Tormod's shoulder and the soft movement of his hand as he smoothed Eloise's skirt while Amaryllis watched from behind.

The door opened and the maid came in with a tray, cups, and a hot tisane. Amaryllis set it on the table and poured some for Eloise immediately, giving it to her and passing her a cushion so that she might rest more easily.

Charlotte made some harmless observation about a social event she had read of in the London *Illustrated News*. Tormod seized on it gratefully, and after they had all drunk a little of the tisane, Charlotte and Caroline took their leave, followed by Amaryllis.

"Poor Eloise," Amaryllis said as soon as they were in the street. "She does look most poorly. I had not expected her to take it quite so badly. I have no idea what can have caused such a tragedy, but since Eloise was the last person to see poor Mina before she died, I cannot but wonder if perhaps she knows something." Her eyes widened. "Oh! Told her in the greatest of confidence, of course! Which must place her in a most dreadful dilemma, poor creature! Knowing something vital, and not being able to tell it! I should not care to be in such a position."

Charlotte had begun to wonder the same thing, especially in view of Tormod's decision to take her away from Rutland Place into the country, where Pitt could not easily question her.

"Indeed," she said noncommittally. "Confidences are always a most difficult matter when there is strong reason to believe it might be morally right to divulge what you know. The burden is even heavier if the person who entrusted you is dead, and therefore cannot release you. One cannot envy anyone so placed. If that indeed is the case. We must not leap to conclusions and risk spreading gossip." She flashed Amaryllis a freezing smile. "That would be quite irresponsible. It may simply be that Eloise is more compassionate than we are. I am very sorry, but I did not know Mrs. Spencer-Brown very well." She left the implication in the air.

Amaryllis did not miss it. "Quite. And some of us display our emotions while others prefer to keep a certain reserve—a dignity as befits the death of a friend. After all, one does not wish to become the center of attention. It is poor Mina who is dead, not one of us!"

Charlotte smiled more widely, feeling as if she were baring her teeth.

"How sensitive of you, Mrs. Denbigh. I am sure you will be a great comfort to everyone. I am charmed to have met you." They had come to Amaryllis' gateway.

"How kind," Amaryllis answered. "I'm sure I enjoyed it also." She turned and, lifting her skirts, climbed the steps.

"Charlotte!" Caroline said sharply under her breath. "Really! Sometimes I am quite embarrassed for you. I thought now that you were married you might have improved a little!"

"I have improved," Charlotte replied as she walked. "I lie much better. I used to fumble before, and now I can smile as well as anyone, and lie through my teeth. I can't bear that woman!"

"So I gathered!" Caroline said dryly.

"Neither can you."

"No, but I manage to keep it under considerably better control!"

Charlotte gave her a look that was unreadable, and stepped off the pavement to cross the road.

Then, suddenly, she noticed the lean, elegant figure of a man coming out of a gateway on the far side of the street. Even before he turned she knew him, knew the straight back, the grace of his head, the way his coat sat upon his shoulders. It was Paul Alaric, the Frenchman from Paragon Walk about whom everyone thought so much and actually knew so little.

He walked over to them easily, a half smile on his face, and raised his hat. His eyes met Charlotte's with a widening of surprise, and then a flash that might have been pleasure or amusement—or even only the courtesy of remembering a most agreeable acquaintance with whom one had shared profound emotions of danger and pity. But naturally he spoke to Caroline first, since she was the elder woman.

"Good afternoon, Mrs. Ellison." His voice was exactly as Charlotte had remembered: soft, the pronunciation exquisitely correct, more beautiful than that of most men for whom English was their mother tongue.

Caroline stood in the middle of the road, her skirt still held in her hand. She swallowed before she spoke, and her voice was rather high.

"Good afternoon, Monsieur Alaric. A very pleasant day. I don't think you have met my daughter Mrs. Pitt."

For an instant he hesitated, his eyes meeting Charlotte's very directly while a host of memories flashed through her mind—memories of fear and conflicting passions. Then he bowed very slightly, the decision made.

"How do you do, Mrs. Pitt."

"I am quite well, thank you, Monsieur," she replied

levelly. "Although I was distressed at the tragedy that has so recently happened."

"Mrs. Spencer-Brown." His face wiped clean of polite trivia and his voice dropped. "Yes. I'm afraid I can think of no answer which is not tragic. I have been struggling within myself to find any reason for such an ugly and useless thing to have happened, and I cannot."

Compulsion drove Charlotte to pursue it, even though good taste might have demanded that she say something sympathetic and change the subject.

"Then you do not think it could have been an accident?" she asked. Caroline was beside her now, and she was acutely conscious of her, of the tight muscles of her body, of her eyes fixed on Alaric's face.

There was gentleness in him, and something like a light of bitter humor, as if for a second her candor had aroused some other emotion in him.

"No, Mrs. Pitt," he said. "I wish I could. But one does not take a dose of medicine that has not been prescribed for one, nor drink from an unlabeled bottle, unless one is very foolish, and Mrs. Spencer-Brown was not foolish in the least. She was an extremely practical woman. Do you not think so, Mrs. Ellison?" He turned toward Caroline and his face softened into a smile.

The color rose up Caroline's cheeks. "Yes, yes, indeed I do. In fact, I cannot recall ever knowing of Mina doing anything—ill-considered."

Charlotte was surprised; she had not received the impression that Mina was especially intelligent. Indeed, the conversation they had had, as she recalled it, had been mostly trivial, concerned with things of the utmost unimportance.

"Really?" she said with rather more skepticism than she had intended. She did not wish to be rude. "Perhaps I did not know her well enough. But I would have thought it quite possible her mind could have been occupied with some other concern, and she might have made an error."

"You are confusing intelligence with common sense, Charlotte," Caroline said spiritedly. "Mina was not fond of study, nor did she concern herself with some of the very odd affairs that you do." She was too discreet to name them, but a slight lowering of her eyelids and a sidelong glance made Charlotte decide that she was referring to her political convictions with regard to Reform Bills in Parliament, Poor Laws, and the like. "But she was well aware of her own skills," Caroline continued, "and how best to use them. And she had far too much native wit to make mistakes—of any sort. Do you not think so, Monsieur Alaric?"

He glanced down the street over their shoulders into some distance they could not see before turning to face Charlotte.

"We are looking for a genteel way of saying that Mrs. Spencer-Brown had a very fine instinct for survival, Mrs. Pitt," he replied. "She knew the rules, she knew what could be said and what could not—what could be done. She was never careless, never moved by passion before sense. She did appear trivial on occasion, because that is the socially acceptable way. To talk intelligently of serious subjects is not considered attractive in a woman." He smiled fleetingly; Caroline could not know they had talked before. "At least not by most men. But underneath the prattle Mina was a skilled and prudent woman, who knew precisely what she wanted and what she could have."

Charlotte stared at him, trying to control her thoughts.

"You make that sound a little sinister," she said slowly. "Calculating?"

Caroline took her arm. "Nonsense. One has to use some sense in order to survive! Monsieur Alaric means only that she was not flighty, the sort of silly creature who does not take any care what she is doing. Is that not so?" She looked at him, her face glowing in the cool air, her eyes bright. Charlotte was surprised—and jarringly afraid—to see how lovely she still was. The color, the brilliance, the blood under the skin had nothing to do with the March wind; it was the presence of this man, with his dark head and strong, straight back, standing in the road talking gently about death, and his pity for the tragedy around it.

"Then I fear it may have been suicide!" Charlotte said suddenly and rather loudly. "Perhaps the poor woman got herself into an affair of the heart, became involved with someone other than her husband, and the situation was unbearable to her. I can see very easily how that could happen." She did not have the boldness to look at either of them, and there was absolute silence in the street, not even the sound of a bird or of distant hooves.

"Such adventures very often end in disaster," she continued after a harsh breath. "Of one sort or another. Maybe she preferred death to the scandal that might have accompanied such a thing becoming public!"

Caroline stood frozen.

"Do you think either she, or any man, would allow such a matter to become public?" Alaric asked with an expression Charlotte could not fathom.

"I have no idea," she said with defiance she instantly regretted, but she plunged on. He had always had the ability to make her speak incautiously. "Perhaps an indiscreet letter, or a love token? People who are infatuated are often very foolish, even normally sensible people!"

Caroline was so rigid Charlotte could feel her behind her shoulder like a column of ice.

"You are right," Caroline said in a low voice. "But death seems a terrible price to pay for such a folly."

"It is!" For the first time Charlotte looked fully at her; then she turned to Alaric and found his eyes dark and bright, and unreadable, but understanding her as clearly as if they could see inside her head.

"But then when we embark on such affaires," Charlotte continued with a tightening of her throat, "we seldom see the price at the end until it is time to pay." She swallowed and suddenly tried to sound light, as if it were all just speculation, and nothing to do with anything real. "At least so I have observed." Surely he must also be remembering Paragon Walk and their first meeting? Did he still live there now?

His face relaxed fractionally and his lips moved in the smallest smile. "Let us hope we are wrong and there is some less desperate explanation. I would not care to think of any-one suffering so."

She recalled herself. All that was long past. "Nor I. And I am sure you would not either, Mama." She closed her hand over Caroline's. "We had better be returning home, now that we have paid our duty calls. Papa will be expecting us for tea."

Caroline opened her mouth as if to speak, then closed it again; but even so Charlotte had to pull her.

"Good day, Monsieur Alaric," Charlotte said briskly. "I am delighted to have made your acquaintance."

He bowed and raised his hat.

"And I yours, Mrs. Pitt. Good afternoon, Mrs. Ellison."

"Good afternoon, Monsieur Alaric."

They walked a few paces, Charlotte still pulling Caro-line uncomfortably by the arm.

"Charlotte, I despair of you sometimes!" Caroline shut her eyes to block out the scene.

"Do you!" Charlotte said tartly without relaxing her pace. "Mama, there is no need for a great deal of words between us that will only hurt. We understand each other. And you do not need to tell me that Papa is not at home either. I know that."

Caroline did not reply. The wind was sharper and she tucked her head down into her collar.

Charlotte knew she had been abrupt, even cruel, but she was very badly frightened. Paul Alaric was not some light affaire, a man full of pretty phrases and little gestures to please, a taste of romance to brighten the monotony of a thirty-year marriage. He was hard and real; there was power in him and emotion, a suggestion of things beyond reach, exciting and perhaps infinitely beautiful. Charlotte herself was still tingling from the meeting.

Chapter Five

Charlotte did not tell Pitt of her feelings regarding Paul Alaric and Caroline, or indeed that he was someone she had known previously; in fact, she could not have put it into words had she desired to. The encounter had left her more confused than ever. She remembered the heat of emotion and the jealousies he had engendered in Paragon Walk, the disquiet he had awoken even in her. She could understand Caroline's infatuation easily. Alaric was far more than merely charming, a handsome face upon which to build a dream; he had a power to surprise, to disturb, and to remain in the memory long after parting. It would be blind to dismiss him as a flirtation that would wear itself out.

She could not explain it to Pitt, and she did not wish to have to try.

But of course she had to tell him that Tormod and Eloise Lagarde planned to leave Rutland Place the following day, so that if he wished to speak to them about Mina's death, he would have to do so immediately.

Since they had been the last people he knew of to see

Mina alive, there was a great deal Pitt wished to ask them, although he had not yet formed in his mind any satisfactory way of wording his thoughts, which were still confused, conscious only of unexplained tragedy. But chance allowed him no time to juggle with polite sympathies and suggestions. At quarter past nine, the earliest time at which it would be remotely civil to call, he was on the icy doorstep facing a startled footman, whose tie sat askew and whose polished boots were marred with mud.

"Yes, sir?" the man said, his mouth hanging open.

"Inspector Pitt," Pitt said. "May I speak with Mr. Lagarde, if you please? And then with Miss Lagarde when it is convenient?"

"It ain't convenient." In his consternation the footman forgot the grammar the butler had been at pains to instill in him. "They're going down to the country today. They ain't—they is not receiving no one. Miss Lagarde aren't well."

"I'm very sorry Miss Lagarde is unwell," Pitt said, refusing to be edged off the step. "But I am from the police, and I am obliged to make inquiries about the death of Mrs. Spencer-Brown, who I believe was known to Mr. and Miss Lagarde quite closely. I am sure they would wish to be of every assistance they could."

"Oh! Well—" The footman had obviously not foreseen this situation, nor had the butler prepared him for anything of this sort.

"Perhaps it would be less conspicuous for me to wait somewhere other than on the doorstep," Pitt said, glancing back into the street with the implicit suggestion that the rest of the Place knew his identity, and therefore his business.

"Oh!" The footman realized the impending catastrophe. "Of course, you'd best come into the morning room. There's no fire there—" Then he recollected that Pitt was the police, and explanations, let alone fires, were unnecessary for such persons. "You just wait in there." He opened the door and watched Pitt go in. "I'll tell the master you're here. Now don't you go a-wandering around! I'll come back and tell you what's what!"

Pitt smiled to himself as the door closed. He bore no rancor. He knew the boy's job depended on his proper observance of social niceties, and that an irritable butler, ill-served, could cost him very dear. There would be no recourse, no opportunity for explanations, and little tolerance of mistakes. To have the police in the house was most unfortunate, but to keep them at the front door arguing for all the world to see would be unpardonable. Pitt had seen a good deal of life belowstairs, beginning with his own parents' experience when his father had been gamekeeper on a large country estate. As a boy, Pitt had run through the house with the master's son, an only child glad of any playmate. Pitt had been quick to learn, to ape the manners and the speech, and to copy the school lessons. He knew the rules on both sides of the green baize door.

Tormod came quickly. Pitt had barely had time to look at the gentle landscape paintings on the walls and the old rosewood desk with its marquetry inlays before he heard the step on the polished floor outside the room.

Tormod was rather what he had expected: broad-shouldered, wearing a beautifully cut coat, his collar a little high. He had dark hair swept back from a broad white brow and a full mouth with a wide lower lip.

"Pitt?" he said formally. "Don't know what I can tell you. I really haven't the faintest idea what can have happened to poor Mina—Mrs. Spencer-Brown. If she had any anxiety or fear, unfortunately she did not confide it to either my sister or myself."

It was a blank wall, and Pitt had no idea how he was going to make the slightest impression on it. Yet this was the only human clue he had.

"But she did call on you that last day, and left within an hour or so of her death?" he said quietly. His mind was racing, searching for something pertinent to ask, anything that might crack the smooth composure and reveal a hint of the passion that must have been there—unless it really had been only a chance and ridiculous accident.

"Oh, yes," Tormod said with a rueful little shrug. "But

even with the wisdom of hindsight, I still cannot think of anything she said which would point to why she should take her own life. She seemed quite composed and in normally good spirits. I have been trying to think what we talked of, but only commonplaces come back to me." He looked at Pitt with a half smile. "Fashion, menus for the dinner table, some silly Society jokes—all the most ordinary things one talks about when one is passing the time and has nothing real to say. Pleasant, but one only partially listens."

Pitt knew the type of conversation perfectly well. Life was full of just such pointless exchanges. The fact that one spoke was what mattered; the words were immaterial. Could it really be that Mina had had no idea whatsoever that she had less than an hour left to live? Had accident occurred like lightning out of a still sky? No storm, no rumble of far thunder, no oppression mounting before? Murder was not like that. Even a lunatic had reasons for killing: insanity built its slow heat like spring thawing the long winter snows, till suddenly the one more gallon became too much and the dams burst with wild, destructive violence.

But Pitt had seen death caused by madmen, and they did not use poison—not on a woman alone in her own withdrawing room, neatly laid on the chaise longue.

If this was murder, it was perfectly sane—and there was sane reason behind it.

"I wonder," he said aloud, reverting back to the subject. "Could Mrs. Spencer-Brown have had some trouble on her mind and desired to confide it to you but, when faced with the necessity of expressing it in words, have found herself unable to? Might she have spoken only of commonplaces for just that reason?"

Tormod appeared to consider the possibility, his eyes blank as he examined his memory.

"I suppose so," he said at last. "I don't believe it myself. She did not seem other than her usual self. I mean, she was not agitated, as far as I can recall, or unconcerned with the conversation, as one might be if one were seeking an opportunity to speak of something else."

"But you said yourself that you were only half listening," Pitt pointed out.

Tormod smiled, pulling his face into a comic line.

"Well"—he stretched his hands out, palms up—"who listens to every word of women's conversation? To tell the truth, I had intended to be out, but my plans had been canceled at the last moment, or I should not even have been at home. One has to be civil, but how interested can one be in what color Lady Whoever wore to the ball or what Mrs. So-and-So said at the soirée? It's women's concern. I just didn't feel that it was anything different from usual. I heard no change of tone, caught nothing of anxiety—that's what I mean."

Pitt could only sympathize. It must have required hard discipline to remain courteous throughout. Only the rigid doctrine of good manners above all—from nanny's knee, through tutors and public school—had instilled a pattern of self-control that would allow Tormod to do so with apparent grace. All the same, Pitt took the opportunity it gave him.

"Then perhaps your sister may have observed something, heard some nuance that only a woman would understand?" he asked quickly.

Tormod raised his eyebrows a little, whether at the suggestion or at Pitt's use of words.

He hesitated. "I would rather you did not trouble her, Inspector," he said slowly. "The death has been a severe shock to her. In fact, I am taking her away from Rutland Place for a little while, to recover. The associations are most unpleasant. My sister and I are orphans. Death has hit us hard in the past, and I'm afraid Eloise still finds it difficult to bear. I suppose it may be that Mina did confide something to her that day. I was not present all the time. It may be that Eloise feels she should have understood how desperate the poor woman was, and done something, and that grieves her additionally. Although, in truth, if someone is determined to take their own life, one cannot do anything to prevent them—only put off the time of the inevitable."

Then he brightened. "I'll tell you what—I shall ask

Eloise. She will confide in me if there is anything—that I promise you—and I shall report it to you if it has any bearing whatsoever on Mina's death. Will you accept that? I'm sure you would not wish to distress anyone more than is absolutely necessary."

Pitt was torn. He remembered all the white, stricken faces he had ever seen of people who had encountered death, especially sudden and violent death. Those faces came back to him each time it occurred again: the surprise, the hurt, the slow acceptance that one cannot evade truth as the shock wears off and the reality remains, like growing cold, creeping deeper and deeper.

But he could not afford to let Tormod Lagarde make his judgments for him.

"No, I'm afraid that won't do."

He saw Tormod's face change, the mouth set hard and the eyes chill.

"I'm quite happy that you should be present," Pitt continued without changing his own expression or his voice. A smile remained fixed on his lips. "In fact, if you prefer to ask her yourself, I'm quite agreeable. I understand your concern that she should not be harassed or reminded of other tragedies. But since I know facts that you cannot know about Mrs. Spencer-Brown's death, I must hear Miss Lagarde's answers for myself, and not as you interpret them to me with the best intention in the world."

Tormod met his eyes, stared at him for a few moments in surprise, then took a step backward and, with a swing of his arm, reached for the bell rope.

"Ask Miss Lagarde to come into the morning room, will you Bevan?" he said when the butler appeared.

"Thank you," Pitt said, acknowledging the concession.

Tormod did not reply, turning instead to look out of the window at the gray drizzle that was beginning to thicken the air and dull the outlines of the houses across the Place. The laurel leaves outside hung glistening drops from their points.

When Eloise arrived, she was pale but perfectly composed. She kept her shawl close around her, and met Pitt's gaze candidly.

As soon as the door opened, Tormod went to her, putting his arm around her shoulders.

"Eloise, darling, Inspector Pitt has to ask you some questions about poor Mina. I'm sure you understand that since we were the last people to see her, he feels we may know something of her state of mind just before she died."

"Of course," Eloise said calmly. She sat down on the sofa and regarded Pitt steadily, only the bare interest of courtesy in her face. The reality of death was seemingly greater than any curiosity.

"There's no need to be afraid," Tormod said to her gently.

"Afraid?" She seemed surprised. "I'm not afraid." She lifted her head to look at Pitt. "But I don't think I can tell you anything that is of value."

Tormod glanced at him warningly, then back at Eloise.

"Do you remember I left you for a while?" he asked her, his voice very soft, almost as if encouraging a child. "You had been speaking of little things until then—fashion and gossip. Did she confide any other matter to you when you were alone? Anything of the heart? A love, or a fear? Perhaps someone she was becoming fond of?"

Eloise's mouth moved in a fraction of a smile. "If you mean did she love someone other than her husband," she said without expression in her voice, "I have no reason to think so. She certainly did not speak of it to me—then or at any other time. I'm not sure if she believed in love of the storybook kind. She believed in passions—lust and pity, and loneliness—but they are quite different things, not really love. They pass when the hunger is satisfied, or the need for pity removed—or when one grows exhausted with loneliness. These things are not love."

"Eloise!" Tormod's arm tightened around her and his hand held the flesh of her arm so hard it made white marks on her skin that Pitt could see even through the muslin of her dress. "I'm so sorry!" His voice was soft, a whisper. "I had no idea Mina would speak of such things to you or I would never have left you alone with her." He swung around to stare at Pitt. "There's your answer, Inspector! Mrs. Spencer-Brown was a woman who was disillusioned in some tragic way, and she wished to unburden herself of it to someone. Unfortunately she chose my sister, an unmarried girl—which I find hard to forgive, except that she must have been desperate! God have pity on her!

"Now I think you have learned enough from us. I'm taking Eloise away from here, away from Rutland Place, until the worst of the shock is over, and she can rest in the country and put this from her mind. I don't know what Mrs. Spencer-Brown indicated to her about her private agonies, but I will not permit you to press her any further. It is obviously a—an intimate and extremely painful subject. I trust you are gentleman sufficient to understand that?"

"Tormod—" Eloise began.

"No, my dear, the Inspector can discover whatever else he needs to know in some other fashion. Poor Mina seems unquestionably to have taken her own life. There was nothing you could have done about it, and I will not have you blame yourself in any way at all! We may never know what it was that she could no longer bear, and perhaps it is better that we should not. A person's most terrible griefs should be buried decently with them. There are things that lie so close to the heart of a person, every decency of man or God demands they remain private!" He lifted his head and glared at Pitt, defying him to contend.

Pitt looked at them sitting side by side on the sofa. He would get nothing more from Eloise, and in truth he was inclined to agree that Mina's suffering, whatever it was, deserved to be buried with her, not turned over, weighed, and measured by other hands, even the impersonal ones of the police.

He stood up. "Quite," he said succinctly. "Once I am sure that it was simply a tragedy and there has been no crime, even of negligence, then it would be far better if we all left the matter to be forgotten in kinder memories."

Tormod relaxed, his shoulders easing, the fabric of his coat falling back to its natural lines. He stood up also and extended his hand, holding Pitt's in a hard grip.

"I'm glad you see it so. Good day to you, Inspector."

"Good day, Mr. Lagarde." Pitt turned a little. "Miss Lagarde. I hope your stay in the country is pleasant."

She smiled at him with uncertainty, something that struck her with doubt, even a presage of fear.

"Thank you," she said in little more than a whisper.

Outside in the street Pitt walked slowly along, trying to compose his thoughts. Everything so far indicated some private grief, nursed to herself, that had finally overwhelmed Mina Spencer-Brown and driven her to take, quite deliberately, an overdose of something she already possessed. Probably it would prove to be her husband's medicine containing the belladonna, which Dr. Mulgrew had spoken of.

But before he allowed it to rest, he must ask the other women who had known her. If anyone was aware of her secret, it would be one of them, either from some imparted confidence or merely from observation. He had learned how much a relatively idle woman could perceive in others simply because she had no business and few duties to occupy her. People were her whole concern: relationships, secrets, those to be told and those to be kept.

He called on Ambrosine Charrington first, because she was the farthest away and he wanted to walk. In spite of the thickening rain he was not yet ready to face anyone else. Once, he even stopped altogether as a ginger cat stalked across the footpath in front of him, shook himself in disgust at the wet, and slipped into the shelter of the shrubbery. Perhaps, Pitt thought, he should not disturb the slow settling of grief. Maybe it was no subject for police, and he should go now, turn and walk away, catch the omnibus back to the police station, and deal with some theft or forgery until Mulgrew and the police surgeon put in their reports.

Still thinking about it, without having consciously made any decision, he began to walk again. The rain was gathering in vehemence and ran in cold streaks inside his collar and down his flesh, making him shudder. He was glad to reach the Charringtons' doorstep.

The butler received him with faint displeasure, as if he were a stray driven in by the inclement weather rather than a person who had any place there. Pitt considered the hair plastered over his forehead, the wet trousers flapping around his ankles, and the one bootlace broken, and decided that the butler's look of disapproval was not unwarranted.

Pitt forced himself to smile. "Inspector Pitt, from the police," he announced.

"Indeed!" The butler's look of polite patience vanished like sun behind a cloud.

"I would like to see Mrs. Charrington, if you please," Pitt continued. "It is with regard to the death of Mrs. Spencer-Brown."

"I don't believe—" the butler began, then looked more closely at Pitt's face and realized protestations were only going to prolong the interview, not end it. "If you come into the morning room, I will see if Mrs. Charrington is at home." It was a fiction Pitt was well used to. It would be discourteous to say, "I will ask her if she will see you," although he had been told so bluntly often enough.

He had barely sat down when the butler returned to escort him to the withdrawing room, where there was a fine fire dancing in the grate and three bowls of flowers in jardinières by the wall.

Ambrosine sat bolt upright on a green brocade love seat and looked Pitt over from hair to boots with interest.

"Good morning, Inspector. Do be good enough to sit down and remove your coat. You seem more than a little wet."

He obeyed with pleasure, handing the offending garment to the butler, then arranging himself in an armchair so as to absorb the full benefit of the fire.

"Thank you, ma'am," he said with feeling.

The butler retired, closing the door behind him, and Ambrosine raised her fine eyebrows.

"I am told you are inquiring into poor Mrs. Spencer-Brown's death," she said. "I am afraid I know nothing whatsoever of interest. In fact, how little I know is quite amazing in itself. I would have expected to hear something. One has to be remarkably clever to keep a secret in Society, you know. There are many things that are not spoken of which would be in unforgivable taste to mention, but you will usually find that people know, all the same. There is a certain smugness in the face!" She looked at him to see if he understood, and was evidently satisfied that he did. "It is infinitely pleasing to know secrets, especially when others are aware that you do—and they do not."

She frowned. "But I have not observed this attitude lately in anyone but Mina herself! And I never really knew whether she had any great knowledge or merely wished us to think so!"

He was equally puzzled. "Do you not think that someone might be prepared to speak now that a death is involved," he said, "to avoid misunderstandings, and perhaps even injustice?"

She gave a weary little smile. "What an optimist you are, Inspector. You make me feel very old—or at least as if you must be very young. Death is the very best excuse of all to hide things forever. Few people have the least objection to injustice—the world is run on it. And, after all, it is part of the creed: *'De mortuis nil nisi bonum.'* "

He waited for her to explain, although he thought he knew what she meant.

" 'Speak no ill of the dead,' " she said bleakly. "Of course I mean Society's creed, not the Church's. A very charitable idea, at first glance, but it leaves all the weight of the blame upon the living—which, of course, is what it is designed to do. Whoever took any joy from hunting a dead fox?"

"The blame for what?" he asked her soberly, forcing himself not to be diverted from the issue of Mina.

"That depends upon whom we are discussing," she replied. "In the case of Mina, I really do not know. It is a field in which I would have expected you to be far more knowledgeable than I. Why are you concerned in the matter at all? To die is not a crime. Of course I appreciate that to kill oneself is—but since it is obviously quite unprosecutable, I fail to see your involvement."

"My only interest is to make certain that that is what it is," he answered. "A matter of her having taken her own life. No one appears to know of any reason whatsoever why she should have done so."

"No," she said thoughtfully. "We know so little about each other, I sometimes wonder if we even know why we do the important things. I don't suppose it is the reason that appears—like money, or love."

"Mrs. Spencer-Brown seems to have been very well provided for." He tried a more direct approach. "Do you suppose it could have been anything to do with an affaire of love?"

Her mouth quivered with a suppressed smile.

"How delicate of you, Inspector. I have no idea about that, either. I'm sorry. If she had a lover, then she was more discreet than I gave her credit for."

"Perhaps she loved someone who did not return her feelings?" he suggested.

"Possibly. But if all the people who ever did were to kill themselves, half of London would be occupied burying the other half!" She dismissed it with a lift of her fingers. "Mina was not a melancholy romantic, you know. She was a highly practical person, and fully acquainted with the realities of life. And she was thirty-five, not eighteen!"

"People of thirty-five can fall in love." He smiled very slightly.

She looked him up and down, judging him correctly to within a year.

"Of course they can," she agreed, with the shadow of an answering smile. "People can fall in love at any age at all. But at thirty-five they have probably had the experience several times before and do not mistake it for the end of the world when it goes amiss."

"Then why do you think Mrs. Spencer-Brown killed

herself, Mrs. Charrington?" He surprised himself by being so candid.

"I? You really wish for my opinion, Inspector?"

"I do."

"I am disinclined to believe that she did. Mina was far too practical not to find some way out of whatever misfortune she had got herself into. She was not an emotional woman, and I never knew anyone less hysterical."

"An accident?"

"Not of her making. I should think an idiotic maid moved bottles or boxes, or mixed two things together to save room and created a poison by mistake. I daresay you will never find out, unless your policeman removed all the containers in the house before the servants had any opportunity to destroy or empty them. If I were you, I shouldn't worry myself—there is nothing whatsoever you can do about it, either to undo it or to prevent it happening again somewhere else, to somebody else."

"A domestic accident?"

"I would think so. If you had ever been responsible for the running of a large house, Inspector, you would know what extraordinary things can happen. If you were aware what some cooks do, and what other strange bodies find their way into the larder, I daresay you would never eat again!"

He stood up, concealing an unseemly impulse to laugh that welled up inside him. There was something in her he liked enormously.

"Thank you, ma'am. If that is indeed what happened, then I expect you are right—I shall never know."

She rang the bell for the butler to show Pitt out.

"It is one of the marks of wisdom to learn to leave alone that which you cannot help," she said gently. "You will do more harm than good threshing all the fine chaff to discover a grain of truth. A lot of people will be frightened, perhaps made unemployable in the future, and you will still not have helped anyone."

* * *

He called on Theodora von Schenck and found her an utterly different kind of woman: handsome in her own way, but entirely lacking the aristocratic beauty of Ambrosine or the ethereal delicacy of Eloise. But more surprising than her appearance was the fact that, like Charlotte, she was busy with quite ordinary household chores. When Pitt arrived, she was counting linen and sorting into a pile the things that required mending or replacement. In fact, she did not seem to be ashamed that she had put some aside to be cut down into smaller articles, such as pillowcases from worn sheets, and linen cloths for drying and polishing from those pieces that were smaller or more worn.

However, for all her frankness, she was unable to offer him any assistance about the reasons for Mina's death. She found the idea of suicide pitiful, expressing her sorrow that anyone should reach such depths of despair, but she did not deny that sometimes it did happen. On the other hand, since she had not known Mina well, she was aware of nothing at all to bring her to such a state. Theodora herself was a widow with two children, which reduced her social connections considerably, and she preferred to devote her time to her home and children rather than making social calls or attending soirées and such functions; therefore she heard little gossip.

Pitt left no wiser, and certainly no happier. If he could feel certain that there was some unresolved tragedy, as Tormod Lagarde had seemed convinced, then he would be satisfied to leave it decently alone. On the other hand, Ambrosine Charrington had been sure that such a thing was utterly out of character. If it had been some preposterous accident, should he persist until he had done all he could to discover precisely what? Did he owe it to Mina herself? To be buried in a suicide's grave was a disgrace, a stigma not easy to bear for her survivors. And did he perhaps owe it to Alston Spencer-Brown to show him that his wife had not been so unhappy as to prefer death to life? Might not Spencer-Brown go on torturing himself with hurt and confusion in the belief that she had loved someone else and found life insupportable without him? And other people—would they believe something secret and perhaps obscure about Alston that had driven his wife to such an end?

Was it possible that no matter how ugly, or how expensive, the facts were better? The truth deals only one wound, but suspicions a thousand.

Because Theodora had mentioned that Amaryllis and she were sisters, Amaryllis Denbigh was a complete surprise to Pitt. Without giving it conscious thought, he had been expecting someone similar, and it was a faintly unpleasant readjustment to meet a woman younger, not only in years but jarringly so in fashion, manner, and deportment.

She met him with cool civility, but the spark of interest was in her eyes and in the suppressed tightness of her body. He never for a moment feared that she might decline to talk. There was something hungry in her, something seeking, and yet at the same time contemptuous of him. She had not forgotten that he was a policeman.

"Of course I understand your situation, Inspector—Pitt?" She sat down and arranged her skirts with white fingers that stroked the silk delicately; he could almost feel its rippling softness himself, as if it slid cool beneath his own skin.

"Thank you, ma'am." He eased himself into the chair across the small table from her.

"You are obliged to satisfy yourself that there has been no wrong done," she reasoned. "And naturally that requires you to discover the truth. I wish I could be of more assistance to you." Her eyes did not leave his face, and he had the feeling she knew every line of it, every shade. "But I fear I know very little." She smiled coolly. "I have only impressions, and it would be less than fair to represent them as facts."

"I sympathize." He found the words hard to say, for no reason that he could frame. He made an effort to concentrate his mind upon Mina, and his reason for being here. "Yet if anyone had known facts, surely they would have prevented the tragedy? It is precisely because there are only impressions and understandings that have come with the wisdom of hindsight that these things occur so startlingly, and we are left with mysteries and perhaps unjust beliefs." He hoped he was not being sententious, but he was trying to follow her own line of reasoning and convince her to speak. He believed he could judge what to trust and what to discard as malicious or unrelated.

"I had not thought of it like that." Her eyes were round and blue and very direct. She must have looked much like this in feature and expression when she was still in pigtails and dresses to her knees: the same frankness, the same slightly bold interest, the same softness of cheek and throat. "Of course you are quite right!"

"Then perhaps you would be kind enough to tell me of your impressions?" he invited, disliking himself for it even as he spoke. He despised the sort of mischievous speculation that he was encouraging—indeed would listen to with the same eagerness as a gossip selecting dirt to relish and refine before whispering it with laughter and deprecation to the next hungry ear.

She was too subtle to excuse herself again; to do so would imply she needed excuse. Instead she fixed her eyes on a bowl of flowers on a side table against the wall and began to speak.

"Of course Mina—that is, Mrs. Spencer-Brown—was very fond of Mr. Lagarde, as I expect you know." She did not look back at him. The temptation was there; he saw it in the tightening of her neck, but she resisted it. "I do not, for one moment, mean to imply anything improper. But there are always people who will misunderstand even the most innocent of friendships. I have wondered once or twice if there was someone who so misunderstood Mina's regard, and perhaps was caused great unhappiness by it."

"Such as who?" he asked, a little surprised. It was a possibility he had not thought of: a simple misunderstanding leading to jealousy. He had only considered an unrequited love.

"Well, I suppose the obvious answer is Mr. Spencer-Brown," she replied, facing him at last. "But then the truth is not always the obvious, is it?"

"No," he agreed hastily. "But if not him, then who?"

She breathed a deep sigh and appeared to reflect for a few moments.

"I really don't know!" She lifted her head suddenly as if she had newly made up her mind about something. "I imagine it is possible—" She stopped. "Well, all sorts of other things—other people? I know Inigo Charrington was very attached to Eloise at one time. She would not even consider him. I've no idea why! He seems pleasing enough, but to her it was as if he did not exist in that sense. She was civil enough to him, naturally. But then one is!"

"I don't see what that has to do with Mrs. Spencer-Brown's death," he said frankly.

"No." She gave him a wide, blue look. "Neither do I. I expect it has nothing at all. I am only seeking possibilities, people who might have said something at one time or another which could have given rise to misunderstanding. I did tell you, Inspector, that I knew nothing! You asked me for my impressions."

"And your impression is that Mrs. Spencer-Brown was in normally good spirits as far as you knew?" Without intending to, he had used Tormod's words.

"Oh yes. If something happened to distress her, it must have occurred quite suddenly, without any warning. Maybe she learned something appalling?" Again her eyes were wide and round.

"Mr. Lagarde says she was not at all upset when she left his house," he pointed out. "And from the hour her servants have reported, it appears she went straight home."

"Then perhaps she met someone in the street? Or there was a letter waiting for her when she arrived?"

A letter was something that had not occurred to him. He should have asked the servants if there had been any messages. Perhaps Harris had thought of it.

It was too late to cover his mistake; she had seen it in his face. Her smile became surer.

"If she destroyed it, as indeed would be the natural thing," she said softly, "then we shall never know what it contained. And perhaps that is best, do you not think?"

"Not if it was blackmail, ma'am!" he said tartly; he was angry with himself, and with her for seeing what he had not, and for the feeling he had that it amused her.

"Blackmail!" She looked startled. "What a terrible idea! I can hardly bear to think you are right. Poor Mina! Poor, poor woman." She took a deep breath and tightened her fingers on the silk across her thighs, clasping till the knuckles shone pale. "But I suppose you know more about these things than we do. It would be childish to close one's eyes. The truth will not go away for ignoring it, or we could get rid of everything unpleasant simply by refusing to look at it. You must have patience with us, Inspector, if we see only reluctantly, and more slowly than we should. We have been used to the easier things in life, and such ugliness cannot always be acknowledged without a little period of adjustment. Perhaps even some force?"

He knew what she said was true, and his reason applauded her. Perhaps he had been unfair in his judgment. Prejudice was not confined to the privileged. He knew it in himself: the bitter aftertaste of opinions forced back and found unjust, formed in envy or fear, and the need to rationalize hate.

"Of course." He stood up. He wanted no more of the interview. She had already given him more than enough to consider. And he had mentioned blackmail rather to shock her than because he really thought it a possibility. Now he was obliged to recognize it. "As yet I know of no truth, pleasant or unpleasant, so the less that is said the less pain that will be caused. It may well have been no more than a tragic accident."

Her face was quite calm, almost serene, with its pink and white coloring and girlish lines.

"I do hope so. Anything else will increase the distress for everyone. Good day to you, Inspector."

"Good day, Mrs. Denbigh."

He had put the matter out of his mind and was working on a number of fires, two of which were in his area and were probably arson, when at half past four in the afternoon a constable with black hair plastered neatly to his head with water knocked on his door and announced that there was a visitor, a gentleman of quality.

"Who is it?" Pitt was expecting no one, and his immediate thought was that the man had been misdirected from the Chief Superintendent's office and they would be able to be rid of him with a few words of assistance.

"A Mr. Charrington, sir," the constable answered. "A Mr. Lovell Charrington, of Rutland Place."

Pitt put the paper he was reading aside, facedown, on the desk.

"Ask him to come in," he said with a feeling of misgiving. He could imagine no reason at all why Lovell Charrington should come to the police station, unless it was to impart something both secret and urgent. Regarding any ordinary event, he could either have sent for Pitt to attend upon him or simply waited until he returned in the ordinary course of the investigation.

Lovell Charrington came in with his hat still on, beaded with rain, and his umbrella folded but untied, hanging from his hand. His face was pale, and there was a drop of water on the end of his nose.

Pitt stood up. "Good afternoon, sir. What can I do for you?"

"You are Inspector Pitt, I believe?" Lovell said stiffly. Pitt had the impression that he did not mean to be rude, simply that he was awkward, torn between desire to say something difficult for him and a natural revulsion at the place. Almost certainly he had never been inside a police station before, and horrifying ideas of sin and squalor were burning in his imagination.

"Yes, sir." Pitt tried to help him. "Would you like to sit down?" He indicated the hard-backed wooden chair to one side of the desk. "Is it something to do with the death of Mrs. Spencer-Brown?"

Lovell sat reluctantly. "Yes. Yes, I have been—considering—weighing in my mind whether it was correct that I should speak to you or not." It was remarkable how he managed to look alarmed and faintly pompous at the same time—like a rooster that has caught itself crowing loudly at high noon: acutely self-conscious. "One desires to do one's duty, however painful!" He fixed Pitt with a solemn stare.

Pitt was embarrassed for him. He cleared his throat and tried to think of something harmless to say that did not stick in his mouth with hypocrisy.

"Of course," he answered. "Not always easy."

"Quite." Lovell coughed. "Quite so."

"What is it you wish to say, Mr. Charrington?"

Lovell coughed again and fished in his pocket for a handkerchief.

"You have quite the wrong word. I do not *wish* to say it, Inspector; I feel an obligation, which is quite different!"

"Indeed." Pitt breathed out patiently. "Of course it is. Excuse my clumsiness. What is it you feel that we should know?"

"Mrs. Spencer-Brown . . ." Lovell sniffed and kept the handkerchief knotted up in his fingers for a moment before folding it and replacing it in his pocket. "Mrs. Spencer-Brown was not a happy woman, Inspector. Indeed I would go so far as to say, speaking frankly, that she was somewhat neurotic!" He spoke the word as if it were faintly obscene, something to be kept between men.

Pitt was startled, and he had difficulty in preventing its showing in his face. Everyone else had said the opposite, that Mina was unusually pragmatic, adjusted very precisely to reality.

"Indeed?" He was aware of repeating himself, but he was confused. "What makes you say that, Mr. Charrington?"

"What? Oh—well, for goodness' sake, man." Now Lovell showed impatience. "I've had years of observing the woman. Live in the same street, you know. Friend of my wife. Been in her house and had her in mine. Know her husband, poor man. Very unstable woman, given to strong emotional fancies. Lot of women are, of course. I accept that, it's in their nature."

Pitt had found most women, especially in Society, to have fancies of an astoundingly practical nature, and to be most excellently equipped to distinguish reality from romance. It was men who married a pretty face or a flattering tongue. Women—and Charlotte had showed him a number of examples—far more often chose a pleasant nature and a healthy pocket.

"Romance?" Pitt said, blinking.

"Quite," Lovell said. "Quite so. Live in daydreams, not used to the harsh facts of life. Not suited for it. Different from men. Poor Mina Spencer-Brown conceived a romantic attachment for young Tormod Lagarde. He is a decent man, of course, upright! Knew she was a married woman, and years older than he is into the bargain—"

"I thought she was about thirty-five?" Pitt interrupted.

"So she was, I believe." Lovell's eyes opened wide and sharp. "Good heavens, man, Lagarde is only twenty-eight. Be looking for a girl of nineteen or twenty when he decides to marry. Far more suitable. Don't want a woman set in her ways—no chance to correct her then. One must guide a woman, you know, mold her character the right way! Anyhow, all that's beside the point. Mrs. Spencer-Brown was already married. Stands to reason she realized she was making a fool of herself, and was afraid her husband would find out—and she couldn't bear it anymore." He cleared his throat. "Had to tell you. Damned unpleasant, but can't have you nosing around asking questions and raising suspicions against innocent people. Most unfortunate, the whole affair. Pathetic. Great deal of suffering. Poor woman. Very foolish, but terrible price to pay. Nothing good about it." He sniffed very slightly and dabbed at his nose.

"There very seldom is," Pitt said dryly. "How do you come to know about this affection of Mrs. Spencer-Brown's for Mr. Lagarde, sir?"

"What?"

Pitt repeated the question.

Lovell's face soured sharply.

"That is a highly indelicate question, Inspector—er—Pitt!"

"I am obliged to ask it, sir." Pitt controlled himself with difficulty; he wanted to shake this man out of his narrow, idiotic little shell—and yet part of him knew it would be useless and cruel.

"I observed it, of course!" Lovell snapped. "I have already told you that I have known Mrs. Spencer-Brown for several years. I have seen her over a vast number of social occasions. Do you think I go around with my eyes closed?"

Pitt avoided the question. "Has anyone else remarked this—affection, Mr. Charrington?" he asked instead.

"If no one else has spoken of it to you, Inspector, it is out of delicacy, not ignorance. One does not discuss other people's affairs, especially painful ones, with strangers." A small muscle twitched in his cheek. "I dislike intensely having to tell you myself, but I recognize it as my duty to save any further distress among those who are still living. I had hoped you would understand and appreciate that! I am sorry I appear to have been mistaken." He stood up and hitched the shoulders straight on his jacket by pulling on both lapels. "I trust, however, that you will still comprehend and fulfill your own responsibility in the matter?"

"I hope so, sir." Pitt pushed his chair back and stood up also. "Constable McInnes will show you out. Thank you for coming, and being so frank."

He was still sitting looking at the closed door, the reports of the arson untouched and facedown, when Constable McInnes returned twenty minutes later.

"What is it?" Pitt said irritably. Charrington had disconcerted him. What he had said about Mina jarred against everything else he had heard. Certainly Caroline had told him of the affection for Tormod Lagarde, but hand in hand with the conviction that Mina was unusually levelheaded. Now Charrington said she was flighty and romantic.

"Well, what is it?" he demanded again.

"The reports from the doctor, sir." McInnes held out several sheets of paper.

"Doctor?" For a moment Pitt could not think what he meant.

"On Mrs. Spencer-Brown, sir. She died of poisoning. Of belladonna, sir—a right mass of it."

"You read the report?" Pitt said, stating the obvious.

McInnes colored pink. "I just glanced at it, sir. Interested, like—because . . ." He tailed off, unable to think of a good excuse.

Pitt held out his hand for it. "Thank you." He looked down and his eye traveled over the copperplate writing quickly. On examination, it had proved that Wilhelmina Spencer-Brown had died of heart failure, owing to a massive dose of belladonna, which, since she had not eaten since a light breakfast, appeared to have been consumed in some ginger-flavored tonic cordial, the only substance in the stomach at the time of death.

Harris had taken the box of medicinal powder supplied to Alston Spencer-Brown by Dr. Mulgrew, and it was still three-quarters full. The total amount absent, including the dosages Spencer-Brown said he had taken, was considerably less than that recovered in the autopsy.

Whatever had killed Mina was not a dose of medicine, taken either accidentally or by her own intention. It came from some other, unknown source.

Chapter Six

Charlotte spent a miserable day turning over in her mind what she should do about Caroline and Paul Alaric. Three times she decided quite definitely that it was not so very serious and she would do best to take Pitt's advice and leave it alone. Caroline would not thank her for interfering, and Charlotte might only cause them both embarrassment, and make the whole matter seem more than it really was.

And then four times she remembered Caroline's face, with the high glow in her skin, the tautness of her body, and the little gulp of excitement as she had spoken to Paul Alaric in the street. And she could still picture him perfectly herself, looking elegant and standing very straight, his eyes clear, his voice soft. She had another vivid recollection of his speech, his diction casually perfect, each consonant distinct, as if he had thought of everything before he spoke and had intended it exactly as it came.

Yes, quite definitely, she must do something, and quickly—unless it was too late even now!

She had already baked a complete batch of bread without any salt, and had hurt Gracie's feelings by telling her to do the kitchen floor when she had just finished it. Now it was three in the afternoon, and she had turned one of Pitt's shirt collars and stitched it back the same way it had been in the first place.

She tore it out crossly, using a few words she would have been ashamed to have had overheard, and decided to write to her sister Emily immediately and request that she call upon her as soon as she received the letter, whether it was convenient or not. Emily, who had married Lord Ashworth at just about the time Charlotte had married Pitt, might well have to cancel some interesting social engagement without notice; the journey itself, however, would simply be a matter of calling the carriage and stepping in. And Charlotte had gone to Emily quickly enough when that dreadful business had happened in Paragon Walk when Emily was expecting her baby. It was indelicate to remind her of it, but at the moment she could not afford polite invitations.

She found notepaper and wrote:

> Dear Emily,
> I have been calling upon Mama more frequently in the last two weeks, and something quite appalling has happened which may hurt her irreparably if we do not step in and take some action to prevent it. I would prefer not to put it into writing, as it is a long and complicated affair. I feel I must explain it to you in person, and ask your advice as to what we may do before a tragedy occurs and it is too late to do anything!
> I know that you are busy, but new events have transpired which make it urgent that we act without delay. Therefore please cancel any plans you may have and call upon me as soon as you receive this. We both know from the past in Paragon Walk, and other places, that when disaster strikes it does not wait upon the decent end of soirées and other such enjoyments.
> There has already been one death.
>
> Your loving sister,
> Charlotte.

She folded it up, put it into an envelope, and addressed it to Lady Ashworth, Paragon Walk, London, and sent Gracie to put it in the postbox immediately.

She had exaggerated, and she knew it. Emily might well be angry, even accuse her of lying by implication. There was no reason whatever to suppose that Mina's death had anything to do with Caroline, or that Caroline herself was in any danger.

But if she had simply written that Caroline was running grave risk of making a fool of herself over a man, even Paul Alaric, it would have little effect. Of course, if their father found out it would hurt him deeply—he would be quite unable to understand. The fact that he had in times past taken at least one romance considerably further would be to him completely different. What was acceptable for a man to do, providing he was discreet, had nothing whatsoever to do with what that same man's wife might do. And, to be honest, Caroline was not even being particularly discreet! All of which would not fetch Emily in any haste, simply because she would not believe it.

Whereas mention of death, and a rather unsubtle reminder of the hideous events at Paragon Walk, would almost certainly bring her as fast as her carriage could negotiate the streets.

And indeed it did. Emily knocked very sharply on the front door before noon the following day.

Charlotte opened it herself.

Emily looked elegant, even at that hour, her fair hair swept fashionably high under a delicious hat, and a dress of the limpid shade of green that suited her best.

She pushed her way in past Charlotte and marched down to the kitchen, where Gracie bobbed a quick curtsy and fled upstairs to tidy the nursery.

"Well?" Emily demanded. "What on earth has happened? For goodness' sake, tell me!"

Charlotte was genuinely pleased to see her; it had been some little while since they had spent any time together. She put her arms around her in a swift hug.

Emily responded warmly but with impatience.

"What has happened?" she repeated urgently. "Who is dead? How? And what has it to do with Mama?"

"Sit down." Charlotte pointed to one of the kitchen chairs. "It's quite a long story, and it won't make a lot of sense unless I tell it from the beginning. Would you like some luncheon?"

"If you insist. But tell me who is dead, before I explode! And what has it to do with Mama? From the way you wrote, she is in danger herself."

"A woman called Mina Spencer-Brown is dead. At first it looked like suicide, but now Thomas says it is almost certainly murder. I have onion soup—would you like some?"

"No, I would not! Whatever possessed you to cook onion soup?"

"I felt like it. I've wanted onion soup for days now."

Emily regarded her with a look of pain.

"If you had to have a craving because of your condition, couldn't you have made it for something a little more civilized? Really, Charlotte! Onions! They are socially impossible! Where on earth can we go calling after onion soup?"

"I can't help it. At least they are not out of season, or ridiculously expensive. You can afford to have a craving for fresh apricots or pheasant under glass if you wish, but I cannot."

Emily's face tightened. "Who is Mina Spencer-Brown? And what has she to do with Mama? Charlotte, if you have got me here simply because you want to meddle in one of Thomas' cases"—she took a deep breath and pulled a face—"I would love to have an excuse to interfere! Murder is much more exciting than Society, even if it terrifies me sick at times and makes me weep because the solution is always so wretchedly sad." She clenched her fist on the table. "I do think you might have told me the truth, instead of a pack of silly stories about Mama. I put off a really rather good luncheon to come here. And you offer me boiled onion soup!"

Memories flickered through Charlotte's mind for a moment: the terrible corpse in the closed garden in Callander

Square; and standing side by side with Emily, paralyzed with fright, when Paul Alaric found them at the end of the murders in Paragon Walk. Then she remembered the present again, and all the tingle and beating of the blood vanished.

"It is to do with Mama," she said soberly. She served the soup and bread and sat down. "It will need salting. I forgot. Do you recall Monsieur Alaric?"

"Don't be a fool!" Emily said with raised eyebrows. She reached for the salt and sprinkled a little. "How could I possibly forget him—even if he were not still my neighbor? He is one of the most charming men I have ever met. He can converse upon almost any subject as if he were interested. Why on earth does Society consider it fashionable to affect to be bored? It is really very tedious." She smiled. "You know, I never really knew if he was aware quite how fascinated we all were by him, did you? How much do you think it was merely the challenge of his being a mystery, and that each of us wished to outdo the other by winning his attentions?"

"Only partly." Charlotte had him so clearly in her mind even now, here in her own kitchen, it had to be something more than that. "He was able to laugh at us and yet at the same time make us believe that he liked us."

"Indeed?" Emily's eyes widened and her delicate nose flared a little. "I find that a most infuriating mixture. And I am perfectly sure that Selena at least desired of him a great deal more than simply to be 'liked'! Friendship does not arouse that kind of excitement and discomfort in anyone!"

"He has become acquainted with Mama." Charlotte hoped for a considerable reaction from Emily. She was disappointed: Emily was not interested.

"This soup is really rather nice with salt in it," she remarked with surprise. "But I shall have to sit at the far side of the room and shout at everyone. You might have thought of that! What if Mama has met Monsieur Alaric? Society is very small."

"Mama carries a picture of him in her locket."

That had the desired effect. Emily dropped her spoon and stared, appalled.

"What did you say? I don't believe it! She couldn't be so—so idiotic!"

"She was."

Emily shut her eyes in relief. "But she stopped!"

"No. The locket was lost—probably stolen. A lot of small things have been stolen from around Rutland Place—a silver buttonhook, a gold chain, a snuffbox."

"But that's awful!" Emily's eyes were wide and dark with anguish. "Charlotte, it's simply dreadful! I know the servant problem is bad, but this is preposterous. One owes it to one's friends to see at least that they are honest. What if someone finds this locket? And knows it is Mama's with that—Frenchman—in it! What would they say? What would Papa think?"

"Exactly," Charlotte said. "And now Mina Spencer-Brown is dead—probably murdered—almost next door to Mama. But she still doesn't mean to stop seeing him. I've tried to dissuade her, and it has been exactly as if she had not heard me."

"Haven't you pointed out to her—" Emily began incredulously.

"Of course I have!" Charlotte cut her off before she could finish. "But did you ever take any notice of advice when you were in love?"

Emily's face fell. "Don't be ridiculous! What on earth do you mean, 'in love'? Mama is fifty-two! And she is married—"

"That's just years," Charlotte said sharply, waving away the unimportance of time with her soup spoon. "I don't suppose one feels any different. And to imagine that being married prevents you from falling in love is too naïve for words. If you are going to grasp at Society with both hands, Emily, at least practice some of its realism as well as its sophistry and silly manners!"

Emily shut her eyes and pushed her soup dish away.

"Charlotte, it's awful!" she said in a tight, pained voice. "It would be total disaster. Have you any idea what happens to a woman who is known to be—without morals? Oh, it might be all right if it were with some earl or duke or something, and one was important enough oneself—but for someone like Mama—never! Papa could even divorce her! Oh, dear heaven! It would be the end for all of us. I should never be received anywhere again!"

"Is that all you care about?" Charlotte said furiously. "Being invited out? Can't you think about Mama? And how do you imagine Papa would feel? Not to mention whatever it is that has happened to Mina Spencer-Brown!"

Emily's face was white, anger lost in a sudden sense of shame for her own thoughts.

"You can't possibly think Mama had anything to do with murder," she said, lowering her voice considerably. "That's inconceivable."

"Of course I don't," Charlotte said. "But it's perfectly conceivable, even probable, that the murder had something to do with the thefts. And that isn't all. Mama said she has had the feeling for some time that someone has been watching her, spying on her. That could have something to do with the murder as well."

Two spots of color appeared in Emily's cheeks.

"Why didn't you tell me about this before?" Her indignation was back again, embarrassment forgotten. "You should have sent for me straightaway. I don't care how clever you think you are, you should not have tried it on your own. Look what a mess you have let it grow into! You have an overblown opinion of yourself, Charlotte. Just because you have stumbled on the truth in one or two of Thomas' cases, you think you are so clever nobody can deceive you. And look what you have allowed to happen now!"

"I didn't know it was murder until the day before I wrote to you." Charlotte kept her temper with difficulty. She knew Emily was frightened, and she was also aware at the back of her mind that perhaps she had been a little overconfident of her own abilities. It might really have been better if she had called Emily sooner, at least about Caroline and Paul Alaric.

Emily reached for her soup dish again.

"This is cold. I don't know why you can't have a craving

for something reasonable, like pickles. When I was carrying, I wanted strawberry jam. I had it with everything. Will you add some more hot from the pan to this, please?"

Charlotte stood up and ladled out some for both of them. She put Emily's in front of her, then sat down to her own.

"What shall we do?" she asked quietly.

Emily looked back at her, all the anger evaporated. She was aware of her own selfishness, but it was unnecessary for either of them that she should say so.

"Well, we had better go immediately, this afternoon, and persuade Mama of the danger she is in, and stop her from seeing Monsieur Alaric again—except in the most casual way, as it is unavoidable, of course. We do not want to be obvious. It would occasion talk. Then in case it has anything to do with the thefts, and somebody has this wretched locket, we had better see if we can find out who killed the woman—Spencer-Brown. I have enough money. I can buy the locket back if it is blackmail."

Charlotte was surprised. "Would you do that?"

Emily's blue eyes widened. "Of course I would! We should buy back the locket first, then call in the police. It wouldn't matter what they said afterwards—without the locket, nobody would believe them. They would only damn themselves the further for malice. We would destroy the picture, and Mama would deny it. Monsieur Alaric would hardly contradict! Even if he is foreign, he is most certainly a gentleman." A shadow passed over Emily's face. "Unless, of course, it was he who killed Mrs. Spencer-Brown."

That Paul Alaric could be the murderer was an idea peculiarly repugnant to Charlotte. She had never really thought of him in that light, even in Paragon Walk, and it was sharp and ugly to do so now.

"Oh, I don't think it could be he!" she said involuntarily.

Emily's stare was very straight. "Why not?"

Then perception flashed across her face. She knew her sister too well for comfort; indeed she had always had a disconcertingly acute judgment of most people, both about what they wanted and, even more uncomfortably, why they wanted it. It was a facility, coupled with a sharp realism in her desires and the restraint to keep a still tongue in her head, that had led to her considerable success in Society. Charlotte had far more imagination, but it lacked a bridle. She failed to take account of social conventions, and therefore many of the motives of others eluded her. It was only when the darker, more elemental and tragic passions were involved that she understood instinctively, and often with a sharp and painful wave of pity.

"Why not?" Emily repeated, finishing her soup. "Do you think that because he is handsome he is therefore decent? Don't be such a child! You ought to know better than to imagine that simply because someone is attractive he is not capable of the most facile and disgusting things as well. Handsome people are often extremely selfish. To be able to charm others is very dangerous to the character. It comes as a shock, sometimes an unacceptable one, to find there is something you want and you may not have it. He would not be the first simply to take it! If he has been brought up to believe he has only to smile and people will do as he wishes— For heaven's sake, Charlotte, remember Selena! She was totally spoiled by having been told she was a beauty!"

"You don't need to belabor the point," Charlotte interrupted her angrily. "I understand you perfectly. I have met spoiled people too! And I have not forgotten how everyone twittered over Monsieur Alaric. He had only to show up and half the women in the Walk made fools of themselves!"

Emily gave her a dry look, her own memories less than entirely comfortable.

"Then you had better put on your best dress, and we shall go and call on Mama right away," she said briskly. "Before she goes out, or receives anyone else. We can hardly say what we have to unless we are alone."

Caroline received them with surprise and delight.
"My dears, how marvelous! Do come in and sit down.

How wonderful to see you both!" She was dressed in the softest lavender-pink dress, high to the throat, with a fichu of lace falling gently. At any other time Charlotte would have envied her it; a gown like that would have suited her wonderfully and, far more important than the mere look of it, would have made her feel beautiful. Now all she could think of was how flushed Caroline was, how gaiety and even excitement bubbled just beneath the surface.

She glanced across at Emily and saw the chill of shock in her eyes.

"Emily, do sit over here where I can see you," Caroline said cheerfully. "You haven't been here for ages—at least it seems like ages. It is far too early for tea, and I suppose you have had luncheon already?"

"Onion soup," Emily said with a little wrinkle of her nose.

Caroline's face fell. "Oh, my dear! Whatever for?"

Emily reached for her bag, opened it, and took out her perfume. She touched herself liberally with it and then offered it to Charlotte.

"Mama, Charlotte tells me you have had some tragic happenings here lately," she began, ignoring the question of the soup. "I'm so sorry. I wish you had written me. I would like to have been here to offer some comfort to you."

Considering how radiant Caroline looked, the remark seemed somewhat misplaced. Charlotte had never seen anyone less distressed.

Caroline recollected herself rapidly. "Oh yes, Mina Spencer-Brown. Very sad indeed—in fact, quite tragic. I cannot think what drove her to it. I wish I had been able to help. I feel awfully guilty, but I had no idea at all there was anything wrong."

Charlotte was conscious of the minutes ticking away, mindful that early callers might come at any time after three.

"She didn't kill herself," she said brutally. "She was murdered."

There was total silence. The light died from Caroline's

face, and her body hunched into itself; suddenly she looked thinner.

"Murdered?" She repeated the word. "How could you know? Are you trying to frighten me, Charlotte?"

It was precisely what she was trying to do, but to admit it would rob at least half its effect.

"Thomas told me, of course," she answered. "She died of belladonna poisoning, but the dose was far more than there had been in the house. It must have come from somewhere outside. No one else would give her poison for her to kill herself, so it can only have been murder, can't it?"

"I don't understand." Caroline shook her head. "Why should anyone kill Mina? She did no harm to anyone. She didn't have any money to leave, nor was she in line to inherit anything, so far as I know." There was confusion in her face. "It doesn't make any sense. Alston is the last sort of man to—to be having an affair with another woman and wish to— No, it's ridiculous!" Her voice regained its conviction and she looked up. "Thomas must have made a mistake— there is another explanation. We simply have not found it yet." She sat a little straighter in her chair. "She must have brought it from somewhere. I'm sure if he looks—"

"Thomas is an excellent policeman and he does not make mistakes," Emily said, to Charlotte's amazement. It was a very sweeping statement, and less than true, but Emily continued regardless: "He will have thought of all those things. If he says it is murder, then it is! We had best face it, and conduct ourselves accordingly." She opened her eyes wide and stared at Caroline, then shifted them a little, unable to look at her and deal the final blow. "And of course that means police all over the place, investigating everything and everyone! There won't be any secrets left in the entire neighborhood."

Caroline did not immediately understand. She saw the unpleasantness of it; indeed she could hardly have forgotten Cater Street, and she saw the dangers to those closely involved with Mina, but not her own peril.

Emily sat back, her face tight with pity, feeling a sense of guilt because she did not intend to be the one hurt.

"Mama," she said slowly, "Charlotte says you have lost a pendant, and that it is of such a nature that you would prefer, if you were not the one to find it, that it was not found at all. This is a time when the utmost discretion is necessary. Even quite innocent acts can look very odd if they become public and everyone in Society begins to discuss them. Stories frequently grow in the telling, you know."

They always grow in the telling, Charlotte thought miserably, and almost without exception for the worse—unless, of course, one is telling them oneself! She wondered now if she had done the right thing in bringing Emily here. She might have said the same things herself, but sitting and looking on, listening, it sounded so much harsher than she would have wished. Indeed it had a ring of selfishness to it, as if it were Emily's reputation that was the first fear and Charlotte were merely self-righteous and inquisitive, carried away with her own imagination of herself as a detective.

They had not been very subtle.

She looked across at Emily and saw the pink in her skin, warm even up to her eyes, and she knew that Emily was suddenly conscious of it too.

Charlotte leaned forward and clasped Caroline's hands. They were stiff, and she made no effort to respond.

"Mama!" Charlotte said. "We must find out all we can about Mina's death, so that the investigation can be over with before there is time for Thomas, or anyone else, to start thinking about other people's lives! She must have been killed for some reason—either love or hate, jealousy, greed—something!" She let out her breath in a sharp little noise. "Or most probably fear. Mina was clever, you said that. She was worldly wise, she observed a lot. Maybe she knew something about somebody that was worth killing to hide. There is a thief here, that is inescapable. Perhaps Mina knew who the thief was and was foolish enough to let the person see that she knew. Or maybe she was the thief herself and stole something someone would kill to retrieve."

Emily rushed in, glad to have something practical to say to overlay the emotions. "For goodness' sake, hasn't Thomas searched the house? He should have thought of that! It's simple enough!"

"Of course he has!" Charlotte snapped, then realized how her voice sounded. She did not need to defend Thomas; Emily thought well enough of him and, in her own way, liked him considerably. "They didn't find anything," she continued. "At least not anything they could understand to be important. But if we ask questions and investigate a little, we may perceive things that they could not. People are not going to tell the police more than they can help, are they?"

"Of course not!" Emily said eagerly. "But they will talk to us! And we can hear things Thomas would not—inflections, lies—because we know the people. That's quite definitely what we must do! Mama, we shall come calling with you this afternoon, immediately! Where shall we begin?"

Caroline smiled bleakly. There was no point in fighting.

"With Alston Spencer-Brown," Charlotte replied for her. "We shall express our deepest sympathy and shock. It would be quite appropriate. We will be overcome with the tragedy and not able to think of anything else."

"Of course," Emily said, standing up and pulling her skirt into the order she wished it. "I am quite desolated."

"You didn't even know her!" Caroline pointed out.

Emily looked at her coolly.

"One must be practical, Mama. I have met her at several soirées. I was most fond of her. Indeed I am convinced we were just at the beginning of a long and intimate friendship. He is not to know the difference. What did she look like? I will appear foolish if I do not recognize a portrait or a photograph. Although I could always say I was shortsighted— But I don't wish to do that. Then I should have to fall over things to make it seem true."

Caroline shut her eyes and put her fingers wearily over them.

"She was about your height," she said, "but very slender, almost thin, and she had a very long neck. She looked younger than she was. She was fair, with an excellent complexion."

"What about her features, and her hair?"

"Oh, she had regular enough features—a little small, perhaps? And very soft hair, sort of light mouse. She was really quite charming, when she chose. And she dressed excellently, nearly always in pale shades, especially creams. Very clever of her. It gave her an air of delicate innocence that appeals to men."

"Good," Emily said. "Then we are ready to go. We don't want to be there with a whole lot of other people. We must not stay too long or we will make him suspicious, but we must see him alone. Goodness! I hope he is receiving? He hasn't taken to his bed or anything?"

"I don't think so." Caroline stood up reluctantly. "I suppose I would have heard if he had. Servants always talk."

Charlotte saw the hesitation in her, the desire even now to escape the necessity.

"You must come, Mama. We can hardly go alone. It would be most awkward. You are the only one who knows him."

"I am coming," Caroline said wearily. "But I won't pretend I wish to. This whole thing is horribly ugly, and I wish we had nothing to do with it. I wish it had been suicide and we could let her rest in peace—be sorry, but not keep on thinking about it."

"I daresay!" Emily said a little sharply. "But we can't. And if we wish to have an acceptable outcome to the affair, then we must make it for ourselves! Charlotte is perfectly right."

Charlotte resented the implication that the whole thing was her idea, but there was nothing to be gained by arguing now. She followed them out obediently.

Alston Spencer-Brown received them in a traditionally darkened room. All the blinds were drawn halfway down the windows, and there was black crêpe around the mirror, several of the photographs, and on the piano. He himself was dressed in the soberest clothes, the only touch of relief the white of his shirt.

"How kind of you to call," he said in a small voice. He looked stunned, shorter and narrower than Charlotte had imagined him.

"The least we could do," Caroline murmured unhappily as they accepted the seats he offered. "We were very fond of Mina."

Alston looked a little questioningly at Emily, obviously not sure who she was or why she was there.

Emily lied without blinking an eye; she was very good at it.

"Indeed we were," she said with a sad smile. "Very fond. I met her at several soirées and she was quite charming. We were just getting to know one another and found we had so much in common. She was such a discerning person."

"Indeed she was," Alston said with a lift of surprise that Emily should have noticed. "A most perceptive woman."

"Exactly." Emily put a wealth of understanding into the word. "She saw so much that passed by other, less sensitive people."

"Do you think so?" Charlotte looked from one to the other of them.

"Oh yes." Alston nodded. "I'm afraid poor Mina was frequently too astute for her own happiness. She was able to see in others traits and qualities that were not always attractive." He shook his head. "Not always to their credit." He sighed heavily and stared from Emily to Caroline, and back again. "I daresay you observed that yourselves?"

"Of course." Emily sat straight-backed, rather prim. "But one cannot help a certain"—she hesitated delicately—"wisdom in the ways of the world if one has the intelligence to possess it. I'm sure I never heard Mina speak ill of people, for all that. She was not a gossip!"

"No," he said flatly. "No, she knew how to keep her own counsel, poor creature. Perhaps that was her undoing."

Charlotte took up the thread before the conversation

became maudlin. Mina had had a sly tongue, even if Emily had not had the wit to guess as much.

"But it is almost impossible not to hear things." Charlotte was surprised to hear her voice continue in precisely the same tone. "And to see them also, if one lives in a small area where everyone sees everyone else. I remember quite clearly poor Mrs. Spencer-Brown speaking with great sympathy"— she gulped on the words. Hypocrite!—"of the death of Mrs. Charrington's daughter. That must have been a dreadful shock, and one cannot help but wonder what awful event occurred, even if only to know what comfort to offer."

Caroline sat up at a sharp poke from Emily.

"Yes, indeed," Caroline said. "No one knows what it was that struck her down so suddenly. Quite appalling. I recall Mina's mentioning it."

"She was very perceptive," Alston repeated. "She knew there was something terribly wrong there—far more than met the eye. Most people were fooled, you know, but not Mina." There was a perverse ring of pride in him. "She noticed everything." His face put on a sober look. "Of course she never spoke, except to me. But she knew that the Charringtons had some tragedy that they dared not speak of. She said to me more than once that she would not be surprised if Ottilie met her death by violence! Of course the family would conceal it if it happened somewhere else, where we did not see— I mean, if it were—shameful!"

Charlotte's mind raced. Did he mean another murder? Murder by a lover, perhaps? Or had Ottilie died bearing an illegitimate child—or, worse than that, as the result of a badly executed abortion? Or could she have been found in some appalling place, a man's bedroom—or even a brothel?

Could one die of a socially vile disease at such a young age?

She thought not.

Surely death by such things was long and very slow, a matter of years?

But one could discover one had contracted it—and

perhaps even be quietly suffocated by one's own family before the ravages became obvious!

They were obscene thoughts, but not impossible. And any one of them worth killing for—if Mina had been foolish enough to let her knowledge be seen.

Emily was talking again, trying to draw out more details without betraying a vulgar curiosity. They had passed from Ottilie Charrington before it became too indiscreet, and were now discussing Theodora von Schenck. Charlotte and Caroline had prepared Emily thoroughly.

"Of course," Emily said, nodding sagaciously, "mysteries always make for gossip. It is bound to follow. I cannot blame Mina in the least. I confess to wondering myself how Theodora has so improved her circumstances. You must admit—it lacks an explanation?" She leaned forward expectantly. "It is only human to speculate! You must not feel badly for it."

Charlotte blushed for her and, at the same time, felt a little tingle of pride. She really was very adroit.

Alston rose to the temptation perfectly.

"Oh, that is where Mina was so perceptive," he said with an air of sad satisfaction. "She did not speak of it, because she was very discreet, you know—not in the least uncharitable. But she saw a great deal, and it is my private belief that she knew the truth—about a number of things!" He sat back, looking from one to another of them.

Emily's eyes widened at the marvel. "Do you really think so? You know she never whispered a word of it! Oh, how I admire her restraint!"

An ugly, squalid idea intruded into Charlotte's mind and would not be dismissed. She too sat forward, staring at Alston, her face hot with the repugnance of the thought inside her.

"She must have been very observant," she said quietly. "She must have seen a great deal."

"Oh yes," Alston said. "It was remarkable how much she saw. I am afraid a great deal must have passed by me without my having the least idea of it." Suddenly memories overwhelmed him and he was riddled with guilt because his blindness might have held him from preventing the ultimate tragedy. If only he also had seen and understood, then Mina might not have been murdered. It was plain in his face, in the puckering and downturn of his mouth and the evasion of his eyes as they filled with embarrassing tears.

Charlotte could not bear it. Even though she thought she knew the truth, and there was as much anger as pity in her for Mina, she leaned forward and without self-consciousness put her hand on Alston's sleeve.

"But as you remarked, and indeed as we all know," she said firmly, "she was no gossip. She was far too wise to repeat her observations. I am sure you are the only one who had any idea of her—perceptions."

"Do you think so?" He looked at her eagerly, seeking to be absolved from the blame for blindness. "I should so dislike to think she—she gossiped! One should—prevent such things."

"Of course," she reassured. "Do you not agree, Mama? Emily?"

"Oh yes," they answered, although she knew from their eyes that they had only a partial idea of what they were supposed to mean by it.

Charlotte took her hand from his sleeve and stood up. Now that she had learned as much as he knew, she wanted to leave; it seemed indecent to stay here muttering sympathy that did not help, knowing that none of them really cared, except quite impersonally, as they would have for anyone.

Emily stayed firmly in her seat.

"You must take great care of yourself," she said with concern, looking directly at Alston. "Of course you cannot go out for some time. It would not be appropriate, and I am sure you would have no desire to." Emily knew her social conventions perfectly. "But you must not permit yourself to become ill."

Caroline stiffened, her hands tightening on the arms of her chair. She stared across at Charlotte.

Charlotte felt her own muscles knot. Was Emily hinting at another murder?

Alston's eyes widened, and his grief was swallowed entirely by fear.

Before anyone could collect decent words to say that would not make the appalling thought irretrievable, the parlormaid opened the door and announced that Monsieur Alaric had called and would Mr. Spencer-Brown receive him?

Alston muttered something incoherent, which the girl took to be assent, and after a moment's agonized silence in which Charlotte glanced at Emily but dared not look at Caroline, Paul Alaric came in.

"Good afternoon. . . ." He hesitated; obviously the maid had not warned him that there were other guests. "Mrs. Ellison, Mrs. Pitt." He turned to Emily, but before he could speak, Alston rose hastily to the occasion, collecting himself in some relief at a clear-cut social duty.

"Lady Ashworth, may I present Monsieur Paul Alaric." He turned to Alaric. "Lady Ashworth is Mrs. Ellison's younger daughter."

Alaric shot a glance at Charlotte, brilliant with inquiry; then in perfect soberness he took the hand Emily offered him.

"How charming to see you, Lady Ashworth. I hope you are well?"

"Quite well, thank you," Emily replied coolly. "We called to express our sympathy to Mr. Spencer-Brown. Since we have done so, perhaps we should allow you to pay your visit uninhibited by the necessity of making courteous conversation with us." She rose gracefully and gave him a smile that was barely more than good manners.

Charlotte rose also; she had been on the point of excusing them when the parlormaid had come to announce Alaric.

"Come, Mama," she said briskly. "Perhaps we may call upon Mrs. Charrington? I did so like her."

But Caroline remained seated. "Really, my dear." She leaned back in her chair and smiled. "If we depart the moment Monsieur Alaric arrives, he will think us most uncivil.

There is plenty of time yet for other calls."

Emily caught Charlotte's eye with a sudden appreciation of the perverseness that faced them. Then she turned
back to her mother.

"I'm sure Monsieur Alaric will not think ill of us." This
time she flashed a charming smile at him. "It is sensibility for
Mr. Spencer-Brown that makes us withdraw, and not a lack of
wish for Monsieur Alaric's company. We must think first of
others, and not of ourselves. Is that not so, Charlotte?"

"Of course it is," Charlotte agreed quickly. "I am sure
that if I were feeling distressed there would be times when the
company of my own sex would be especially valuable to me."
She also turned and smiled at Alaric, and was a little disconcerted to see his eyes, bright and faintly puzzled, regarding
her so closely.

"I should be flattered beyond the point of vanity,
ma'am, to believe any man would prefer my company to
yours," he said with a softness in his voice, although whether
it was irony or merely humor she could not tell.

"Then perhaps a little of each?" Charlotte suggested
with her eyebrows raised. "Even the sweetest things become
boring after a while and one longs for a variety."

"The sweetest things," he murmured, and this time
she knew unquestionably that he was laughing at her, although there was nothing to show it in his face and she believed it was lost upon everyone else in the room.

"Let alone those with considerable acid to them," she
said.

Alston had not followed the conversation, but his innate good manners overrode his confusion. There was an
ease in convention, the comfort of knowing the rules.

"I cannot imagine wishing you to leave, any of you."
His gesture embraced them all. "Please do remain a little
longer. You have been so kind."

Caroline accepted immediately, and there was nothing
Charlotte or Emily could do but reseat themselves and,
with as much grace as they could muster, begin a new conversation.

Caroline made it easy for them; from being merely polite and silently sympathetic, suddenly she was glowing, her intensity reaching out until it could be felt throughout the room.

"We were just encouraging Mr. Spencer-Brown to take the best care of himself," she said warmly, looking from Alston to Alaric. "It is so easy in one's grief for someone one has loved to forget oneself. I am sure you will be able to help him more than we can."

"That is why I called," Alaric said. "Social gatherings are unacceptable, naturally, but to remain alone inside the house makes everything harder to bear." He turned to Alston. "I thought in the next few days you might like to come for a carriage ride? It can be very pleasant if the weather is fine, and you would not be required to meet anyone."

"Do you think I should?" Alston seemed uncertain.

"Why not? Everyone must bear grief in his own manner, and those who wish you well will not grudge you whatever ease you can find. Music pleases me, and contemplating the great works of art, whose beauty survives the life and death of their creators to reach out to all pain and all aspiration. I would be happy to accompany you to any gallery you choose—or anywhere else."

"Do you not think people might expect me to remain in?" Alston frowned anxiously. "At least until after the funeral? That is not for several days yet, you know. Friday. Yes." He blinked. "Of course you know. How foolish of me."

"Would you care for me to ride with you?" Alaric asked quietly. "I shall not be in the least offended if you would like to be alone, but I rather think if I were in such a situation, I should prefer not to be."

The crease ironed out across Alston's brow. "Would you? That really is most generous of you."

Charlotte was thinking the same thing, and it annoyed her. She would much rather have disapproved of Paul Alaric, and have had grounds in her mind for doing so. She glanced sideways at Caroline and saw the radiance in her eyes, the softness of approval.

Then she looked at Emily and knew that she had seen it also.

"How kind of you," Emily said with an edge to her voice that had far more to do with her own fears than any concern for Alston. "I am sure it is a most excellent act. Companionship is invaluable at such a time. I recall when I was bereaved, it was the company of my mother and my sister that gave me the most comfort."

Charlotte had no idea what she was talking about—surely not Sarah's death? That had affected them all equally—but she knew of no other bereavement.

Emily continued, regardless: "And I see no reason why you should not take a small drive if Monsieur Alaric is good enough to offer his company for that also. No one of any sensibility at all—no one who could possibly matter—would misunderstand that." She lifted her chin. "People do misconstrue some associations, of course, but that is more often so when it is a friendship between a lady and a gentleman. Then people are bound to talk, no matter how innocent it may be in truth. Do you not agree, Monsieur Alaric?"

Charlotte watched him closely to see if she could detect in his face even the faintest degree of comprehension of what they really meant, the purpose under their superficial words.

He remained completely at ease; seemingly his attention was still upon Alston.

"There are always those who will think evil, Lady Ashworth," he answered her. "Whatever the circumstances. One cannot possibly afford to cater to all of them. One must satisfy one's own conscience and observe the most obvious conventions so as not to offend unnecessarily. I believe that is all. Beyond that, I think one should please oneself." He turned to Charlotte, his eyes penetrating, as if he understood in some sense that she would have said exactly the same, were she to be truthful. "Do you not agree, Mrs. Pitt?"

She was caught in a dilemma. She hated equivocation, and her own tongue had caused enough social disasters to make anything but concurrence with him laughable. Also she would like to have been agreeable because there was a quality in him far beyond elegance, or even intellect, which drew her—a reserve of emotion as yet unreached that fascinated, like a thunderstorm, or the splendor of a rising wind far out at sea: dangerous and overwhelmingly beautiful.

She shut her eyes, then opened them wide.

"I think that can be a very selfish indulgence, Monsieur Alaric," she said with primness that made her sick even as she was speaking. "Much as one would like to on occasion, one cannot ignore Society. If it were ever to be only oneself who paid the price for outraging people's sensibilities, no matter how misplaced, it would be quite a different matter. But it is not. Gossip also hurts the innocent, more often than not. We are none of us alone. There are families upon whom every stain rubs off. The notion that you can please yourself without harming others is an illusion, and a most immature one. Too many people use it as an excuse for all manner of self-indulgences, and then plead ignorance and total amazement when others are dragged down with them, as if it could not have been foreseen with an ounce of sense!" She stopped for breath, not daring to look at any of them, least of all at Alaric.

"Bravo," Emily whispered so softly that to the others it must have seemed as if she were no more than sighing.

"Charlotte!" Caroline was stunned, unable to think what to say.

"How very perceptive of you." Emily rushed in to fill the hot silence. "And you have expressed it so well! It is a subject which has long needed some plain speaking! We delude ourselves so often to give us excuse for all sorts of behavior. Perhaps I should not, since you are my sister, but I do so commend your honesty!"

Since it was a precept Charlotte had been the last to obey in her own life, Emily's remark could only be ironic, although there was nothing but translucent candor in her blue eyes now.

Charlotte beamed at her, daggers in her mind.

"Thank you," she said sweetly. "You flatter me." She stood up. "And now I, at least, must leave or I shall not have left myself time to call upon Mrs. Charrington, and I do find her so charming. Do you care to come with me, Mama? Or shall I tell her that you felt it your duty to remain here with Mr. Spencer-Brown—and Monsieur Alaric?"

Since it was manifestly ridiculous for Caroline to think anything of the sort, she had no alternative but to rise as well.

"Of course not," she said tartly. "I should be delighted to come with you. I am very fond of Ambrosine and would like very much to call upon her. I must introduce her to Emily. Or do you know her already as well?" she added waspishly.

Emily was not in the least deterred. "No, I don't believe I do. But Charlotte has spoken of her so kindly, I have been looking forward to meeting her."

That was also untrue: Charlotte had never mentioned her, but it was an excellent parting line.

Alaric stood up, very straight, shoulders beautifully square, a flicker of the old laughter in his eyes, seeing them all so clearly, as a foreigner sometimes does.

"You will find her unique," he said with a little bow. "And above all things, never, ever a bore."

"Such a rare quality," Charlotte murmured, blushing. "Never to be boring."

Caroline lost her temper in frustration and reached out to kick Charlotte underneath her skirts. She missed, but the second time she caught her sharply on the ankle. The corners of her mouth lifted with satisfaction. "Quite," she said. Then she looked at Alston, who had also risen to bid them goodbye. "If there is anything we can do, please do let me know." Curiously she did not mention Edward, except by implication. "We are so close by and would be happy in any help or comfort we could offer—perhaps in practical arrangements?"

"How very kind of you," Alston replied. "I should be most grateful."

Charlotte looked straight at Alaric and met his eyes. She took a deep breath.

"I'm sure if you felt my father could offer you any help with regard to your assistance at the funeral, he would be delighted to do so." She lifted her chin. "Perhaps he should call upon you and see what would be convenient? We have suffered bereavements ourselves, and he is a most sensitive person. I am quite convinced you would like him." She did not look away, although she could feel the heat creeping up her face.

At last she was rewarded by an answering flash of understanding in the depths of Alaric's eyes, and a slow color under his skin.

"Indeed." His voice was very quiet. "I respect your purpose, Mrs. Pitt. I shall consider it gravely."

She tried to smile, and failed. "Thank you."

They said their formal farewells and walked to the entrance where the parlormaid was waiting, Alston having rung for her. Both doors were opened so that they might pass through without being forced into single file. Charlotte turned as they stepped into the hall and found to her considerable embarrassment that Paul Alaric was still facing them, and his eyes, wide and black, were not on Caroline, or Emily, who had also looked back, but upon herself.

The last thing she wanted was to look at Caroline, yet she found herself doing precisely that. The gaze that met hers was of one woman to another, no more; they might never have met before. The only element there was the sudden and complete knowledge of rivalry.

Chapter Seven

Charlotte could hardly wait until Pitt returned. She made the easiest of meals, placed it in the oven to cook itself, and then flitted from one job to another, accomplishing nothing. It was quarter past six when at last she heard the front door open, and she instantly dropped the linen cloth in her hand and ran from the kitchen to meet him. Usually she forced herself to let him come to the warmth of the big cooking range, take off his coat, and sit down before speaking to him of the day, but this time she shouted as soon as his foot was in the passage.

"Thomas! Thomas, I saw Alston Spencer-Brown today, and I discovered something!" She ran down the corridor and grasped at both his hands. "I think I know something about Mina—perhaps why she was killed!"

He was wet and tired, and not in the best of moods. His superiors were still clinging to the belief that it must have been suicide while the balance of her mind was upset by some private distress. It could all be so much more decently disposed of, and without turning over a lot of people's lives to investigate affairs that were far preferably left alone. Uncovering causes for enmity was always an ugly and unpopular occupation, and seldom profited the career of whoever undertook it—at least not if he was of a rank sufficiently advanced that there was no validity in the shield that he was merely following orders.

Pitt's superior, Dudley Athelstan, was a younger son who had married well and had an ambition that fed on its own success. He had spent the latter part of the day trying to persuade Pitt that there was no case to investigate. There were any number of ways an unbalanced woman might come by sufficient poison to take her own life if that was what she had determined to do. When Pitt had left him, Athelstan had been in growing ill-humor because he could not convince even himself, let alone Pitt and Sergeant Harris, that the matter had been answered beyond reasonable doubt, for no chemist or apothecary could be found who had sold such a substance, and certainly no doctor had prescribed it, no matter how diligently they had searched.

Now Pitt started to undo his coat. It was dripping in the hallway, and the day before he had received a very wounded and sober criticism from Gracie about the amount of labor it took to get the floor to its degree of polish, without inconsiderate people spilling water all over it.

"Why did you go and see Alston Spencer-Brown?" he inquired a little sourly. "He's surely nothing to do with you, or your mother?"

Charlotte could feel the irritation in him as if he had brought the cold in from the street, but she was too excited to take heed.

"The murder is to do with Mama," she said briskly, taking the coat and putting it on a hook to drip further, instead of carrying it through to the kitchen to dry. "We have to get the locket back. Anyway, Emily wanted to visit Mama, and I went with her!" If the flame of the gas lamp in the hallway had been brighter, he might have seen her blush at the half-truth. She turned and walked smartly back to the kitchen and the fire. "Mama went to call upon him to express her sympathy," she explained. "Anyway, that's not important!" She swung around and faced him. "I know at least one good reason why Mina Spencer-Brown might have been killed—maybe two!" She waited, glowing with excitement.

"I can think of a dozen," he said soberly. "But no proof for any of them. It never lacked possibilities, but they are not enough. Superintendent Athelstan wants the case closed. Suicide leaves them decently alone with their grief."

"Not possibilities," she burst out with impatience. "I mean real reasons! Do you remember I told you Mama said she felt as if she were being followed, watched all the time?"

"No," he said honestly.

"I told you! Mama was aware of someone—most of the time! And Ambrosine Charrington said the same thing. Well, I believe it was Mina! She spied on people—she was what is called a Peeping Tom. Alston said so, in a roundabout sort of way—although of course he didn't realize what he was meaning. Don't you see, Thomas? If she followed someone with a secret, a real secret, she may have learned something that was worth killing over. And I know from Alston of at least two possibilities!"

He sat down and took off his wet boots. "What?"

"Don't you believe me?" She had expected him to receive the news eagerly, and now he looked as if he were listening only to humor her.

He was too tired to be polite.

"I think your mother's affaire is probably not as serious as you imagine. Plenty of people have a little flirtation, especially Society women who have little else to do. You should know that by now. I expect it's all dropped handkerchiefs and bunches of flowers—about as real as a piece of embroidery. And I daresay if anyone was watching her, it was only out of boredom. You are making too much of it, Charlotte. If she were not your mother, you would take no notice."

She restrained herself with great difficulty. For a moment she considered losing her temper, telling him that the outward show might be trivial but the feeling underneath was as real and as potentially violent as anything conducted in the back streets, or in less naturally restricted levels of Society.

Then she realized how tired he was, how discouraged by Athelstan's desire to hide or ignore what did not suit his ambition. Anger would communicate nothing.

"Would you like a cup of tea?" she said instead, looking at his wet feet and the white skin of his hands where the cold had numbed the circulation. Without waiting for an answer, she topped up the kettle and moved it from the back of the stove onto the front.

After a few moments' silence while he put on dry socks, he looked up.

"What are these two possibilities?"

She heated the teapot and measured out the tea.

"Theodora von Schenck has an income, lately acquired, which nobody can account for. Her husband left her nothing, nor did anyone else, apparently. When she came to Rutland Place, she had nothing but the house. Now she has coats with sable collars, and Mina perhaps put forward some very interesting speculations as to where they might have come from."

"Like what?" he inquired.

She jiggled the teapot impatiently while the kettle blew faint halfhearted whiffs of steam, hot but not yet boiling.

"A brothel," Charlotte answered. "Or a lover. Or blackmail? There are all sorts of things worth killing to hide, where money is concerned. Maybe Theodora was blackmailing people with Mina's information and they had a fight over the money."

He smiled sourly. "Indeed. Your Mina seems to have had a most uncharitable turn of imagination, and a tongue to go with it. Are you sure that is what she said, and not what you are thinking for her?"

"Alston remarked several times on how perceptive she was of other people's characters, especially the less pleasant aspects of them. But he also said that she never spoke of them to anyone but him." She reached for the kettle at last. "However, that is the less likely possibility of the two, I think. The other possibility I remember Mina mentioning myself, and with a kind of relish, as if she knew something." She poured the water onto the tea and put on the lid, then brought the pot to the table and set it on the polished pewter stand. She let it brew while she went on: "It has to do with the death of Ottilie Charrington, which was sudden and unexplained. One week she was in perfect health, and the next the family returned from a holiday in the country and said she was dead. Just like that! No one ever said from what cause, no one was invited to any funeral, and she was never mentioned again. Mina apparently hinted that there was something very shameful about it—perhaps a badly done abortion?" She shivered and thought of Jemima asleep upstairs in her pink cot. "Or she was murdered by a lover, or in some unbearable place, like a brothel. Or possibly even she did something so terrible that her own family murdered her to keep it silent!"

Pitt looked at her gravely, without speaking.

She poured the tea and passed him his cup.

"I know it sounds violent, and unlikely," she went on. "But then I suppose murder always is unlikely—until it actually happens. And Mina was murdered, wasn't she? You know now that she didn't kill herself."

"No." He sipped the tea and burned his mouth; his hands were too numb for him to have realized its heat. "No, I think someone else put poison into the cordial wine we found in her stomach in the autopsy. We found the dregs in the empty bottle in her bedroom, and a glass. It was just chance she took it when she did; it could have been anytime she felt like it. It could have been anyone who put it there, anytime."

"Not if they wanted to silence her," Charlotte pointed out. "If you are afraid of someone, you want them dead before they speak, which means as soon as possible. Thomas, I really do believe she was a Peeping Tom. The more I think about it, the more it makes sense. She peeped once too often and saw something that cost her her life." She stared down into her tea, watching the vapor curl off it and rise gently. "I wonder if people who get murdered are usually unpleasant, if they have some flaw in them that invites murder? I mean people that aren't killed for money, of course. Like Shakespearean tragic heroes—one fatal deformity of soul that mars all the rest that might have been good." She stirred her tea, although there was no sugar in it. The steam curled thicker. "Curiosity killed the cat. If Mina had not wanted to know so much about everybody . . . I wonder if she knew about Monsieur Alaric, and Mama's locket?" Oddly enough, she was not afraid. Caroline was foolish, but there was neither the viciousness nor the fear in her to make her kill. And Paul Alaric had no reason to.

He looked up sharply, and too late she realized she had not mentioned Alaric's name before. Of course Pitt could not have forgotten him from Paragon Walk. At one time they had suspected him of murder . . . or worse!

"Alaric?" he said slowly, searching her face.

She felt herself flush, and was furious. It was Caroline who was behaving foolishly; she, Charlotte, had done nothing indiscreet.

"Monsieur Alaric is the man whose picture Mama has in the locket," she said defensively, looking straight back at him. And then because his eyes were too clear, too wise, she turned away and stirred her sugarless tea vigorously once again. She tried to sound casual. "Did I not mention that?"

"No." She knew he was still watching her. "No—you didn't."

"Oh." She kept her eyes on the swirling tea. "Well, he is."

There were several moments of silence.

"Indeed?" he said at last. "Well, I'm afraid we didn't find the locket—or any of the other stolen things, for that matter. And if Mina was a Peeping Tom, stealing for the sake of a sick need to know about other people, to possess something of them—" He saw her shudder, and he gave a sigh. "Isn't that what you are saying? That she was abnormal, perverted?"

"I suppose so."

He tried his tea again. "And of course there is the other possibility," he added. "Maybe she knew who the thief was."

"How tragic, and ridiculous!" she said with sudden

anger. "Someone dying over a few silly things like a locket and a buttonhook!"

"Lots of people have died for less." The rookeries came to his mind with their teeming misery and need. "Some for a shilling, some by accident for something they didn't have, or in mistake for somebody else."

She sipped her tea. "Are you going to investigate it?" she said at last.

"There's no choice. I'll see what I can find out about Ottilie Charrington. Poor soul! I hate digging through other people's wretched tragedies. It must be bad enough to lose a daughter, without the police unburying every indiscretion, putting every love or hate under a magnifying glass. No one wants to be seen so clearly!"

But the following morning the necessity was just as plain. If Charlotte was right and Mina had been inquiring, peeping at other people, then it was more than probable that some knowledge gained that way had been the cause of her death. He had heard before of people, outwardly normal people, often respectable, who were diseased with a compulsion to watch others, to pry into intimate things, to follow, to lift curtains aside, even to open letters and listen at doors. This compulsion always led to dislike and fear, often to imprisonment. It was inevitable that one day it would bring about murder also.

He could hardly start by going directly to the Charringtons. There was no excuse for him to question them about their daughter's death so long after the event unless he were to tell them of his suspicions, and that was obviously impossible at this point. It might be slander, at best. And on so tenuous a thread they would have no obligation to answer him even so.

Instead he went back to Mulgrew. The doctor had attended most of the families of Rutland Place, and if he had not known Ottilie himself, he would almost certainly be able to tell Pitt who had.

"Filthy day!" Mulgrew greeted him cheerfully. "Owe

you a couple of handkerchiefs. Obliged to you. Act of a gentleman. How are you? Come in and dry yourself." He waved his arms to conduct Pitt along the hallway. "Street's like a river, or perhaps I should say a gutter! What's wrong now? Not sick, are you? Can't cure a cold, you know. Or backache. No one can! At least if someone can, I've not met him!" He led the way back to an overcrowded room full of photographs and mementos, bookcases on every wall, cascades of papers and folios sliding off tables and stools. A large Labrador lay asleep in front of the fire.

"No, I'm not sick." Pitt followed him with a feeling of relief, even elation. Suddenly the ugly things became more bearable, the darkness he must probe less full of shapeless fear, but rather known things, things that could be endured.

"Sit down." Mulgrew waved an arm widely. "Oh, tip the cat off. She always gets on there the moment my back is turned. Pity she has so much white in her—damn white hairs stick to my pants. Don't mind, do you?"

Pitt eased the little animal off the chair and sat down smiling.

"Not at all. Thank you."

Mulgrew sat opposite him.

"Well, if you're not sick, what is it? Not Mina Spencer-Brown again? Thought we proved she died of belladonna?"

The little cat curled itself around Pitt's legs, purring gently, then hopped up onto his knees and wound itself into a knot, face hidden, and fell asleep instantly.

Pitt touched it with pleasure. Charlotte had wanted a cat. He must get her one, one like this.

"Are you physician to the Charringtons as well?" he asked.

Mulgrew's eyes opened wide in surprise.

"Throw her off if you want," he said, pointing to the cat. "Yes, I am. Why? Nothing wrong with any of them, is there?"

"Not so far as I know. Except that their daughter died. Did you know her?"

"Ottilie? Yes, lovely girl." His face retreated quite suddenly into lines of heavy sorrow. "One of the saddest things I know, her death. Miss her. Lovely girl."

Pitt was aware of a genuine grief, not the professional sadness of a doctor who loses a patient, but a sense of personal bereavement, of some happiness that no longer existed. He was embarrassed to have to continue. He had not expected emotion; he had been prepared only for thought, academic investigation. The mystery of murder was ephemeral, even paltry; it was the emotions, the fire of pain, and the long wastelands afterward that were real.

His hands found the cat's warm little body again, and he stroked it softly, comforting himself as much as pleasing the animal.

"What caused her death?" he asked.

Mulgrew looked up. "I don't know. She didn't die here. Somewhere in the country—Hertfordshire."

"But you were the family physician. Didn't they tell you what it was?"

"No. They said very little. Didn't seem to want to talk about it. Natural, I suppose. Shock. Grief takes people differently."

"It was very sudden, I understand?"

Mulgrew was looking into the fire, his eyes away from Pitt's, seeing something he could not share.

"Yes. No warning at all."

"And they didn't tell you what it was?"

"No."

"Didn't you ask?"

"I suppose I must have. All I can really remember was the shock, and how nobody spoke of it, almost as if by not putting it into words they could undo it, stop it from being real. I didn't press them. How could I?"

"But as far as you know she was perfectly well at the time she left Rutland Place?" Pitt inquired.

Mulgrew looked at him at last.

"One of the healthiest I know. Why? Obviously it matters to you or you wouldn't be here asking so many questions.

Do you imagine it has something to do with Mrs. Spencer-Brown?"

"I don't know. It's one of several possibilities."

"What kind of possibility?" Mulgrew's face creased in pain. "Ottilie was eccentric, even in bad taste to many, but there was nothing evil in her. She was one of the most truly generous people I ever knew. I mean generous with her time—she was never too busy to listen if she thought someone needed to talk. And generous with her praise—she didn't grudge appreciation, or envy other people's successes."

So Mulgrew had loved her, in whatever manner. Pitt did not need to know more: the warmth in Mulgrew's voice told of the loss still hurting him, twisting an emptiness inside.

It made Pitt's own thoughts, prompted by Charlotte, the more painful. It was sharp enough for him to lie. He needed to think about it a little, come to it by degrees. He did not look at Mulgrew when he spoke.

"From evidence I've just heard"—he measured his words slowly—"it seems possible that Mina Spencer-Brown was inordinately curious about other people's affairs, that she listened, and peeped. Does that seem likely to you?"

Mulgrew's eyes widened and he stared at Pitt, but he did not answer for several minutes. The fire crackled, and on Pitt's knees the cat woke and started kneading him gently with her claws. Absentmindedly he eased her up to rest on his jacket, where she could not reach her claws through to his flesh.

"Yes," Mulgrew said at last. "Never occurred to me before, but she was a watcher, never missed a thing. Sometimes people do that. Knowledge gives them an illusion of power, I suppose. It becomes compulsive. Mina could have been one of them. Intelligent woman, but an empty life—one stupid, prattling party after another. Poor creature." He leaned forward and put another piece of coal on the fire. "All day, every day, and not really necessary anywhere. What a bloody stupid thing to die for—some piece of information acquired through idiotic curiosity, no use to you at all." He turned his face away from the firelight. "And you think it had something to do with Ottilie Charrington?"

"I don't know. Apparently, Mina thought her death was a mystery, hinting that there was a great deal more to it than had been told and that she knew what it was."

"Stupid, sad, cruel woman," Mulgrew said quietly. "What on earth did she imagine it was?"

"I don't know. The possibilities are legion." He did not want to spell them out and hurt this man still more, but he had to mention at least one, if only to discount it. "A badly done abortion, for example?"

Mulgrew did not move.

"I believe not," he said very levelly. "I cannot swear to it, but I believe not. Do you have to pursue it?"

"At least enough to satisfy myself it is wrong."

"Then ask her brother Inigo Charrington. They were always close. Don't ask Lovell. He's a pompous idiot—can't see further than the quality of print on a calling card! Ottilie drove him frantic. She used to sing songs from the music halls—God only knows where she learned them! Sang one on a Sunday once—drinking song, it was, something about beer—not even a decent claret! Ambrosine called me in. She thought Lovell was going to take a seizure. Purple to the hair, he was, poor fool."

At any other time Pitt would have laughed. But the knowledge that Ottilie was dead, perhaps murdered, robbed the anecdote of any humor.

"Pity," he said quietly. "We get so many of our priorities wrong and never know it until afterwards, when it doesn't matter anymore. Thank you. I'll speak to Inigo." He stood up and put the little cat on the warm spot where he had been sitting. She stretched and curled up again, totally content.

Mulgrew shot to his feet. "But that can't be all! If Mina, wretched woman, was a Peeping Tom, she must have seen other things—God knows what! Affaires, at least! There's more than one butler around here should lose his job, that I know of—and more than one parlormaid, if her mistress knew of it!"

Pitt pulled a face. "I daresay. I'll have to look at them all. By the way, did you know there is a sneak thief in Rutland Place?"

"Oh God, that too! No, I didn't know, but it doesn't surprise me. It happens every now and then."

"Not a servant. One of the residents."

"Oh, my God!" Mulgrew's face fell. "Are you sure?"

"Beyond reasonable doubt."

"What a wretched business. I suppose it couldn't have been Mina herself?"

"Yes, it could. Or it could have been her murderer."

"I thought my job was foul at times. I'd a damned sight rather have it than yours."

"I think I would too, at the moment," Pitt said. "Unfortunately we can't chop and change. I couldn't do yours, even if you were willing to trade. Thanks for your help."

"Come back if I can do anything." Mulgrew put out his hand, and Pitt clasped it hard. A few minutes later he was outside again in the rain.

It took him two and a half hours to find Inigo Charrington, by which time it was past noon and Inigo was at the dining table in his club. Pitt was obliged to wait in the smoking room, under the disapproving eye of a dyspeptic steward who kept clearing his throat with irritating persistence, till Pitt found he was counting the seconds each time, waiting for him to do it again.

Finally, Inigo came in and was informed in hushed tones of Pitt's presence. He came over to him, his face a mixture of amusement at the steward's dilemma—and his own as other eyes were raised to stare at him—and apprehension about what Pitt might want.

"Inspector Pitt?" He dropped rather sharply into the chair opposite. "From the police?"

"Yes, sir." Pitt regarded him with interest. He was slender, not more than thirty at the most, with an odd, quicksilver face and auburn hair.

"Something else happened?" Inigo said anxiously.

"No, sir." Pitt regretted having alarmed him. Somehow he could not picture him having murdered his sister, or Mina either, to keep a scandal quiet. There was too much sheer humor in his face. "No, nothing at all, that I am aware of. But we have still not found any satisfactory answer as to how Mrs. Spencer-Brown met her death. There seems no explanation, so far, that makes either accident or suicide possible."

"Oh." Inigo sat back a little. "I suppose that means it could only have been murder. Poor soul."

"Indeed. And I daresay a great deal more pain will be caused before the business is finished."

Inigo looked at him gravely. "I imagine so. What do you want me for? I don't think I know anything. I certainly didn't know Mina very well." His mouth turned down in a sour smile. "I didn't have any reason to kill her. Although I suppose you can hardly take my word for that! I wouldn't be likely to tell you so if I had!"

Pitt found himself smiling back. "Hardly. What I was hoping for was information." He could not afford to be direct. Inigo was far too quick; he would anticipate suspicion and cover any trace of real worth.

"About Mina? You'd do much better asking some of the women—even my mother. She's rather absentminded at times, and she gets her gossip a little twisted, but underneath it all she's a pretty shrewd judge of character. She may get her facts wrong, but her feelings are invariably right."

"I shall ask her," Pitt said. "But she might speak considerably more freely to me if I had approached you first. Normally ladies such as Mrs. Charrington do not confide their opinions of their neighbors to the police."

Inigo's face softened into mercurial laughter, gone in an instant.

"Very tactfully put, Inspector. I imagine they don't. Although Mama has a taste for the bizarre. I'll mention it to her this evening. She might surprise you and tell you all sorts of things. Although quite honestly, she isn't really a gossip.

Not enough malice in her. She used to like to shock people occasionally when she was younger. Got bored with everyone repeating the same rubbish evening after evening at the same parties—just different dresses and different houses, but all the same conversations. Bit like Tillie."

"Tillie?" Pitt was lost.

"My sister—Ottilie. Better not repeat that. My father used to go into an apoplexy when I called her Tillie when we were children."

"And she liked to shock people?" Pitt quickly asked.

"Loved it. Never heard anyone laugh like Tillie. It was beautiful, rich, the sort of laughter that you have to join in with even if you have no idea what was funny."

"She sounds like a delightful person. I'm sorry I shall not meet her." He found it was far more than a sympathetic platitude; he meant what he said. Ottilie was something good that he had missed.

Inigo's eyes widened for a moment as if he did not understand; then he let out a little sigh.

"Oh. Yes. You would have liked her. Everything seems rather colder now she's gone, not the same color in things. But that isn't what you're here for. What do you want to know?"

"I understand she died very suddenly?"

"Yes. Why?"

"It must have been a great shock. I'm sorry."

"Thank you."

"Those fevers can be very sudden—no warning," he tried experimentally.

"What? Oh yes, very. But this must be wasting your time. What about Mina Spencer-Brown? She certainly didn't die of a fever. And Tillie wasn't given belladonna for treatment, I can assure you. Anyway, we were in the country at the time, not here."

"You have a country house?"

"Abbots Langley, in Hertfordshire." He smiled. "But you won't find any belladonna there. We all have excellent digestions—need to, some of the cooks we've had! If Papa chooses them, we have all soups and sauces, and if Mama does, then pies and pastries."

Pitt felt intrusive. How could anyone like being a Peeping Tom?

"I wasn't thinking of belladonna," he said honestly. "I am looking for reasons. Somewhere Mrs. Spencer-Brown must have given somebody cause to want her dead. Finding the belladonna is less important."

"Is it?" Inigo's eyebrows rose. "Don't you want to know who, more than why?"

"Of course I do. But anyone could make belladonna out of deadly nightshade. There's plenty of it about in these old gardens. It could have been picked anywhere. It's not like strychnine or cyanide that most people would have to buy."

Inigo winced. "What a terrible thought—going out to get something to kill people." He paused for a moment. "But I honestly haven't any idea why someone should kill Mina. I didn't especially like her. I always thought she was too"—he searched for the word he wanted—"too deliberate, too clever. All head and no heart. She was thinking all the time, never missed anything. I prefer people who are either stupider or less permanently interested. Then if I do something idiotic it can be decently forgotten." He smiled a little crookedly. "But you hardly go out and distill poison for someone because you don't like them very much. I couldn't even say I disliked her—just that I was not entirely comfortable when she was there, which wasn't very often."

It all fitted so easily with what Charlotte had said, slid into the pattern and coalesced: a watcher, a listener, adding everything together in her mind, working out answers, understanding things that were intimate.

But how, and for whom, had "not entirely comfortable" changed into "intolerable"?

He wanted to think of a useful question, something to make Inigo believe he was asking about Mina, not Ottilie.

"I never saw her alive. Was she attractive—to men?"

Inigo's face creased with spontaneous laughter.

"Not very subtle, Inspector. No, she wasn't—not to me. I like something a little less schooled, and with more humor. If you ask around the Place, no doubt you will be told my taste runs to the warmhearted, slightly eccentric, for entertainment. And if I were to marry—I really don't know who the woman would be. Someone I really liked—certainly not Mina!"

"You mistake me," Pitt said with a dry smile. "I was thinking of a possible lover, even a rejected one. They say hell hath no fury like a woman scorned, but I've found men take it no less kindly, especially vain and successful men. There are many people who believe that loving someone puts the person into some sort of debt to you and gives you certain rights. More than one man has killed a woman because he thought she wasted herself on someone unworthy of her—someone other than himself, that is. I've known men with the notion that they somehow owned a woman's virtue, and if she stained it she had offended not against herself or against God—but against him!"

Inigo stared into the polished surface of the table and smiled very slowly over something he was not prepared to share with Pitt, something at the same time funny and bitter.

"Oh, indeed," he said sincerely. "I believe in feudal times if a woman lost her virginity she had to pay a fine to the lord of the manor, because she was then worth much less to him come the time someone wished to marry her and naturally had to pay the lord for the privilege. We haven't changed so much! We're far too genteel to pay in money, of course, but we still pay!"

Pitt would like to have known what he meant, but to ask would have been vulgar, and he probably would not have been answered.

"Could she have had a lover?" He went back to the original question. "Or an admirer?"

Inigo thought for a few moments before replying.

"Mina? I've never considered it, but I suppose she could have. The oddest people do."

"Why do you say that? She looked as if she had been at least attractive, if not even beautiful."

Inigo seemed surprised himself. "Just her personality. She didn't seem to have any fire, any—gentleness. But then you said an admirer, didn't you? She was very delicate; she had a femininity about her that would have been just what appealed to some—a sort of austere purity. And she always dressed to suit it." He smiled apologetically. "But it is pointless asking me who, because I have no idea."

"Thank you." Pitt stood up. "I can't think of anything else to ask you. It was most courteous of you to see me, especially here."

"Hardly." Inigo stood up as well. "Your presenting yourself didn't give me a great deal of choice. I had either to see you or to look like a pompous ass—or, worse than that, as if I had something to hide."

It had been intentional, and Pitt would not insult him by denying it.

He did not go to see Ambrosine Charrington the following day, but instead packed a gladstone bag with clean shirt and socks and took the train from Euston Station to Abbots Langley to see what he could discover about Ottilie Charrington's death.

He spent two days, and the more he learned the more confused he became. He had no trouble in locating the house, for the Charringtons were well known and respected.

He ate a comfortable lunch at the inn, then walked to the local parish churchyard, but there were no Charringtons buried there—neither Ottilie nor anyone else.

"Oh, they've only been here for twenty years, going on," the sexton told him reasonably. "They're newcomers. You won't find any of 'em here. Buried in London somewhere, like as not."

"But the daughter?" Pitt asked. "She died here little over a year ago!"

"Maybe so, but she ain't buried here," the sexton assured him. "Look for yourself! And I've been to every funeral here in the last twenty-five years. No Charringtons—not a one."

A sudden thought occurred to Pitt.

"How about Catholic or Nonconformist?" he asked. "What other churches are there close by?"

"I know every funeral as goes on in this neighborhood," the sexton said vehemently. "It's my job. And the Charringtons weren't any of them outlandish things. They was gentry—Church of England, like everybody else who knows what's good for them. Church here every Sunday they're in the village. If she'd been buried anywhere around here, it would be in this churchyard. Reckon as you must be mistaken and she died up in London somewhere. Leastways, if she died here, they took her back to London to bury her. Family vault, likely. Lie alongside your own, that's what I always say. Eternity's a mighty time."

"Don't you believe in the Resurrection?" Pitt said curiously.

The sexton's face puckered with disgust at any man who would be so crass as to introduce abstract matters of doctrine into the practicalities of life and death.

"Now what kind of a question is that?" he demanded. "You know when that's going to be, do you? Grave's a long time, a very long time. Should be done proper. You'll be a lot longer in it than any grand house here!"

That was a point beyond argument. Pitt thanked him and set out to find the local doctor.

The doctor knew the Charringtons, but he had not attended Ottilie in her last illness, nor had he written any death certificate.

The following midday, by which time Pitt had seen servants, neighbors, and the postmistress, he caught the train back to London convinced that Ottilie Charrington had been in Abbots Langley on the week of her death but that she had not died there. The booking clerk at the station recalled seeing her on one or two occasions, but he could not swear when; and although she had bought a ticket to London, he did not know if she had returned.

It seemed an inescapable conclusion that she had died not in Abbots Langley but somewhere unknown, and of some cause unknown.

Now Pitt could not avoid seeing Ambrosine and Lovell Charrington any longer. Even Superintendent Athelstan, much as it pained him, could think of no argument to avoid it, and an appointment was duly made—politely, as if it were a courtesy. However, it was not as Pitt had intended: He would rather have been casual, and preferably have seen Lovell and then Ambrosine separately. But when he had reported on his visit to Abbots Langley, Athelstan had taken the matter into his own hands.

Lovell received Pitt in the withdrawing room. Ambrosine was not present.

"Yes, Inspector?" he said coolly. "I cannot think what else I can tell you about the unfortunate business. I have already done my duty and informed you fully of everything I knew. Poor Mrs. Spencer-Brown was most unstable, sad as it makes me to have to say so. I do not interest myself in other people's private lives. Therefore I have no idea what particular crisis may have precipitated the tragedy."

"No, sir," Pitt said. They were both still standing, Lovell stiff and unprepared to offer any sop to comfort. "No, sir, but it now seems beyond doubt that Mrs. Spencer-Brown did not take her own life. She was murdered."

"Indeed?" Lovell's face was white, and he suddenly reached for the chair behind him. "I suppose you are quite sure? You have not been too hasty, leaped to conclusions? Why should anyone murder her? That is ridiculous! She was a respectable woman!"

Pitt sat down too. "I have no reason to doubt that, sir." He decided to lie, at least by implication; there was no other way he could think of to approach the subject. "Sometimes even the most innocent people are killed."

"Someone insane?" Lovell grasped at the easiest explanation. Insanity was like disease—indiscriminate. Had not Prince Albert himself died of typhus? "Of course. That must be the answer. I am afraid I have seen no strangers about the area, and all our servants are chosen most carefully. We always follow up references."

"Very wise," Pitt heard himself agree, hypocrisy dry in his mouth. "I believe you very tragically lost your own daughter, sir?"

Lovell's face closed over in tight defense, almost hostility.

"Indeed. It is a subject I prefer not to discuss, and it has no relation whatever to the death of Mrs. Spencer-Brown."

"Then you know more of Mrs. Spencer-Brown's death than I do, sir," Pitt replied levelly. "Because as yet I have no knowledge as to what caused it, or who, let alone why."

Lovell's skin was white, drawn in painful lines around his mouth and jaw. Cords of muscle stood out in his neck, making his high collar sit oddly.

"My daughter was not murdered, sir, if that is what you imagine. There is no question of it. Therefore it can have no connection. Do not let your professional ambition give you to see murder where there is nothing but simple tragedy."

"What did cause her death, sir?" Pitt kept his voice low, aware of the pain he must be inflicting; consciousness of it was stronger than the gulf of feeling and belief between the two men.

"An illness," Lovell replied. "Quite sudden. But it was not poison. If that has occurred to you as a connection, then you are quite mistaken. You would do better to employ your time investigating Mrs. Spencer-Brown rather than going over other people's family losses. And I refuse to permit you to trouble my wife with these idiotic questions. She has suffered enough. You can have no idea what you are doing!"

"I have a daughter, sir." Pitt was reminding himself as much as this stiff little man in front of him. What if Jemima had died suddenly, without warning to the emotions—full of life one day, and nothing but a vivid, beautiful, and agonizing memory the next? Would he now find it intolerable to discuss it as Lovell did?

He could not guess. It was tragedy beyond the ability of the mind to conjure.

And yet Mina had been someone's daughter too.

"Where did she die, sir?"

Lovell stared at him. "At our house in Hertfordshire. What possible concern is it of yours?"

"And where is she buried, sir?"

Lovell's face flushed scarlet. "I refuse to answer any more questions! This is monstrous impertinence, and grossly offensive! You are paid to discover the cause of Mina Spencer-Brown's death, not to exercise your infernal curiosity about my family and its bereavements. If you have anything to ask me about the matter, then do so! I shall do my best to answer you, according to my duty. Otherwise I request that you leave my house immediately, and do not return unless you have legitimate business here! Do you understand me, sir?"

"Yes, Mr. Charrington," Pitt said very softly. "I understand you perfectly. Was your daughter friendly with Mrs. Spencer-Brown?"

"Not particularly. I think they were no more than civil to one another. There was a considerable difference in their ages."

A completely random thought occurred to Pitt.

"Was your daughter well acquainted with Mr. Lagarde?"

"They had known each other for some time," Lovell replied stiffly. "But there was no"—he hesitated while he chose his word—"no fondness between them. Most unfortunate. It would have been an excellent match. My wife and I tried to encourage her, but Ottilie had no—" He stopped, his face hardening again. "That is hardly pertinent to your inquiry, Inspector. Indeed, it is not pertinent to anything at all now. Forgive me, but I think you are wasting both your time and mine. There is nothing I can tell you. I bid you good day."

Pitt considered whether to argue, to insist, but he did not believe that Lovell would tell him anything more.

He stood up. "Thank you for your assistance. I hope it will not be necessary to trouble you again. Good day, sir."

"I hope not indeed." Lovell rose. "The footman will show you out."

Rutland Place was pale with watery sun. In one or two gardens green daffodil leaves stood like bayonets, yellow banners of bloom held above them. He wished people would not plant them in ranks, like an army.

Whether Mina Spencer-Brown had been right about the ugliness of its nature or not, there was certainly a mystery about Ottilie Charrington's death. She had neither died nor been buried where her family claimed.

Why should they lie? What really had killed her, and where?

The answer could only be that there was something so painful, or so appalling, that they dared not tell the truth.

Chapter Eight

For three days there was no progress at all. Pitt followed up every material clue he could find, and Sergeant Harris questioned servants, both kitchen and outdoor. No one told them anything that seemed to be of importance. It became more and more apparent that Mina had been, as Charlotte guessed, an obsessive watcher. Little scraps of information, impressions gathered here and there gradually confirmed it. But what had she seen? Surely something more damning than merely the identity of a petty thief?

Then on the afternoon of the fourth day, a little after one o'clock, Charlotte was standing in the parlor opening the French doors onto the small back garden, breathing in the air that at last had warmth in it and the smell of sweet earth, when Gracie came in at a trot, her heels scuffing up the new rug.

"Oh, Mrs. Pitt, ma'am, there's a letter come for you by special footman, in a carriage and all, and he says it's terrible urgent. And please, ma'am, the carriage is still standing there in the street as large as life, and ever so grand!" She held out the envelope at arm's length for Charlotte to take.

A glance was sufficient to see that it was Caroline's writing. Charlotte tore the envelope open and read:

> *My dear Charlotte,*
> *The most appalling thing has happened. I hardly know how to tell you, it seems so utterly tragic.*
> *As you know, Eloise Lagarde was most distressed by Mina's death and the circumstances of it, and Tormod took her to their country house to rest and recover her spirits.*
> *My dear Charlotte, they have returned this morning after the most dreadful accident I have ever known! I feel quite sick to think of it, it is almost past enduring. While out driving, returning from a picnic one evening with friends, poor Tormod was at the reins of the carriage and he slipped from the box and fell, right under the wheels. As if that in itself was not terrible enough, a group of friends were right behind them. It was past dusk, and they did not see what had happened! Charlotte, they drove straight over him! Horses and carriage!*
> *That poor young man, hardly older than yourself, is crippled beyond any hope! He lies on his bed in Rutland Place and, for all we can believe or pray, will do so for the rest of his life!*
> *I am so distressed I cannot think what to say or do. How can we help? What response is there in the face of such total tragedy?*
> *I felt you would wish to know as soon as possible, and I have sent the carriage for you, in case you wish to come this afternoon. I would dearly like your company, even if only to share with someone my shock at such pain. Your father is at business and shall be dining out this evening, and Grandmama is of no comfort at all.*
> *I have also written to Emily and sent the letter by messenger.*
>
> *Your loving mother,*
Caroline Ellison.

Charlotte read the letter a second time, not that she doubted she had understood it, but to give herself time to allow its meaning, with the weight of pain it carried, to sink into her consciousness.

She tried to imagine the night, the dark road, Tormod Lagarde as she had last seen him, with his high, pale brow and wave of black hair, standing on the driving box; then perhaps a horse swerving, an unexpected turn in the road, and suddenly he was lying in the mud, the carriage above him, the noise and the rattle, the wheels passing over a leg or an arm, the crushing weight, bones snapped. A moment's silence, the night sky, and then the smashing, pummeling hooves of the other carriage and the crushing weight, agony as his body was broken—

Dear God! Better, infinitely more merciful, if he had been killed outright, simply never to have known sensibility or light again.

"Ma'am?" Gracie's voice came urgently. "Ma'am? Are you all right? You look terrible white! I think as you ought to sit down. I'll get the salts, and a good cup of tea!" She turned to go, determined to rise to the occasion and do something useful.

"No!" Charlotte said at last. "No, thank you, Gracie. It's all right. I'm not going to faint. It is most terrible news, but it is an acquaintance, not a member of my family or a close friend. I shall go and call upon my mother this afternoon. It is a friend of hers. I cannot say how long I shall be. I must put on something more suitable than this dress. It is far too cheerful. I have a dark dress which is quite smart. If the master comes home before I do, please show him this letter. I'll put it in the desk."

"You look terrible pale, ma'am," Gracie said anxiously. "I think as you should have a nice cup of tea before you goes anywhere. And shall I ask the footman if he'd like one too?"

Charlotte had forgotten the footman; indeed her mind had slipped back to the past and she had not even remembered that the carriage was not her own.

"Yes, yes, please do that. That would be excellent. I shall go upstairs and change, and you may bring my cup of tea there. Tell the footman I shall not be long."

"Yes, ma'am."

Caroline was very somber when Charlotte was shown in. For the first time since Mina's death, she was dressed in black and there was no lace at her throat.

"Thank you for coming so soon," she said the moment the maid had closed the door. "Whatever is happening to Rutland Place? It is one unspeakable tragedy after another!" She seemed unable to sit down; she held her hands tightly together and stood in the middle of the floor. "Perhaps it is wicked of me to say so, but I feel as if in a way this is even worse than poor Mina! It is only what the servants say, and I should not listen to it, but it is the only way of hearing anything," she excused herself quite honestly. "According to Maddock, poor Tormod is"—she took a breath—"completely crushed! His back and his legs are broken."

"It's not wicked, Mama." Charlotte shook her head in a tiny gesture, putting out her arm to touch Caroline. "If you have any faith, death cannot be so terrible—only, on occasion, the manner of it. And surely it would have been better, if he is as dreadfully injured as they say, that he should have died quickly? If he cannot recover? And I would not trust to Maddock for that. I daresay he got it from the cook, and she from one of the maids, who will have had it from an errand boy, and so on. Do you intend to call, to express your sympathies?"

Caroline's head came up quickly. "Oh yes, I feel that would only be civil. One would not stay, of course, but even if only to acknowledge that one is aware and to offer any help that may be possible. Poor Eloise! She will be quite shattered. They are very close. They have always been so fond of each other."

Charlotte tried to imagine what it would be like to love someone so dearly and have to watch him day after day, mutilated beyond reparation, awake and sane, and be unable to help. But imagination stopped short of any sort of reality. She could remember Sarah's death, of course, but that had been quick—violent and horrible, to be sure—but thank God, there had been no lingering, no stretching out of pain day after day.

"What can we possibly do?" she asked helplessly. "Just to call and say we are sorry seems so wretchedly trivial."

"There isn't anything else," Caroline answered quietly. "Don't try to think of everything today. Perhaps in the future there may be something—at least companionship."

Charlotte received that in silence. The sunlight streaming across the carpet, picking out the garlands of flowers, seemed remote, more like a memory than anything present. The bowl of pink tulips on the table looked stiff, like an ornamental design, hieratic and foreign.

The maid opened the door. "Lady Ashworth, ma'am." The maid bobbed a curtsy, and immediately behind her Emily came in, looking pale and less than her usually immaculate self.

"Mama, what a fearful thing! How ever did it happen?" She caught hold of Charlotte's arm. "How did you hear? Thomas is not here, is he? I mean it's nothing—"

"No, of course not!" Charlotte said quickly. "Mama sent the carriage for me."

Caroline shook her head in confusion. "It was an accident. They were out driving. It was fine, and they had had a picnic somewhere and returned late, by a longer and more pleasant way. It's all perfectly ridiculous!" For the first time there was anger in her voice as the futility of it struck her. "It need never have happened! A skittish horse, I suppose, or some wild animal cutting across a country road, frightening them. Or maybe it was an overhanging branch from some tree."

"Well, that's what one keeps woodsmen for!" Emily said in an explosion of impatience. "To see that there are no overhanging branches across carriageways." Then equally quickly her anger vanished. "What can we do to help? I don't really see what there is, except one's sympathy. And little use that will be!"

"It is still better than nothing." Caroline moved toward the door. "At least Eloise will not feel that we are indifferent, and then if there comes a time when she wishes something, even if it is only company, she will know that we are ready."

Emily sighed. "I suppose so. It seems like offering a bucket to bail out the sea!"

"Sometimes merely to know you are not alone is some comfort," Charlotte said, as much to herself as to them. Out in the hallway Maddock was waiting.

"Shall you be returning for afternoon tea, ma'am?" he inquired, holding Caroline's coat for her.

"Oh yes." Caroline nodded and allowed him to put it around her shoulders. "We are merely going to call upon Miss Lagarde. We will hardly be long."

"Indeed," Maddock said gravely. "A most terrible tragedy. Sometimes these young men drive most rashly. I have always believed that racing was a highly dangerous and foolish exercise. Most conveyances are not designed for it."

"Were they racing?" Charlotte asked quickly, turning to face him.

Maddock's features were without expression. He was a servant and knew his place, but he had also been with the Ellisons since Charlotte was a young girl. Little she did could surprise him.

"That is what they are suggesting, Miss Charlotte," he replied impassively. "Although it would seem a somewhat foolish occupation along a country road, and almost bound to cause injury to someone, even if only the horses. But I have no idea if it is true or merely backstairs speculation. One cannot prevent servants from exercising their imaginations about such a disaster. No amount of chastisement will silence them."

"No, of course not," Caroline said. "I wouldn't waste time trying—as long as it is not quite irresponsible." She raised her eyebrows a little. "And they are not neglecting their duties!"

Maddock looked faintly hurt. "Naturally, ma'am, I have never permitted that in my house."

"No, of course not." Caroline was mildly apologetic

for having thoughtlessly insulted his integrity.

Emily was standing at the door, and the footman opened it for her. The carriage outside was already waiting.

The distance to the Lagardes' was only a few hundred yards, but the day was wet and the footpath running with water, and this was the most formal of calls. Charlotte climbed in and sat in silence. What on earth could she say to Eloise? How could a person reach from her own happiness and safety across such a gulf?

None of them spoke before the carriage stopped again and the footman handed them down. Then he remained standing at the horses' heads, waiting in the street as a mute sign to other callers that they were there.

A parlormaid, minus her usual white cap, opened the door and said in a tight little voice that she would inquire whether Miss Lagarde would receive them. It was some five minutes before she returned and conducted them into the morning room at the back of the house, overlooking the rain-swept garden. Eloise rose from the sofa to greet them.

It was excruciating to look at her. The translucent skin was as white as tissue paper, with the same lifeless look. Her eyes were sunken and enormous, seeming to stretch till the bruises beneath were part of them. Her hair was immaculate, but had obviously been dressed by the maid, as had she; her clothes were delicate and neat, but she wore them as if they were artificial, winding-sheets on a body for which the spirit no longer had any use. She seemed even thinner, her laced-in waist more fragile. The shawl Charlotte had previously seen her wear was gone, as if she no longer cared if she was cold or not.

"Mrs. Ellison." Her voice was completely flat. "How kind of you to call." She might have been reading a foreign language, without any comprehension of its meaning. "Lady Ashworth, Mrs. Pitt. Please do sit down."

Uncomfortably they obeyed. Charlotte felt her hands chill, and yet her face hot with a sense of embarrassment at having intruded into something too exquisitely painful even for the rituals of pride and the need for privacy to cover. She was overwhelmed by anguish like this; it filled the room.

Charlotte was stunned into silence. Even Caroline fumbled for words and found none. Only Emily's unrelenting social discipline carried her through.

"No expression of our sympathy could possibly meet such distress as you must feel," she said quietly. "But do be assured we grieve for you, and in time if there is anything we may do to be of comfort, we would be only too willing."

"Thank you," Eloise replied without expression. "That is generous of you." It was as if she were hardly aware of them, only of the need to reply or at least to acknowledge each time someone spoke. Her sentences were formal, things she had prepared herself to say.

Charlotte searched her mind for anything at all that did not sound idiotic.

"Perhaps presently you would care for a little company," she suggested. "Or if you have somewhere to go, perhaps you would prefer not to go alone?" It was a suggestion for Emily or Caroline rather than herself, since she had neither frequent opportunity to visit Rutland Place nor a carriage available.

Eloise's eyes met hers for a moment, then slid away into something frighteningly like complete vacancy, as if all the world she knew was inside her head.

"Thank you. Yes, I expect that may be. Although I fear I shall hardly be pleasant company."

"My dear, that is not at all true," Caroline said. She lifted her hands as if to reach forward, but there was some barrier around Eloise, an almost tangible remoteness, and she let them fall again without touching her. "I have never known you anything but sympathetic," she finished helplessly.

"Sympathetic!" Eloise repeated the word, and for the first time there was emotion in her voice, but it was hard, stained with irony. "Do you think so?"

Caroline could do nothing but nod.

Silence closed in on them again, stretching as long as they would suffer it to exist.

Again Charlotte racked her mind to think of something

to say, just for the sake of sound. But it would be offensive, almost prurient, to inquire how Tormod was faring, or what the doctor might have said. And yet to speak of anything else was unthinkable.

The moments ticked on. The room seemed to grow enormous and the rain outside far away; even the sound of it was removed. The nightmare horses galloped through all their minds, the wheels crashed.

Eventually, when Charlotte was just about to say something, however absurd, to break the pressure, the maid returned to announce Amaryllis Denbigh. Much as Charlotte disliked Amaryllis, she felt a rush of gratitude merely to be relieved of the burden.

Amaryllis came a few steps behind the maid. She stood in the doorway and stared from one to the other of them aghast, although surely she must have seen the carriage outside.

Her eyes fastened on Charlotte accusingly. She was white-faced, and her usually lush hair was awry and the pink salve on her lips smudged.

"Mrs. Pitt! I had not expected to find you here!"

There was no civil reply to this, so Charlotte attributed it to natural distress and ignored it altogether.

"I am sure you have called in sympathy, as we have," she said levelly. She waited a second or two for Eloise to say something; then, as she did not, Charlotte added, "Please do sit down. This sofa is most comfortable."

"How can you talk of comfort at such a time?" Amaryllis demanded in a sudden gust of fury. "Tormod will get better, of course! But he is in agony." She shut her eyes and hot tears ran down her cheeks. "Absolute agony! And you sit there as if you were at a soirée and talk about comfort!"

Charlotte felt anger and pain well up inside her, because Amaryllis spoke out of her own passion, without thought for the pain she must be causing Eloise.

"Then stand, if you prefer to," she said tartly. "If you imagine it will be of some conceivable service, I'm sure no one will mind."

Amaryllis seized a chair and sat down, her silk skirts everywhere.

"At least if he will get better, then that is hope," Emily said, trying to ease the electric harshness a little.

Amaryllis swung round, opened her mouth, then closed it again.

Eloise was sitting perfectly motionless, her face blank, her hands lifeless in her lap.

"He will not," she said without a shadow of expression, as if she had faced death itself and grown accustomed to it and accepted it without hope. "He will never stand again."

"That's not true!" Amaryllis' voice rose almost to a shriek. "How dare you say anything so dreadful? That is a lie! A lie! He will stand, and in time he will walk. He will! I know it." She stood up, went over to Eloise, and stopped in front of her, shaking with emotion, but Eloise neither looked up nor flinched.

"You are dreaming," Eloise said very quietly. "One day you will know the truth. However long it takes, it is always there, and it will come to you."

"You're wrong! You're wrong!" The color flamed up Amaryllis' face. "I don't know why you're saying all this. You have your own reasons—God in heaven knows what they are!" There was accusation in her voice, shrill and ugly—frightened. "He will get better. I refuse to give in, to surrender!"

Eloise looked at her as if she were transparent or of no importance, as if she were unreal, as inconsequential as a magic-lantern slide.

"If that is what you wish to believe," she said quietly, "then do so. It really makes no difference to anyone, except I would ask you not to keep repeating it, especially if the time should come when Tormod is well enough to receive you."

Amaryllis' body became rigid, her arms like wood, her bosom high.

"You want him to lie there!" she cried, almost gulping the words. "You evil woman! You want to keep him a prisoner here! Just you and he, all the rest of his life! You're mad!

You're never going to let him go—you—"

Suddenly Charlotte woke into action. She jumped to her feet and slapped Amaryllis sharply across the face.

"Don't be idiotic!" she said furiously. "And so utterly selfish! Who on earth do you imagine you are helping, standing there shrieking like a servant girl? Pull yourself together and remember that it is Eloise and not you who has to bear the hardship of this! It is she who has cared about him all her life! Can you possibly believe that poor Mr. Lagarde wishes to have his sister subjected to abuse on top of everything else? The doctor is the only one who can say whether he will recover or not, and false hope is more painful than learning to accept with patience the truth, whatever it may be, and await the outcome!"

Amaryllis stared at her. Quite possibly it was the first time in her life anyone had struck her, and she was too appalled to react. And the insult that she had behaved like a servant was a mortal one!

Emily stood up also and took Charlotte aside, then guided Amaryllis back to her seat. Eloise sat through it all as if she had neither seen nor heard them, absorbed in her own thoughts. They could have been shadows passing across the lawn for any mark they made upon her mind.

"It is natural you should be shocked," Emily said to Amaryllis with a supreme effort at calmness. "But these dreadful things affect people in different ways. And you must remember that Eloise has spoken with the doctor and knows what he has said. It would be best if we were all to await his advice. I daresay Mr. Lagarde needs as little disturbance as can be." She turned to Eloise. "Is that not so?"

Eloise was still looking at the floor.

"Yes." She raised her eyebrows a little, almost with surprise. "Yes, we should not distress him with our feelings. Rest—that is what Dr. Mulgrew said. Time. Time will tell."

"Is he to call again soon?" Caroline inquired. "Would you care to have someone with you when he does, my dear?"

For the first time Eloise smiled very faintly, as if at last she had heard not only the words, but their meaning.

"That is most kind of you. If it is not a trouble? I am expecting him momentarily."

"Of course not. We shall be happy to stay," Caroline assured her, her voice rising with pleasure that there was something they could do.

Amaryllis hesitated when they all turned to look at her, then changed her mind.

"I think there are other calls it would be courteous for us to make while I am in the neighborhood," Emily said. "Charlotte can remain here. Perhaps Mrs. Denbigh would care to come with me?" She spoke with exquisite ease. "I should be most happy for your company."

Amaryllis' eyes widened; obviously it was a contingency she had not foreseen, and she was about to protest, but Caroline grasped the opportunity.

"What an excellent idea." She rose, straightening her skirts to make them fall elegantly behind her. "Charlotte will be delighted to remain here, and I shall accompany you so we may continue with our visiting. I am sure Ambrosine would be pleased to see us. You would be happy to do that, wouldn't you, my dear?" She looked to Charlotte nervously.

"Of course," Charlotte agreed quite sincerely. For once, Mina and the mystery surrounding her death were banished from her mind and she was aware only of Eloise. "I think that is most certainly what you should do. And it is only a step. I can quite easily walk back when it is time."

Amaryllis stood a few moments longer, still trying to think of some acceptable excuse to stay, but nothing came to her and she was obliged to follow Emily out into the hallway as Caroline took her arm and walked with her, and the maid closed the door behind them.

"Don't let her distress you," Charlotte said to Eloise after a moment. She would not be fatuous enough to suggest that what was said was not meant. It was blindingly obvious that it had been fully intended. "I daresay the shock has affected her judgment."

Eloise's face shadowed with a ghost of humor, wraith-like and bitter.

"Her judgment, perhaps," she answered. "But only insofar as previously she would have thought the same, whereas good manners would have prevented her from saying it."

Charlotte slid more comfortably into her seat. Dr. Mulgrew might yet be some time.

"She is not the pleasantest of persons," she observed.

Eloise met her eyes; for the first time she appeared actually to see her, not some inward scene of her own.

"You do not care for her." It was a statement.

"Not a great deal," Charlotte admitted. "Perhaps if I knew her better—" She left the suggestion as a polite fiction.

Eloise stood up and walked slowly over toward the French windows and stood facing the rain.

"I think a great deal of what we like about people is what we do not know but imagine to be there. That way we can believe the unknown is anything we wish."

"Can we?" Charlotte looked at her back, very slender, with shoulders square. "Surely to continue to believe what is not true is impossible, unless you leave reality altogether and sink into madness?"

"Perhaps." Eloise suddenly lost interest again and her voice was weary. "It hardly matters."

Charlotte considered arguing, purely as a principle, but she was overwhelmed by the grief and futility that drowned the room. While she was still struggling to think of anything to say that had meaning, the parlormaid returned to announce that Dr. Mulgrew had arrived.

Shortly afterward, when the doctor was upstairs with Tormod and Eloise was waiting on the landing, the maid returned to ask Charlotte if she would receive Monsieur Alaric until Eloise should reappear.

"Oh." She caught her breath. Of course it would be impossible to refuse. "Yes, please—ask him to come in. I am sure Miss Lagarde would wish it."

"Yes, ma'am." The girl withdrew, and after a moment Paul Alaric appeared, soberly dressed, his face grave.

"Good afternoon, Mrs. Pitt." He showed no surprise, so he must have been forewarned of her presence. "I hope you are well?"

"Quite, thank you, Monsieur. Miss Lagarde is upstairs with the doctor, as I imagine you already know."

"Yes, indeed. How is she?"

"Most terribly distressed," she answered frankly. "I cannot remember having seen anyone look so shocked. I wish there was something we could say or do to comfort—it is frightening to be so helpless."

She had been afraid, almost angry in anticipation of it, that he might say something trite, but he did not.

"I know." His voice was very quiet, his mind seeking to understand the pain. "I really don't feel I can be of any use, but not to call seems so indifferent, as if I did not care."

"Are you a great friend of Mr. Lagarde's?" she inquired with surprise. She had not considered a realm of his life where he might find company with a man as much younger and as relatively slight in his pursuits as Tormod Lagarde. "Please do sit down," she offered as composedly as she could. "I daresay they will be a little while as yet."

"Thank you," he said, moving the skirts of his coat so he did not sit on them. "No, I cannot say that I found much in common with him. But then tragedies of this sort override all trivial differences, don't they?"

She looked up to find his eyes on her, curious and quite devoid of the impersonal glaze she was accustomed to in social conversation. She smiled slightly to show she was calm and grave and composed; then, as an afterthought, she smiled again, to show that she agreed with him.

"I see it has not kept you away," he continued. "It would have been quite excusable for you to have found other business and avoided what can only be painful. You do not know the Lagardes well, I believe? And yet you felt a desire to come?"

"I fear to little enough good," she said with sudden

unhappiness. "Except perhaps that Mama and Emily removed Mrs. Denbigh."

He smiled, and the irony inside him went all the way to his eyes.

"Ah, Amaryllis! Yes, I imagine that was something of a kindness in itself. I don't know why, but there seems to be little love lost between her and Eloise. It would have been a source of considerable pain had they become sisters-in-law."

"You don't know why?" Charlotte was surprised. Surely he could not be so blind! Amaryllis was intensely possessive and her feeling for Tormod was almost devouring in its heat. The thought of living in a household with Eloise would be unbearable to her. When two women shared a house, there was always one who became superior; that it should be Eloise was unlikely, and for Amaryllis intolerable, but if Eloise were driven, however subtly, into a subordinate position, then Tormod would feel a sense of obligation, even of pity, toward her, and that might be worse. No, if Paul Alaric could not see why Amaryllis felt as she did, he was disappointingly lacking in imagination.

Then she looked at his face and realized he had not understood that Eloise would remain with them. But Tormod could hardly leave her alone! She was young and desperately vulnerable—even if it would be socially acceptable, which it was not.

"I had formed the impression that Mrs. Denbigh was extremely fond of Mr. Lagarde," she began. What a ridiculously inadequate use of words for the violence of feeling she had seen in Amaryllis, the appetite of mind and body that boiled so close below the surface.

Slowly he smiled, without pleasure. He had seen it too.

"Perhaps I have too little insight, but a wife and a sister do not seem mutually exclusive."

"Really, Monsieur." Suddenly she was impatient with him. "If you were totally in love with someone, if you can conceive of such a feeling"—the acid of her rage for Caroline dripped through her voice—"would you care to share your daily life with somebody who knew that person infinitely better than you did? Who had a lifetime of memories in common, all the laughter and secrets, the friends, the childhood echoes—"

"All right, Charlotte—I understand." Suddenly he reverted to the moment of friendship they had shared in those terrible days in Paragon Walk when other jealousies and hatreds had seethed into murder. "I have been insensitive, even stupid. I can see that to someone like Amaryllis it would be unendurable. However, if Tormod is as badly injured as I have heard, then the question of marriage will never arise."

It was a statement of a truth that must have been obvious, yet the words fell like ice into the room. They were still silent, each wrapped in his own conception of its enormity, when Eloise returned.

She regarded Alaric without interest, as if she did not recognize him except as a shape, another figure that required acknowledgment.

"Good afternoon, Monsieur Alaric. It is kind of you to call."

The sight of her face, stiff, eyes sunken with shock, affected him more than anything Charlotte could have said. He forgot his manners, a lifetime of polite expressions. There was nothing in him but untutored emotion.

He put out his hand and grasped hers, his other hand touching her arm very gently, as if her skin might bruise.

"Eloise, I'm so sorry. Don't give up hope, my dear. One cannot know what may be possible, with time."

She stood quite still, not moving away from him, although it was not plain whether she was comforted by his closeness or simply oblivious to it.

"I don't know what to hope for," she said simply. "Perhaps that is very wrong of me?"

"No, not wrong," Charlotte said quickly. "You would have to be omniscient to know what is best. You cannot blame yourself, and please do not even think of it."

Eloise shut her eyes and turned away, pulling her arm

from Alaric, leaving him standing confused, aware he was on the outside of some tremendous grief and unable to reach it or share it.

Charlotte felt a certain compassion for him, but her first feeling was for Eloise. She stood up and went to her, putting her arms around her and holding her tightly. Eloise's body was yielding, lifeless, but Charlotte held on to her just the same. Out of the corner of her eye she saw Alaric's face, tight with pity, and then silently he turned and left, closing the door behind him with a tiny click as the latch went home.

Eloise did not move, nor did she weep; it was as if Charlotte were holding a sleepwalker whose nightmare imprisoned her mind and soul elsewhere. Yet Charlotte felt that her presence, the contact of her warmth, was worth something.

Minutes went by. Someone clattered up the back stairs. Rain drove in a gust against the windows. Still neither of them spoke.

At last the door opened and the maid spoke, then was overcome with embarrassment. "Mr. Inigo Charrington, ma'am. Shall I tell him you are not at home?"

"If you would inform Mr. Charrington that Miss Lagarde is not well," Charlotte said quietly. "Ask him to wait in the withdrawing room, and I shall go to him in a few moments."

"Yes, ma'am." The girl withdrew gratefully, without waiting for Eloise to confirm the command.

Charlotte stood for a moment longer, then guided Eloise to the sofa and laid her on it, kneeling beside her.

"Do you not think you would be better to lie down for a while?" she suggested. "Perhaps a dish of tea, or an herbal tisane?"

"If you wish." Eloise obeyed because she had no will to argue.

Charlotte hesitated, still not sure if there was anything else she could do, then accepted at last that it was futile and went to the door.

"Charlotte!"

She turned. For the first time there was expression in Eloise's face, even her eyes.

"Thank you. You have been kind. I may not appear as if I value it, but I do. You are right. Perhaps I shall drink something, and sleep for a little. I feel very tired."

Charlotte felt a surge of relief, as if hard knots inside her had slipped loose.

"I'll tell your maid to see that no one else is admitted for today."

"Thank you."

After delivering the directions to the maid and the footman, Charlotte went into the withdrawing room where Inigo Charrington stood by the mantelshelf, his face creased with anxiety, his coat still over his arm as if he were unsure whether to stay or go.

"Is she all right?" he said without any pretense at formality.

"No," Charlotte replied with equal honesty. "No, she isn't, but I don't know of anything else we can do to help."

"Should you have left her?" Inigo's face creased. "The last thing I want is for my calling to cause further distress."

"I sent the maid for a dish of tisane. Then I think she will rest for a time. Sleep will not alter the facts; she will still have to face them when she awakes, but she may have a little more strength for it."

"It's absolutely bloody!" he said with sudden anger. "First poor Mina, and now this!"

Charlotte was appalled to hear herself reply, "And your own sister—"

"What?" His quicksilver face was blank, almost comically empty.

This time embarrassment made her hold her tongue.

"Oh." Then he realized what she had said. "Oh yes. You mean Ottilie."

She wanted to apologize, to undo her intrusion, but she knew how close it could lie to Mina's death, and murder. And she had learned only too dreadfully how one murder could beget another—and another. Mina was not necessarily the last victim.

"I believe her death was very sudden—I mean, quite unexpected. It must have been a devastating shock." She had meant to be subtle, and ended by sounding crass.

"Unexpected?" Again he repeated her words. "Mrs. Pitt! Of course, how stupid of me. The policeman! But why the interest in Ottilie? She was eccentric, to put it at its mildest, but she certainly never harmed anyone—least of all Mina."

"That is the third time someone has said that she was eccentric," Charlotte said thoughtfully. "Was she really so very unusual?"

"Oh yes." He smiled at memory. "She did some appalling things. Once she got up on the dining table at dinner and sang a bawdy song. I thought Papa would die of it. Thank God no one else was there but the family, and one or two of my friends." His eyes were alight, gleaming with the memory, laughter and softness in them.

"Embarrassing, if it were to be repeated." Charlotte was confused by him; surely no man could act affection so perfectly and be lying? "One cannot afford a great deal of that if one is to remain in Society."

His face was bright, with mockery in it, but no malice, as if he himself were part of the joke.

"You know, Mrs. Pitt, I have the strongest feeling that in spite of your afternoon-tea behavior, you are a good deal more your husband's wife than your mother's daughter! You think we quietly suppressed Ottilie somewhere, don't you? Perhaps imprisoned her in our country house, locked in a disused wing, with an old family retainer to guard her?"

Charlotte felt the crimson heat flood up her face. She was blundering, and yet she must not stop; there would not be another chance.

"Actually, I thought you might have murdered her," she said tartly, furious with herself for her clumsiness. "And perhaps Mina knew it? She was a Peeping Tom, you know. And maybe a thief as well!"

His eyes opened wide in surprise.

"A Peeping Tom, yes, but a thief? Whatever gave you that idea?"

"Several things have gone missing in Rutland Place recently." She could still feel the scarlet under her skin. "None of them are very valuable of themselves, but at least one holds a secret which would be most embarrassing if it were to become known. Perhaps Mina was the thief, and she was killed to retrieve whatever it was?"

"No," he said with conviction. "Whatever she was killed for, it had nothing to do with the thefts. Anyhow, most of the things have been returned. They always are."

She stared at him. "Returned? How do you know?"

He took a long, slow breath. "I do. Just accept that. I have seen the things. Ask the people who lost them, they'll tell you."

"My mother lost something. She did not say she has it back."

"Presumably it was the article containing the embarrassing secret you spoke of, since you are aware of it. Maybe she was afraid you would think she stole it back. You have a highly suspicious mind, Mrs. Pitt!"

"I would hardly suspect my own mother of—" She stopped.

"Killing Mina?" he finished for her. "Perhaps not—but would the police be so well-disposed?"

"Where did Ottilie die? It was not at your country house, as you said."

"Oh." For several minutes he remained silent, standing with one foot on the hearth, and she waited. "Tell you what," he said at last. "Come with me and I'll show you!"

She exploded in frustration. "Don't be ridiculous! If it is something so secret—"

"Bring your own carriage," he interrupted. "And your own footman if you like."

"Policemen do not have carriages!" she snapped. "Or footmen!"

"No, I suppose they don't. Sorry. Bring your mother's.

I'll prove to you we didn't murder Ottilie."

Her mind raced to find a way of accepting that was not wildly foolish. If he or his family had killed Ottilie, and then Mina, they would not balk at killing her just as easily. Yet perhaps she was being offered the solution. And if the stolen articles had really been returned, how did Inigo Charrington know it? Why had Caroline not told her? Anyway, why would a thief take them and then return them? It made no sense—unless it was involved with the murder? Had Mina been the thief, and had the murderer retrieved all the stolen things to mask the recovery of the one thing that would have damned him?

Suddenly the solution came to her. Emily would never permit such an opportunity to escape, and she could provide the means for Charlotte to accept.

"I shall take my sister's carriage," she replied with an assurance she hoped she could justify. "And naturally I shall tell her for what purpose, and who is to accompany me."

"Excellent! Have you considered joining the police force yourself?"

"Don't be impertinent!" she said acidly, but inside excitement was boiling up.

He smiled. "I think you would enjoy it enormously. Actually, I think I might myself. I shall collect you at six o'clock. What you are wearing will be adequate, if you take off that thing from the neck."

"At six o'clock?" She was startled. "Why not now?"

"Because it is barely half past three, and far too early."

She did not understand, but at least by six o'clock she would have had opportunity to make some arrangement with Emily, both to borrow the carriage and to be perfectly sure that Inigo Charrington did not imagine he could harm her in any way and remain at liberty himself.

When she arrived at her mother's house and explained the matter to her sister—out of Caroline's hearing, of course—Emily was aghast. Her immediate reaction was that Inigo had undoubtedly murdered his sister and now intended to do away with Charlotte as well.

"He would hardly be so foolish," Charlotte replied, trying to weight her voice with conviction. "After all, if anything were to happen to me when you all know I am in his company, then he would damn himself completely. I believe he really is going to tell me how Ottilie died and show me some proof of it. I certainly will not believe it without proof!"

"Then I shall come with you," Emily said instantly.

It was only with difficulty that Charlotte succeeded in persuading her that her presence might risk the whole venture. If the nature of Ottilie's death had been such that the family was prepared to have it known, then Pitt would have discovered it in his own attempts. She could think of no satisfactory reason why Inigo was now willing to tell her, except that perhaps fear of the still greater danger of being suspected of murder hung over them. But if it were a matter of desperate embarrassment, even of humiliation, then the fewer people who were aware of it the easier for the family. And also since Charlotte was not of their own social circle, perhaps they would not suffer so acutely for her knowing the truth.

Emily accepted the argument with reluctance, but she was obliged to concede its validity. At least she made no protest about lending both her carriage and her footman. She would take the use of her mother's to return to her home.

Inigo called at six o'clock precisely, dressed in an elegant coat of darkest green with a fine top hat.

It was on the tip of Charlotte's tongue to ask him where on earth they might be going, but she bit back the words, remembering the need for discretion. Caroline had already delivered herself of her opinion of Charlotte's behavior, and she forbore expressing it again in front of Inigo.

Inside the carriage he made sure that she was comfortable, then offered no further remark, but sat silent, a smile curving his mouth, while they drove through gaslit streets Charlotte had not seen before, seemingly toward the heart of the city.

She lost track of time. They turned endless corners till her sense of direction, which had never been good, vanished, and when at last they pulled up she could not have made even a guess where they were.

Inigo climbed out and handed her down. The lamps were brilliant in the street, and some on the front of a large building were of different colors.

"Electric," he said cheerfully. "There are quite a few of them now."

She stared around her. There was music coming from somewhere, and a dozen or more people on the pavement, mostly men, some of whom were in evening dress.

"Where are we?" she asked in bewilderment. "Where is this?"

"It is a music hall, my dear," he said with a sudden, flashing smile. "One of the best. Ada Church is singing here tonight, and she'll pack 'em in."

"A music hall!" Charlotte was stunned. She had been expecting a cemetery, a clinic, or even a madhouse—but a music hall! It was preposterous—like a black farce.

"Come on." He took her arm and pushed her toward the doorway. She thought of resisting; she was both frightened and intensely curious. She had heard of Ada Church—she was said to be very handsome, and had one of the best music hall acts. Even Pitt had once commented that she had beautiful legs—of all things! He had smiled as he said it, and she had recognized that he was teasing, so she had refrained from asking him how he knew!

"Good evening, Mr. Charrington, sir." The doorman raised his hand in a little salute, although his eyes registered surprise at Charlotte. "Good to see you again, sir."

"You've been here before!" Charlotte accused him. "And often!"

"Oh yes."

She stopped, pulling against his arm. "And you have the impertinence to bring me with you! I know I am a policeman's wife, but I do not frequent places like this! I'll have you remember that there are a great many things men may do and women may not! Now you have had your rather cheap joke. I accept that it was tasteless and cruel of me to ask what happened to your sister. You have your revenge, and my apologies. Now please take me home!"

He held on to her arm tightly, too tightly for her to break away.

"Don't be so pompous," he said quietly. "You aren't any good at it. You wanted to know what happened to Ottilie. I'm going to tell you, and prove it. Now stop making a scene and come in. You'll probably even enjoy it, if you let yourself. And if you don't want to be seen here, then don't stand in the entranceway where everybody can look at you making a spectacle of yourself!"

His logic was irrefutable. She jerked her head in the air and sailed in on his arm, looking neither right nor left, and permitted him to seat her at one of the numerous tables in the center of the floor. She was dimly aware of tiers of boxes and balconies, like a theater, of a brilliantly lit stage, of gaudy colors, flounced dresses low off the shoulders, and the black and white of rich men's clothes mixed with the duller browns of those less comfortable, and even the checks of men come from the local streets. Waiters wove their way through the throng, glasses sparkled as they were raised and lowered, and all the time there was the murmur of voices and the lilt of music.

Inigo said nothing, but she was conscious of his bright face watching her, curiosity and laughter so close to the surface she could feel it as if he touched her.

A waiter came over and he ordered champagne, which in itself seemed to amuse him. When it came, he poured, lifted his glass, and toasted her.

"To detectives," he said, his eyes silver in the light. "Would to God all mysteries were so simple."

"I'm beginning to think it is the detectives who are simple!" she replied acidly, but she accepted the champagne and drank it. It was pleasantly sharp, neither sour nor sweet, and she felt less angry after it. When he poured more, she accepted that too.

Presently a juggler came onto the stage, and she watched him without particular interest. She granted that what he was doing was extremely difficult, but it seemed hardly worth the effort. He was followed by a comic who told some very odd jokes, but the audience seemed to find them hilarious. She had a suspicion she had failed to understand the point.

The waiter brought more champagne, and she became aware that she was beginning to find the colors and the music rather pleasing.

A chorus of girls appeared and performed a song she was sure she had heard before, and then a man popped up and twisted himself into the oddest contortions.

At last there was silence and then a roll of drums. The announcer held up his hands.

"Ladies and gentlemen, for your exclusive entertainment and enchantment, the culmination of your entire evening, the quintessence of beauty, of daring, of sheer dazzling delight—Miss Ada Church!"

There was a thunder of applause, even whistles and shouts, and the curtain went up. There was only one woman on the stage, slender with a tiny waist and long, long legs encased in black trousers. A tailcoat and white shirt hid nothing of her figure, and a top hat was perched at a rakish angle on a pile of flaming red hair. She was smiling, and the joy seemed to radiate out of her to fill the whole hall.

"Bravo, Ada!" someone shouted, and there was more clapping. As the orchestra started to play, her rich, throaty voice rang out in a gay, surging, bawdy song. It was less than vulgar, but there was an intimacy to it, full of suggested secrets.

The audience roared its approval and sang the chorus along with her. By the third song, Charlotte found to her horror that she was joining in as well, music swelling up inside her with a pleasant, tingling happiness. Rutland Place seemed a thousand miles away, and she wanted to forget its darkness and its miseries. All that was good was here in the lights and the warmth, singing along with Ada Church, and the vitality that conquered everything.

It would have shocked Caroline rigid, but now Charlotte was singing as loudly as the rest in the rollicking chorus: "Champagne Charlie is my name!"

When at last the curtain came down for the final time, she stopped clapping and turned to find Inigo staring at her. She ought to have felt embarrassed, but somehow she was so exhilarated it did not seem to matter.

He held up the last bottle of champagne, but it was empty. He signaled for the waiter to bring another. Inigo had barely opened it when Charlotte saw Ada Church herself walking toward them, giving a little wave of her arm, but gracefully avoiding the hands stretched out at her. She stopped at their table, and Inigo stood up immediately and offered her his chair.

She kissed him on the cheek, and he slipped an arm around her.

"Hello, darling," she said casually, then turned a dazzling smile on Charlotte.

Inigo bowed very slightly. "Mrs. Pitt, may I present my sister Ottilie? Tillie, this is Charlotte Pitt, the daughter of one of my neighbors, who has rather let her family down by marrying into the police! She fancied we had done away with you, so I brought her here to see that you are in excellent health."

For once, Charlotte was staggered beyond words.

"Done away with me?" Ottilie said incredulously. "How absolutely marvelous! You know, I do believe the thought occurred to Papa, only he didn't have the nerve!" She began to laugh; it rose bubbling in her throat and rang out in rich delight. "How superb!" She clung onto Inigo's arm. "Do you mean the police are actually questioning Papa as to what he did with me, because they suspect him of murder? I do wish I could see his face as he tries to explain himself out of that! He'd almost rather die than tell anyone what I really am!"

Inigo kept his arm around her, but suddenly his humor vanished.

"It's a good deal more than that, Tillie. There has been a murder, a real one. Mina Spencer-Brown was poisoned. She was a Peeping Tom, and it rather looks as if she saw something worth killing to keep secret. Not unnaturally, it occurred to the police that your disappearance might be that something."

Ottilie's laughter vanished instantly, and her hands tightened over his arm, long, slender hands with knuckles white where they gripped the stuff of his sleeve.

"Oh God! You don't think—"

"No," he said quickly, "it's not that. Papa has no idea—and I really don't think Mama cares. In fact, it has occurred to me, looking at her face across the table, that half of her rather wants everyone to know, especially him."

"But you put them back?" she said urgently. "You promised—"

"Of course I did, once I knew where they belonged. No one else knows." He turned to Charlotte. "I'm afraid my mother has a regrettable habit of picking up small things that do not belong to her. I do my best to replace them as soon as possible. I'm also afraid I took rather longer than usual with your mother's locket, because she said nothing about losing it so I didn't know to whom it belonged. I doubt I need to explain all the reasons for that?"

"No," Charlotte said quietly. "No, better not." She was puzzled. She liked Ambrosine Charrington. "Why on earth should she resort to petty stealing?"

Inigo pulled over another chair, and he and Ottilie sat down. Seeing them so close together, Charlotte realized the resemblance was quite marked. There could be no doubt who "Ada Church" was.

"Escape," Ottilie said simply, looking at Charlotte. "Perhaps you can't understand that? But if you had lived with Papa for thirty years, you might. Sometimes you get to feel so imprisoned by other people's ideas and habits and expectations that part of you grows to hate them, and you want to break their ideals, smash them, shock those people into really looking at you for once, reaching through the glass to touch the real flesh beyond."

"It's all right." Charlotte shook her head. "You don't need to explain. I've wanted to stand on the table and scream myself, once or twice, tell everybody what I really thought. Perhaps after thirty years I would have. Do you like it here?" She looked around at the tables, the sea of bodies and faces.

Ottilie smiled, without pretense. "Yes. I love it. I've cried myself to sleep a few times, and I've had long, lonely days—and nights. And a good few times I've thought I was a fool, or worse. But when I hear the music, the people singing with me, and the applause—yes, I love it. I daresay in ten years or fifteen I shall have nothing but vanity and memories, and wish I'd stayed at home and married suitably—but I don't think so."

Charlotte found herself smiling as well; the champagne still glowed inside her.

"You might marry well anyway," she said, and then suddenly her tongue felt awkward, and the next sentence did not sound quite as she had intended it should. "People from music halls sometimes do, so someone said—didn't they?"

Ottilie looked at her brother. "You've been filling her with champagne," she accused.

"Of course. That way she'll have an excuse in the morning. And I daresay not recall quite how much she enjoyed slumming!" He stood up. "Have some yourself, Tillie. I must take Charlotte home before her husband sends half the metropolitan police out for her!"

Charlotte did not hear what he said. The music had started in her head again, and she was happy for him to lead her to the door, collect her cloak, and send for the carriage. The air outside was sharp; its coldness made her feel a little dizzy.

He handed her up and closed the door, and the horses clopped gently through silent streets.

Charlotte began to sing to herself and was still going through the chorus for the seventh time when Inigo helped her down outside her own front door.

"Champagne Charlie is my name!" she sang cheerfully and rather loudly. "Champagne drinking is my game! There is nothing like the fizz, fizz, fizz. I'll drink every drop there is, is, is! I'm the darling"—she hesitated, then remembered—"of the barmaids! And Champagne Charlie is my name!"

The door swung open, and she looked up to see Pitt staring at her, his face white and furious, the gas lamp in the hallway behind him making a halo around his head.

"She's perfectly safe," Inigo said soberly. "I took her to meet my sister—after whom I believe you have been inquiring?"

"I—" Charlotte hiccuped and slid neatly to the floor.

"Sorry," Inigo said with a slight smile. "Good night!"

Charlotte was not even aware of Pitt bending down to pick her up and heave her inside with a comment that would have blistered her ears had she heard it.

Chapter Nine

Charlotte woke up with the most appalling headache she could ever remember. Pitt was standing at the far side of the bedroom opening the curtains, and she could not even see the red flowers on them. The light was painful; she closed her eyes in defense against it, then rolled over to hide her face in the pillow. The movement was a mistake. Hammer blows shivered through her skull and shot round her forehead, tightening the very bones.

She had never felt like this carrying Jemima! A little sickness in the mornings certainly—but never a head as if her brains were trying to beat their way out!

"Good morning." Pitt's voice cut through the thick silence, cold and definitely far from solicitous.

"I feel awful," she said pathetically.

"I'm sure you do," he said.

She sat up very slowly, holding her head with both hands.

"I think I may be sick."

"I shouldn't be in the least surprised." He was distinctly unmoved.

"Thomas!" She hauled herself out of bed, ready to cry with misery and an awful feeling of unexplained rejection. Then suddenly the whole evening returned to her—the music hall, Ottilie, Inigo Charrington, the champagne, and the silly song.

"Oh God!" Her legs folded under her, and she sat down on the edge of the bed sharply. She was still in half her underwear, and there were pins in her hair, uncomfortable, poking into her head. "Oh, Thomas! I'm so sorry!"

"Are you going to be sick?" he asked with only slightly more concern.

"Yes, I think so."

He came over and picked up the chamber pot from under the bed. He put it in her lap for her and pushed back her hair.

"I suppose you realize what could have happened to you?" he said, the ice in his voice changing to anger. "If Inigo Charrington or his father had killed Ottilie, it would have been the simplest thing in the world for them to have killed you too!"

It was several minutes before Charlotte was well enough to defend herself, to explain all her precautions.

"I took Emily's carriage and Emily's footman!" she said at last, gulping to get her breath. "I'm not entirely stupid!"

He took the pot from her and offered her a glass of water and a towel.

"That's a subject I wouldn't try debating just now if I were you," he said sourly. "Do you feel better now?"

"Yes, thank you." She would like to have been dignified, even aloof, but she had placed herself in an impossible position for it. "Everyone knew I was with him! He couldn't have done anything and got away with it, and I made sure he was as aware of that as I."

"Everyone?" His eyebrows rose, and there was a dangerously light tone in his voice.

Mercifully she realized her omission before he was obliged to tell her.

"I mean Mama and Emily," she corrected. It occurred to her to say she had sent the footman with a message for him, but she had never been able to lie to him successfully, and her head was too thick to be able to sort out enough wit to be consistent now. And consistency was vital to a good lie. "I didn't tell you because I thought I should be home before you were." She began to sound indignant. "I didn't know it was going to be a music hall! He simply said he would show me what had happened to Ottilie and prove they had not harmed her!"

"A music hall?" For a moment he forgot to be angry.

She sat upright on the edge of the bed. At least the nausea had gone, and it was easier to achieve a little dignity.

"Well, where did you imagine I had been? I was not in a public house, if that's what you think!"

"And why was it necessary to look for Ottilie Charrington in a music hall?" he said skeptically.

"Because that's where she was," she answered with some satisfaction. "She ran away to go on the halls! She's Ada Church." A sudden memory came back to her. "You know, the one with the nice legs!" she added spitefully.

Pitt had the grace to color. "I saw her professionally," he said tartly.

"Your profession or hers?" Charlotte inquired.

"At least I came home sober!" His voice rose with offended justice.

Her head was splitting, like a boiled egg being sliced off at the top, and she did not in the least wish to quarrel with him any further.

"Thomas, I'm sorry. I really am. I didn't realize it would affect me like this. It was just fizzy and nice. And I went there to find Ottilie Charrington." She pushed her hair back and began to take out the most painful of the pins. "After all, someone killed Mina! If it wasn't the Charringtons, then maybe it was Theodora von Schenck."

He sat down on the end of the bed, his shirttails hanging out, his tie undone.

"Is Ada Church really Ottilie Charrington?" he asked

seriously. "Charlotte, are you absolutely sure? It wasn't some obscure joke?"

"No, I'm sure. For one thing, she looked a lot like Inigo. You could see they were related. And something else I forgot! Ambrosine is the thief! Apparently she's been doing it for some time. Inigo always puts everything back as soon as he can, when he knows who they belong to. I suppose nobody admitted to finding them this time in case you suspected them of having murdered Mina for the things."

"Ambrosine Charrington?" He stared at her, confused and disbelieving. "But why? Why ever should *she* steal things?"

Charlotte took a deep breath. "Do you mind if I lie down again? Grace will look after Jemima. I don't think I can. If I stand up, my head will fall off."

"Why should Ambrosine Charrington steal things?" he repeated.

She tried to remember what Ottilie had said. As far as she could recall, she had understood it very well at the time.

"Because of Lovell." She struggled for a way of explaining it. "He's ossified!" She lay down very carefully, and a little of the pain subsided.

"He's what?"

"Ossified," she said again; the word pleased her. "Gone to bone. He doesn't listen and he doesn't look. I think part of her hates him. After all, her daughter's gone away and they have to pretend she's dead—"

"For heaven's sake, Charlotte, people of that class don't have daughters on the halls! It would be unthinkable to him!"

"I know that!" She pulled the covers closer around her chin. Quite suddenly she was cold. "But that wouldn't stop Ambrosine from loving Ottilie. I've met her. She's really very nice—the sort of person you want to smile at. She makes everything seem a little better. Maybe if Lovell wasn't such a prune she wouldn't have gone on the halls. She might have found it all right just to kick over the traces at home every now and again."

Pitt sat still for a few moments. "Poor Ambrosine," he said presently.

A dreadful thought occurred to Charlotte. She sat bolt upright, dragging all the clothes with her.

"You aren't going to arrest her?" she demanded.

He looked appalled. "No, of course not! I couldn't, even if I wanted to. There's no proof. And Inigo would certainly deny it. Not that I shall ask him." He pulled a face. "Still, it removes the thefts as a motive for Mina's death—although the Charringtons could still have killed her, I suppose."

"Why? Ottilie isn't dead!"

His face took on a look of infinite scorn. "And how do you imagine Lovell would care for it to be known in Society that Ada Church, the toast of the halls, is his daughter? He'd probably sooner be charged with her murder! At least it wouldn't be so damned funny!"

She twisted up her face painfully, torn between irony and frustration. She wanted to laugh, but the very idea hurt.

"What are you going to do?" she asked.

"Write a letter to Dr. Mulgrew."

She did not understand; the answer seemed ridiculous.

"Dr. Mulgrew? Why?"

He smiled at last. "Because he is in love with Ottilie. He might like to know she's alive after all. I don't imagine he'll care very much about her being on the halls. Anyway, he should have the right to find out."

Charlotte leaned back on the pillow with a deep sigh of satisfaction.

"You are interfering," she said pleasantly. She liked to think of Ottilie finding someone who would love her.

He grunted and tucked in his shirttails rather untidily.

"I know that."

Just before eleven o'clock, when Charlotte was still asleep, she dimly heard a knock on the door, and the next moment Emily was beside her.

"What's the matter with you?" Emily demanded. "Gracie wouldn't let me in! Are you ill?"

Charlotte opened her eyes. "She didn't make a very good job of it!" She squinted up at Emily sideways without moving. "I've got a terrible headache."

"Is that all? Never mind that." Emily dismissed it and sat down on the bed. "What happened? What about Ottilie Charrington? How did she die, and did her family do it? If you don't tell me, I shall shake you till you are really sick!"

"Don't touch me! I'm sick now! She isn't dead. She's excellently alive, and singing in the music halls."

"Don't be ridiculous." Emily's face creased with disbelief. "Who told you that?"

"Nobody told me. I went to the music hall and saw her myself. That's why I feel so awful now."

"You what?" Emily was incredulous. "You went to a music hall? What on earth did Thomas say? Honestly!"

"Yes, I did. And Thomas wasn't very pleased." Then memories came back, and Charlotte began to smile. "Yes, I did. With Inigo Charrington, and I drank champagne. Actually it was rather fun, once I got started."

A comical mixture of expressions chased across Emily's face: shock, laughter, and even envy.

"Serves you right you're sick," she said with some satisfaction. "I wish I'd been there! What was she like?"

"Marvelous. She really can sing, and in a way that makes you want to sing with her. She's—so very alive!"

Emily tucked up her legs more comfortably.

"So no one murdered her. Then that can't be why Mina was killed."

"Yes, it could." Charlotte recalled Pitt's argument. "They might have wanted to keep that hidden. After all, she's Ada Church!"

"Well, who is Ada Church?" Emily was puzzled.

"Ottilie is! Don't be stupid!"

"What's that supposed to mean?" Emily was too curious to be offended.

"Ada Church is one of the most famous singers on the halls."

"Is she? I don't know the music halls as well as you do!" There was distinct acid in her tone. "But that would be worth hiding. And there's always Theodora's income to look into. I expect Thomas is doing that. But we still have to do something about Mama and Monsieur Alaric!"

"Oh yes, I forgot about the locket. She has it back."

"She never told me!" Emily was angry, affronted by the callousness of it.

Charlotte sat up very slowly and was surprised that her head felt considerably better.

"She didn't tell me either. Inigo Charrington did. It was his mother who took it, and he put it back."

"Ambrosine Charrington took it? Whatever for? Explain yourself! Charlotte, did you get drunk?"

"Yes, I think I did. On champagne. But that's what he said. I wasn't drunk then." She explained with care what she could remember. "But that doesn't mean Mama can go on with her relationship with Monsieur Alaric."

"No, of course not," Emily said. "We'd better do something, and before it gets any worse. I've been giving it some thought lately, and I've come to a decision. We must try to persuade Papa to pay more attention to her, flatter her more, spend time with her. Then she will have no need of Monsieur Alaric." She looked up at Charlotte, challenging her to argue. She would leave the matter of Ambrosine Charrington and Charlotte's champagne to another time.

Charlotte considered it for a moment or two in silence. It would not be easy to convey to Edward the importance of such a course, and the change it would necessitate in his behavior, without allowing him to understand the reason for their concern, the danger of Caroline beginning a real affaire with Paul Alaric—not just suppressed passion anymore, but something that might end up in the bedroom. She frowned and took a deep breath.

"Oh, not *you!*" Emily said immediately. "I just want you for moral support, to agree with me. Don't you say anything, or you'll bring on a complete disaster."

It was not a time to take issue: defense could wait for a more suitable time.

"When are you going?" Charlotte asked.

"As soon as you have dressed. And you had better wash your face with cold water and pinch your cheeks a bit. You are very pasty."

Charlotte gave her a sour look.

"And you'd better wear something bright," Emily went on. "Do you have a red dress?"

"No, of course I don't." Charlotte crawled out of bed. "Where should I wear a red dress to? I've got a wine-colored skirt and coat."

"Well, put it on and have a cup of tea. Then we'll go and call on Papa. I've arranged it. I know he is at home today, and Mama has a luncheon engagement with a friend of mine."

"Did you arrange that as well?"

"Of course I did!" Emily spoke with deliberate patience, as if to a rather tiresome child. "We don't want her coming home in the middle! Now hurry up and get ready!"

Edward was delighted to have the company of both his daughters and sat at the head of the luncheon table with a smile of complete contentment on his face.

"How very pleasant to see you, my dear," he said to Charlotte. "I'm so glad Emily found you at home and able to come. It seems a long time since I saw you last."

"You have not been home when we have called lately." Charlotte took her cue without waiting for Emily.

"No, I suppose not," Edward said without giving it thought.

"We have been quite frequently," Emily said casually, taking a little roast chicken on her fork. "And then gone out visiting with Mama. Quite an agreeable way to spend one's time, providing one is not required to do too much of it. It can become tedious—the conversations are so much the same."

"I thought it was an occupation you enjoyed?" Edward

looked mildly surprised. He had not considered the matter greatly, merely taken it for granted.

"Oh, we do." Emily ate the chicken and then frowned at him. "But incessant female company has very limited pleasures, you know. I'm sure that if George did not offer me his companionship in the evening and take me to dinner elsewhere occasionally, I should find myself longing for the conversation of some other gentleman. A woman is not at her best unless there is a man she admires to observe her, you know?"

Edward smiled indulgently. He had always found Emily the easiest of his daughters, without being aware that it was largely because she was also the most skilled at judging his moods and masking her own feelings accordingly. Sarah had been too impatient and, being the eldest and the prettiest, a little selfish, and Charlotte was far too blunt and would talk about totally unsuitable things, which embarrassed him.

"George is a fortunate man, my dear," he said, helping himself to more vegetables. "I hope he appreciates it."

"I hope so too." Emily's face suddenly became serious. "It is one of the saddest things that can happen to a woman, Papa, for her husband to lose his regard for her, his desire for her company, his general observance of her well-being. You have no idea how many women I have seen begin to look elsewhere for admiration because their husbands have grown to ignore them."

"To look elsewhere?" He was a little startled. "Really, Emily, I hope you do not mean what that sounds like? I would not care to think of you associating with such women. Others might think the same of you!"

"I should dislike that very much." She was perfectly grave. "I have never given George the least cause for displeasure with my conduct, especially on that subject." She opened her eyes very wide and blue. "And yet, on the other hand, I cannot find it in my heart entirely to blame a woman whose husband has begun to treat her with indifference, if some other man, with pleasant manners and agreeable nature, should find her attractive and tell her so—and she should, in her loneliness, be equally drawn to him—"

"Emily!" Now he was shocked. "Are you condoning adultery? Because that is unfortunately close to what it sounds like!"

"Oh, certainly not!" she said with feeling. "Such a thing will always be wrong. But there are some situations when I cannot find it in me to say that I do not understand." She smiled at him. "Take Monsieur Alaric, the Frenchman, for instance. Such a handsome man, so beautifully mannered, and such an air about him. Do you not agree, Charlotte? I wondered once or twice if perhaps poor Mina was in love with him and not Tormod Lagarde at all. Monsieur Alaric has so much more maturity, don't you think? Even a touch of mystery about him, which is most compelling. I have often wondered if he is really French. We have only assumed it. Now if Alston Spencer-Brown had been devoting too much of his attention to his business affairs, and had begun to grow so accustomed to Mina that he seldom paid her a compliment anymore, or bothered with any little romantic gestures, such as flowers, or a visit to the theater"—she drew breath—"then Monsieur Alaric would only have to flatter her a little, exhibit the merest admiration, and she would be enchanted with him. He would be the answer to all her unhappiness and her feeling of no longer mattering."

"That is no excuse—" he began, but his face was noticeably paler and he had forgotten the chicken. "And you should not speculate about people in such a disgraceful way, Emily! The poor woman is dead and quite unable to defend herself!"

Emily was unperturbed. "I am not suggesting it as an excuse, Papa. One does not need excuses—only reasons." She finished the last of her meal and set down her knife and fork. "Now that poor Mina is dead, I have observed that Monsieur Alaric has found Mama most pleasant and has sought her company to walk with and to talk with." She smiled brightly. "Which shows him to be a man of improving taste! Indeed, Charlotte has said he seems most sympathetic. I do believe Charlotte was quite drawn to him herself."

Charlotte looked across the table at Emily with less than affection. There seemed to be a shade of malicious pleasure in her tone.

"Charming," she agreed, avoiding her father's eye. "But I presume that Mama is not in Mrs. Spencer-Brown's unfortunate situation?"

Edward stared from one to the other of them. Twice he opened his mouth to demand that they speak more clearly what they meant. And twice he decided he did not wish to know.

The maid came and cleared away the dishes and then brought in the pudding.

"It has been some time since we went to the theater," Edward remarked at last, very casually, as if it were a totally new thought. "There must be something new of Gilbert and Sullivan out now. Perhaps we should go and see it."

"An excellent idea," Emily answered, equally lightly. "I can recommend a good jeweler if you have a fancy to give Mama some small keepsake? He has a most romantic turn of mind and is not overly expensive. I know he has quite lovely cameos, because I wished George to buy me one. I always think they are so personal."

"Don't organize me, Emily!"

"I'm sorry, Papa." She smiled at him charmingly. "It was only a suggestion. I am sure you will do much better yourself."

"Thank you." He looked at her with dry humor, but his hands were still tight on his napkin and he sat very upright in his chair.

Emily took a little more pudding.

"This is delicious, Papa," she said sweetly. "It was so nice of you to invite us."

Edward forbore commenting that she had invited herself.

At half past two Edward returned to the city.

"What are you going to do about Mina?" Emily asked as soon as she and Charlotte were alone. "We still have no idea who killed her, or even why."

"Well, the obvious reason is that she snooped once too often," Charlotte answered.

"I had imagined that for myself!" Emily was a little waspish now that the tension of the interview with Edward was over. "But upon whom?"

"It could have been the Charringtons—if not over Ottilie, then maybe over Ambrosine taking things." Charlotte was thinking aloud. "But personally I think Theodora von Schenck is more likely. I can remember Mina making remarks about her income and where it came from. I think maybe she already knew, and she was having fun stirring up our suspicions. Perhaps in time she would even have told us." Her face darkened as the ugliness of the reality opened up in front of her. "That's pathetic, isn't it—seeking to impress people and make yourself interesting by spreading pieces of gossip about people, hinting that you know terrible secrets."

"It's damnably dangerous!" Emily's mouth pulled into a hard, unforgiving line. "Think of the harm she could do to other people, never mind what happened to her! I suppose she hardly deserved to be killed for it, but it's a wicked thing to do nevertheless."

"And pathetic," Charlotte insisted. "She must have had nothing of her own inside herself to be forever staring outwards, needing to know about other people's lives."

"That hardly excuses her!" Emily was angry. "Everybody's unhappy some time or other—we don't all go around prying and repeating!"

Charlotte did not bother to argue. "She was worse than that," she said. "She invented, sowing seeds of all sorts of vicious things. I suppose there is an ugly side to most people's imaginations, if you want to reach for it." She changed her expression entirely. "You were excellent with Papa, but we still have to discourage Monsieur Alaric a little. I have heard he knows Theodora quite well. I shall go and call on him this afternoon and see if he has any idea where her money comes from."

Emily's eyebrows rose. "Indeed? And how do you propose to introduce yourself to such a call, let alone elicit that kind of information from him?"

"I shall throw myself on his mercy." Charlotte made a rapid and rather violent decision.

"You'll do what?" Emily was startled.

"With regard to Mama—you fool!" Charlotte snapped, her face suddenly hot. "I shall contrive to let him know that Papa is aware of the—friendship—and that he does not look kindly on it."

"You never 'contrived' anything in your life!"

"I didn't say I was going to be subtle! Then when I have done that, I shall talk about Mina and how upset everyone is. Why? What are you going to do?"

"If that is what you are going to do, then I shall go and call upon Theodora at the same time, before Monsieur Alaric has an opportunity to warn her, if by chance they are in it together. If there is anything to be in? It will be a little difficult because I don't know her, but if you can go to a music hall with Inigo Charrington, I daresay I shall manage an unintroduced call upon Madame von Schenck!"

"You need not have brought up the music hall again!" Charlotte said sourly. "That was unnecessary."

"Well, don't worry, I shan't tell Thomas you went alone to call on Monsieur Alaric," Emily returned. "In fact, I think you would be wise not to let him know you have any continued interest in the affair at all."

"If you imagine he will suppose I have forgotten it, you hardly know Thomas." Charlotte made a rueful face. "He wouldn't believe it for a moment!"

"Then use a little sense—and at least make sure you stay sober!" Emily responded. "You can take my carriage to Monsieur Alaric's house, and I shall walk. That way it will be marginally more respectable."

"Thank you!"

Charlotte had misgivings as soon as the carriage turned out of Rutland Place, and were it not that she would appear such a fool, she would have called the driver and told him to return her at once.

But she was committed. It was an extraordinary thing to do, and possibly Alaric would misinterpret her motives; her face flushed hot at the thought of it. Caroline was certainly not the only woman to have become so dazzled by him as to have lost all sense of proportion!

By the time the carriage pulled to a stop in Paragon Walk and the footman handed her out, she sincerely hoped that Paul Alaric was not at home and she would be spared the whole affair and could retire with integrity. But fortune was against her—he was not only at home, but received her with pleasure.

"How charming to see you, Charlotte." He stood a little away from her, smiling, and if he was surprised he concealed it entirely. But of course he would; not to do so would be discourteous.

"That is very generous of you, Monsieur Alaric," she replied, then instantly felt stiff. She was barely through the door, and already her interview was not going the way she had intended. Perhaps in France, or wherever he came from— they had all assumed he was French, but no one recalled his saying so—it was less familiar there to use a person's Christian name.

He was still smiling, and she collected her scattered wits with an effort.

"Please forgive my calling upon you without either invitation or having left my card beforehand." That was ridiculous and he knew it as well as she did, but it afforded her a way to begin.

"I am sure the circumstances are quite unusual," he said gently. "May I offer you some refreshment—a dish of tea?"

It would give her something to occupy her hands graciously, and would mean that her stay would be at least half an hour.

"Thank you," she said. "That would be most pleasant." She sat down on the most comfortable-looking chair, and he rang the bell, gave the maid instructions, and then sat opposite her on a simple dark velvet sofa.

The room was unusually spare of ornament; there were great numbers of leatherbound, gold-tooled books in a mahogany case, a soft gray seascape above the mantel, and a Turkish prayer rug so brilliant it was like a cathedral window. The whole was alien . . . and beautiful.

He was sitting easily, still smiling, one leg crossed over the other, but there was a seriousness about his eyes. He knew she would not have come over any trivial or social matter, and he was waiting for her to begin.

Her mouth was dry; all small talk eluded her.

"Emily and I have been dining with Papa," she said rather abruptly.

He did not interrupt, still watching her steadily, frankly.

She took a breath and plunged on. "We were obliged to discuss a rather painful subject—quite apart from Mina's death, or poor Tormod's injury."

A shadow of concern crossed his face. "I'm sorry."

She had very little knowledge how much of the relationship was purely on Caroline's part. She must be careful, as she had so far seen him display nothing beyond extreme courtesy. Either he was far more discreet than Caroline or—more probably—he was unaware of the depth of her feeling. After all, he did not know Caroline as Charlotte did.

She cleared her throat. Now that she must either commit herself or allow the subject to drop and talk of something else, she found it unexpectedly difficult. She was very conscious of him sitting only a few feet away from her.

Once, she had considered him as the leader of a black magic ritual—that seemed preposterous now. But was she crediting him with less vanity and more compassion than he possessed? Might he not enjoy the fascination he held for them, seemingly without effort?

She swallowed and began again, sounding far more pompous than she wished. "It seems that Papa has been too much engaged in his business lately and has not paid the attention to his domestic life that he should. Poor Mama has felt a little neglected, I think. Of course she has not complained. One cannot ask for small signs of affection from one's husband, because even if he responds they are then of no value—you feel you have prompted them yourself, and he does not truly mean them."

"So you and your sister have prompted him?" he suggested, understanding beginning to show in his eyes.

"Quite," she agreed quickly. "We would be deeply distressed to see our family hurt by a misapprehension. In fact, we do not intend to allow it to happen. These things grow out of hand very quickly—new affections form, other parties are drawn in, and before you can undo it, there is . . ."

He was looking directly at her, and she found herself unable to go on. It was quite obvious now that he knew what she meant.

"A domestic tragedy," he finished for her. She noticed with surprise that there was a faint color under his skin, a consciousness of himself—a raw and unpleasing light. Suddenly, with a rush of warmth for him, she realized he had been unaware of his power, underrating its depth completely.

Either he had not understood other women in the past or he had considered their own natures the cause and himself merely the unfortunate catalyst.

"I think tragedy is the appropriate word," she continued. "Perhaps we should look a little more closely at what passions can do. For example, take Mrs. Denbigh. You have seen her? Her despair over Mr. Lagarde would hardly be covered by so gentle and commonplace a term as unhappiness, do you think?"

For several minutes he was silent, and she began to grow uncomfortable as she became aware of his eyes on her. She was very sensitive to being alone in the room with him. Visiting him by herself in his home was a ridiculous thing to have done, and she should have insisted that Emily come with her. Someone was bound to have seen her; there was always a servant about. There would be talk! She had no reputation to lose—Paragon Walk did not care about her—but what about Emily? Someone might have recognized Charlotte from the time when she had stayed with Emily during the murders here.

And what of Paul Alaric himself?

She blushed with discomfort at her own thoughtlessness—and yet she had not wished Emily to accompany her!

Very slowly she raised her eyes to meet his and was startled by the perception in them, a closeness as if he and she had touched, as if her skin had felt a sudden warmth, a tingling.

She must leave. She had said what she came for. Emily's carriage was at the door and would take her back to Rutland Place. She could join Emily at Theodora von Schenck's house.

Thought of Theodora reminded her of the other purpose of her visit. She must force herself to ask him now; the idea of returning was unthinkable.

The maid brought the tea and retired. She took a sip of it gratefully; her mouth was dry and her throat tight.

"Emily has called to see Madame von Schenck," she remarked as conversationally as she was able. "I believe you know her quite well."

He was surprised, and his dark eyes widened. "Moderately. The acquaintance is more a business one than social, although I find her very congenial."

Now it was she who was startled. She had hardly expected him to be so frank.

"Business? What sort of business do you mean?" Then, realizing how blunt that sounded, she went on: "I did not know Madame von Schenck had business. Or did you perhaps know her husband?" She stammered, "I—I mean—"

"No." He smiled faintly at her embarrassment, but there was no unkindness in it. "I did not, although I believe he was a most charming man. So much so that she has never desired to remarry."

Charlotte pretended that she found such a thing hard

to understand, although in truth the thought of remarrying, should anything happen to Pitt, was quite absurd to her.

"Not even for the security of having a husband?" She tried to sound sincere. "After all, she has two children to support."

"And an excellent business head." He was quite openly amused now. "Not in the least a fashionable thing to have, which I imagine is why she is discreet about it. Especially since her particular interest lies in the area of bathroom furniture!" His smile broadened. "Not exactly what the ladies of Rutland Place would find suitable—the design of baths and other such hardware. And she is most imaginative in selling and precise in her finances. I think she has begun to make a considerable profit."

She knew there was a silly smile on her face. It was all so ridiculously harmless, even funny, that she wanted to laugh. She gathered herself and was ready to rise, but before she could frame the words to excuse herself, the maid opened the door again to bring in a choice of cakes and was followed immediately by Caroline.

Charlotte froze, halfway to her feet, the smile dead on her lips.

For an instant Caroline did not see her; her face was turned to Alaric, soft with excitement and pleasure.

Then she saw Charlotte, and every vestige of color bleached out of her skin. She looked at her as she might have at some horned thing risen out of the ground.

There was absolute silence in the room. The maid was too frightened to let go of the trolley.

With a tremendous effort Caroline took a deep breath, and then another.

"I beg your pardon, Monsieur Alaric," she said in a shaking voice. "I appear to have interrupted you. Do excuse me." She stepped backward past the maid and out the door.

Charlotte glanced for a moment at Paul Alaric and saw his face as white and appalled as she knew hers must be, mirroring the same realization and guilt that she felt. Then she ran across the room, pushed the maid aside, and swung the door open.

"Mama!"

Caroline was in the hallway and could not have failed to hear her, but she did not turn her head.

"Mama!"

The footman opened the front door and Caroline walked out into the sun. Charlotte went after her. Snatching her cloak from the footman as she passed, she clattered down the steps and out onto the street.

She caught up with Caroline and took her arm. It was stiff, and Caroline shook her off sharply. She kept her face straight ahead.

"How could you?" she said very quietly. "My own daughter! Is your vanity so much that you would do this to me?"

Charlotte reached for her arm again.

"Don't speak to me." Caroline jerked away roughly. "Don't speak to me, please. Not ever again. I don't wish to know you."

"You're being stupid!" Charlotte said as fiercely as she could without raising her voice for the whole street to hear. "I went there to find out if he knew how Theodora von Schenck got her money!"

"Don't lie to me, Charlotte. I'm perfectly capable of seeing for myself what is going on!"

"Are you?" Charlotte demanded, angry with her mother not for misjudging her but for being so vulnerable, for allowing herself to be swept away by a dream till the awakening threatened everything that really mattered. "Are you, Mama? I think if you could see anything at all, you would know as well as I do that he doesn't love you in the least." She saw the tears in Caroline's eyes, but she had to go on. "It isn't anything to do with me, or any other woman! He is simply unaware that your feeling for him is anything more than pleasant—a little relief from boredom—a courtesy! You have built up a whole romantic vision around him that has nothing to do with the kind of person he is underneath. You don't even know him really! All you see is what you want to!" She held on to Caroline's arm, this time too hard for her to snatch it away.

"I know exactly how you feel!" she went on, keeping up with her. "I did the same with Dominic. I pinned all my romantic ideals onto him, put them over him like a suit of armor, till I had no idea what he was like underneath them. It isn't fair! We haven't the right to dress anyone else in our dreams and expect them to wear them for us! That isn't love! It's infatuation, and it's childish—and dangerous! Just think how unbearably lonely it must be! Would you like to live with someone who didn't even look at or listen to you, but only used you as a figure of fantasy? Someone to pretend about, someone to make responsible for all your emotions so that they are to blame if you are happy or unhappy? You have no right to do that to anyone else."

Caroline stopped and stared at her, tears running down her face.

"Those are terrible things to say, Charlotte," she whispered, her voice difficult and hoarse. "Terrible."

"No, they aren't." Charlotte shook her head hard. "It is just the truth, and when you've looked at it a bit longer you'll find you like it!" Please God that could be true!

"Like it! You tell me I have made a ridiculous fool of myself over a man who doesn't care for me at all, and that even the feeling I had was an illusion, and selfish, nothing to do with love—and I shall come to like that!"

Charlotte threw her arms around her because she wanted to be close to her, share in her pain and comfort her. Besides, looking at her face right now would be an intrusion into privacy too deep to allow forgetting afterward.

"Maybe 'like it' was a silly phrase, but when you see it is true, you will find the lies something you don't even want to remember. But believe me, everyone who was ever capable of passion has made a fool of themselves at least once. We all fall in love with a vision sometime. The thing is to be able to wake up and still love."

For a long time neither of them said anything more, but stood in the footpath with their arms around each other. Then very slowly Caroline began to relax, her body lost its stiffness, and the pain changed from anger to simple weeping.

"I'm so ashamed of myself," she said softly. "So terribly ashamed!"

Charlotte's arms tightened. There was not anything else to say. Time would ease it away, but words could not.

In the distance there was the sound of hooves, someone else making an early visit.

Caroline straightened up and sniffed hard. For a moment her hand lingered in Charlotte's; then she withdrew it and fished in her reticule for a handkerchief.

"I don't think I shall make any more calls this afternoon," she said calmly. "Perhaps you would like to come home for tea?"

"Thank you," Charlotte said. They began to walk again, slowly. "You know, Mina was quite wrong about Theodora. Her money doesn't come from a brothel at all, or blackmail—she has a business for selling bathroom furniture!"

Caroline was stunned. Her eyebrows shot up.

"You mean—"

"Yes, water closets!"

"Oh, Charlotte!"

Chapter Ten

Two days later Pitt was still as confused as ever about who had killed Mina Spencer-Brown. He had a wealth of facts, but no conclusions that were subject to proof—and, worse than that, none that satisfied his own mind.

He stood still on the pavement of Rutland Place in the sun. It was warm there, sheltered from the east wind by the high houses, and he stopped to collect his thoughts before going on to Alston for yet more questioning.

He had been talking to Ambrosine Charrington, and the interview had left him less sure than he had been before he went. It was always possible that Mina had observed Ambrosine in the act of stealing and Ambrosine had been unable to deny it. If that had been so, Mina might have threatened her with exposure.

But would Ambrosine have minded? From what Charlotte had told him, that was far from the case! She might even have been perversely pleased by the disgrace. Ottilie had said it was her motive for doing it in the first place, a desire to shock and distress her husband, to break out of the mold into which he had cast her. Of course she might well not see it so lucidly herself. But he found it impossible to believe she would commit murder to protect a secret she half wanted known.

Did she hate Lovell enough to have allowed Mina to blackmail him? In theory it was possible. It had an irony that would appeal to Ambrosine.

And yet he felt that he would have had some sense of the anger and the tension in Lovell, and of the bitter taste of satisfaction in Ambrosine herself. And he had not. To him she seemed just as elegantly imprisoned as before, and Lovell just as undisturbed in his massive, impregnable security.

Mention of Ottilie had shaken Lovell's composure most markedly, and he had become white-lipped, sweat-browed. He had tried intensely to hide the whole affair. Yet Ambrosine left Pitt entirely comfortable!

Perhaps it was Alston Spencer-Brown after all? Maybe Mina's long-standing involvement with Tormod Lagarde had finally proved too much for him, and when Alston had learned that she was still enamored, he had procured more belladonna from some other doctor, in the city, poured it into the cordial, and left it to do its work.

All Pitt's investigations had pointed to the conclusion that Mina's infatuation with Tormod had been discreet but very real. Many a husband had killed for less, and Alston's ordinary exterior could hide a violent possessiveness, a sense of outrage where murder might seem to him no more than justice.

Pitt was driven back to the facts. The cordial wine was homemade, a mixture of elderberry and currants. People in Rutland Place did not make their own wines! Of course, it was impossible to tell who might have been given some, and if they had used it to mask poison, they would hardly own to its possession now.

The belladonna could have been distilled by anyone, or even crushed from the deadly nightshade plant itself, which, while less common than the brightly flowered woody nightshade, was far more lethal. It did not need the fruit that ripened in the autumn; even the leaves were sufficient. And they might be found in hedgerows or woodlands in any wild area in the southeast of the country.

It was perhaps a little early for a biennial plant, but in a sheltered place—or even blown and taken root in a conservatory or hothouse? A few shoots above the ground would be enough.

The facts proved nothing. Anyone could have given her the bottle, at almost any time. Mina's servants had not seen it before, or any like it, but then one does not always tell servants of cordial wine. It is not drunk at table. Anyone could have picked the nightshade and crushed the leaves. It required no skill, no special knowledge. It was well-known lore that the plant killed; every child was warned. Even its name told as much.

He was driven back again to motive, although you could not damn anyone on motive alone. One man will kill for sixpence, or because he feels he has been insulted. Another will lose reputation, fortune, and love—anything rather than commit murder.

He was still standing in the sun when a hansom cab swung around the far corner and clattered down the Place, jolting to a stop in front of the Lagardes' entrance.

Pitt was close enough to see Dr. Mulgrew practically fall out, clutching his bag, and scramble up the steps. The door opened before he got to it, and Mulgrew disappeared inside.

Pitt hesitated. Natural instinct prompted him to wait there a while and see what should happen next. But then, since there was a man in desperate injury in the house, an emergency call for the doctor was not surprising and probably had nothing whatsoever to do with Mina's death. If Pitt were honest, he would admit that he was using the doctor's arrival as an excuse to put off the next round of questions.

When Pitt got to the Spencer-Browns' Alston was out, which in a way was a relief, although it only postponed what would have to be done another time. He contented himself with talking to the servants again, going over endless recollections, impressions, opinions.

He was still there, sitting in the kitchen accepting with considerable pleasure the cook's offer of luncheon with the rest of the servants, when the scullery door burst open, a maid ran in, and the smells of stew and puddings were dissipated by the scents of sharp wind and earthy vegetables.

"For goodness' sake, Elsie, close that door!" the cook snapped. "Where were you brought up, girl?"

Elsie kicked at the door with one foot, obeying out of habit.

"Mr. Lagarde's dead, Mrs. Abbotts!" she said, her eyes like saucers. "Just died this morning, so May from over the way says! Seen the doctor come, she did, and go again. A mercy, I says! Poor gentleman. So beautiful, he was. Reckon as he was destined to die. Some of us is. Shall I go and shut the blinds?"

"No, you will not!" the cook said tartly. "He didn't die in this house. Mr. Lagarde's passing is not our business. We've enough of our own griefs. You just get on with your work. And if you're late for luncheon you'll go hungry, my girl!"

Elsie scuttled off, and the cook sat down sharply.

"Dead." She regarded Pitt sideways. "I suppose I shouldn't say so, but perhaps it is as well, poor creature. You'll excuse me, Mr. Pitt, but if he was as terrible hurt as they say, could be the Lord's mercy he's gone." She mopped her brow with her apron.

Pitt looked at her, a buxom woman with thick graying hair and an agreeable face, now twisted with a mixture of relief and guilt.

"A nasty shock, all the same," he said quietly. "On top of all else that has happened lately. Bound to upset you. You look a bit poorly. How about a drop of brandy? Do you keep any about the kitchen?"

She looked at him through narrow eyes, suspicion aroused.

"I'm used to such things," he said, reading her thoughts perfectly. "But you aren't. Let me get you some?"

She bridled a little, like a hen fluffing out her feathers.

"Well—if you think— On the top shelf over there, behind the split peas. Don't you let that Mr. Jenkins see it, or he'll have it back in his pantry before you can say 'knife.'"

Pitt hid his smile and stood up to pour a generous measure into a cup and pass it to her.

"How about yourself?" she offered with a little squint.

"No, thank you," he said, and put the bottle back, replacing the split peas. "Strictly for shock. And I'm afraid it's my business to deal with death, on occasion."

She drank the cup to the bottom, and he took it and rinsed it out in the scullery sink.

"Most civil of you, Mr. Pitt," she said with satisfaction. "Pity as we can't help you, but we can't, and that's a fact. We never seen any cordial wine like that, nor any bottle neither. And we don't know anything as to why anyone should want to murder the mistress. I still say as it's someone what's mad!"

He was torn between duty to continue with questions— so far totally unprofitable—and an intense desire to forget the whole thing and abandon himself to the pleasures of Mrs. Abbotts' luncheon. He settled for the luncheon.

Afterward he considered whether to continue his questioning, but the shock of Tormod's death hung heavy over everything. In many houses curtains were drawn, and a silence muffled even the usual civil exchanges till they seemed an indecency.

A little after two o'clock he gave up and returned to the police station. He pulled out all the evidence they had collected to date and began to read it over again, in the somewhat forlorn hope that a new insight would emerge, a relationship between facts that he had overlooked before.

He had discovered nothing by quarter to five, when Harris poked his head around the door and announced Amaryllis Denbigh.

Pitt was startled. He had expected that with the blow of Tormod's death she would be prostrated with grief, even in need of medical care, so fierce had been her anguish over his accident, according to Charlotte. And he trusted Charlotte's judgment of people, if not always of her own behavior! Although in truth he was less outraged by the music hall incident, now that he thought about it, than he intended she should know.

But why on earth was Amaryllis here?

"Shall I send her in, sir?" Harris said irritably. "She looks in a right state to me. You want to be careful of her!"

"Yes, I suppose you'd better. And stay here yourself, in case she faints or becomes hysterical," Pitt said. The thought was an extremely unpleasant one, but he could not afford to deny her entrance. Perhaps at last this was the catalyst, and she might give him the sliver of fact he so desperately needed.

"Yes, Mr. Pitt, sir." Harris withdrew formally, signifying his disapproval, and a moment later followed Amaryllis in.

Amaryllis was white-faced, her eyes glittering, her hands moving over the folds of her skirt, into her muff, and out again over her skirt. She had entered the room with black veiling over her face, but now she threw it off.

"Inspector Pitt!" She was so stiff her body shook.

"Yes, Mrs. Denbigh." He did not like her, yet in spite of himself he was moved to pity. "Please sit down. You must be feeling distressed. May we offer you some refreshment, a cup of tea?"

"No, thank you." She sat down with her back to Harris. "I should like to speak to you in private. What I have to say is very painful."

Pitt hesitated. He did not want to be alone with her; she was obviously on the border of hysteria, and he was afraid of a storm of weeping that would be completely beyond his abilities to deal with. He thought of sending for the police surgeon. His eyes flickered to Harris.

"If you please?" Amaryllis' voice was harsh, rising in a kind of desperation. "This is my duty, Inspector, because it concerns the murder of Mrs. Spencer-Brown, but it is extraordinarily painful for me and I do not wish the added mortification of having to repeat it in front of a sergeant!"

"Of course," Pitt said immediately. He could not draw back now. "Sergeant Harris will wait outside."

Harris stood up with a sour look of warning to Pitt over Amaryllis' shoulder, then went out, closing the door firmly.

"Well, Mrs. Denbigh?" Pitt asked. It was a strange moment. He knew so much about these people, had studied them until they stalked his sleep, and yet now it was she, quite casually walking in here, unasked, who was about to tell him what might be the solution to the whole matter.

Her voice was grating, low, as if the words hurt her.

"I know who killed Mina Spencer-Brown, Mr. Pitt. I did not tell you before because I could not betray a friend. She was dead, and there was nothing to do for her. Now it is different. Tormod is dead too." Her face was white and empty, like an unpainted doll. "There is no reason now to lie. He was too noble. He protected her all her life, but I shan't! Justice can be done. I shall not stand in its way."

"I think you had better explain, Mrs. Denbigh." He wanted to encourage her, yet there was something inexpressibly ugly in the room and he could feel it as surely as damp in the air. "What lies have there been? Who was Mr. Lagarde protecting?"

Her eyes flashed wider. "His sister of course!" Her voice shook. "Eloise."

He was surprised, but he stopped before speaking, masked his feelings, and looked across at her calmly.

"Eloise killed Mrs. Spencer-Brown?"

"Yes."

"How do you know that, Mrs. Denbigh?"

She was breathing in and out so deeply he could see the rise and fall of her bosom.

"I suspected it from the first because I knew how she felt," she began. "She adored her brother, she possessed him—she built her whole life around him. Their parents died when they were both young, and he has always looked after her. To begin with, of course, that was all quite natural. But as time passed and they grew older, she did not let go of the childish dependence. She continued to cling onto him, to go everywhere with him, demand his entire attention. And when he sought any outside interests she would become jealous, pretend to be ill—anything to bring him back to her."

She took a long breath. She was watching Pitt, watching his eyes, his face.

"Of course if Tormod showed any natural affection for any other woman, Eloise was beside herself," she continued. "She never rested until she had driven the woman away, either with lies or by feigning sickness, or else worrying at poor Tormod until he found it hardly worth his while to try anymore. And he was so kindhearted he still protected her, in spite of the cost to himself.

"I'm sure you have found out in all your questions that Mina was very attracted to Tormod? In fact, she was in love with him. It is stupid now to try to cover it with genteel words. It cannot hurt her anymore.

"Naturally that drove Eloise into a frenzy of jealousy. The thought that Tormod would give any of his attention to another woman was more than she could bear. It must have turned the balance of her mind. She poisoned the cordial you have been so assiduously seeking. I have had it offered to me in their house. They bring it from the country with them when they come back from visiting Hertfordshire. I have drunk it on occasion myself."

She was sitting very upright in the chair, her eyes still fixed on Pitt's.

"Mina went to their house that day to visit Eloise, as you already know. Eloise gave her the cordial wine as a parting present. She drank it when she got home—and died—as Eloise had planned that she should.

"Tormod protected her—naturally. He had brought her up from a child. I daresay he felt responsible—although God knows why he should. In time he would have had to have her put away in a sanatorium or somewhere. I think in his heart he knew that. But he could not bear to do it yet.

"Ask anyone who knew them. They will tell you that Eloise hated me also—because Tormod cared for me."

Pitt sat without moving. It all made sense. He remembered Eloise's face, her dark eyes full of inward vision, absorbed in pain. She was the sort of woman who cried out for protection. She seemed as frail as a dream herself, as if she would vanish at a sudden start or a shout. He did not want to think she had receded into madness and murder. And yet he could think of no argument to refute it, nothing false in what Amaryllis had said.

"Thank you, Mrs. Denbigh," he said coldly. "It is late now, but tomorrow I shall go to Rutland Place and investigate fully what you have said." He could not resist adding, "A pity you were not as frank with me before."

There were faint spots of color in her face.

"I couldn't. And it would not have done any good anyway. Tormod would have denied it. He felt responsible for her. She had driven him into that, over the years. She is a parasite! She never wanted him to have any separate being, and she succeeded! She spent her whole life, every day, all day, trying to make sure he felt guilty if he ever did anything without her, went anywhere without her—even if he laughed at a joke without her laughing too!" Her voice was rising again, shrill and hard. "She's mad! You've no idea what it did to him. She destroyed him! She deserves to be locked away—forever and ever!"

"Mrs. Denbigh!" He wanted to silence her, to get rid of that glittering face with its girlishly soft lines and its hollow, hate-bright eyes. "Mrs. Denbigh, please don't distress yourself again! I will go tomorrow and talk to Miss Lagarde. I shall take Sergeant Harris and we shall look for the evidence you say is there. If we find any proof at all, then we shall act accordingly. Now Sergeant Harris will accompany you to your carriage, and I suggest you take some sedative and go to your bed early. This has been a most terrible day for you. You must be exhausted."

She stood in the middle of the floor staring at him, apparently weighing in her mind whether he was going to do as she intended.

"I shall go tomorrow," he acceded a little more sharply.

Without replying, she turned and walked out, closing the door behind her, leaving him alone and unaccountably miserable.

There was no way he could avoid it, this duty that gave him no satisfaction at all, no sense of resolution. But then, murder always brought tragedy.

He dispatched Harris to search yet again, this time particularly bedrooms and dressing rooms, for any cordial wine similar to that which Mina had drunk, or any empty bottles like the one found in Mina's room. He also took the precaution of showing Harris a picture of the deadly night-shade plant, so that he might look for it in the conservatory and outhouses. Neither its presence nor its absence would prove anything, however, except that it was a country plant and would be unusual in the middle of London. But the La-gardes had a country house; there might be nightshade in every hedge or wood in Hertfordshire, for all he knew.

Eloise received him dressed completely in black; the blinds were drawn halfway in traditional mourning, the servants white-faced and somber. She sat on a chaise longue close to the fire, but she looked as if its heat would never again reach her.

"I'm sorry," Pitt said instinctively—not only for his intrusion but for everything, for her loneliness, for death, for being unable to do anything but add to the burden.

She said nothing. What he did, perhaps what anyone did, no longer mattered to her. She was in a desolation beyond his power to touch, for good or ill.

He sat down. He felt ridiculous standing, as if his hands and feet might knock something over.

There was no point in stringing it out, trying to be tactful. That somehow made it worse, almost obscene, as if he did not recognize death.

"Mrs. Spencer-Brown came to see you the day she

died." It was a statement; no one had ever denied it.

"Yes." She was uninterested.

"Did you give her a bottle of cordial wine?"

She was staring into the flames. "Cordial wine? No, I don't think so. Didn't you ask that before?"

"Yes."

"Does it matter?"

"Yes, Miss Lagarde, because the poison was in it."

A smile passed over her face, as shadowy as a ripple of cold wind over water.

"And you think I put it there? I did not."

"But you did give her the wine?"

"I don't remember. I may have. Perhaps she was looking peaked and said she was tired, or something like that. We do have cordial wine. A neighbor in Hertfordshire gives it to us."

"Do you still have any?"

"I expect so. I don't like it, but Tormod did. It's kept in the butler's pantry—it's safe there. It's quite strong."

"Miss Lagarde—" She did not appear to understand the consequence of what they were discussing. She was removed from it, as though it were all a story about someone else. "Miss Lagarde, it is a very serious matter."

She looked up at him at last, and he was stricken by the pain and horror in her eyes—not for him, but for something else, something only she could see. Her expression was devoid of any kind of anger, any hatred—only horror, endless immeasurable horror.

Was this madness he was seeing? Or perhaps the knowledge of madness in one still sane enough to see herself and know what lies ahead, the irrevocable descent into the black corridors of lunacy?

No wonder Tormod had tried to protect her! He yearned to do so himself, to prevent it, to bring her back any way he knew how. He could not think of anything to say. There was nothing large enough to encompass the enormity of what he thought he had seen.

He could not bear it. He stood up. There was no need

to twist the knife with questions. The evidence was what mattered. Without that there was nothing they could do anyway, whatever he knew—or guessed.

"I'm sorry to have disturbed you," he said awkwardly. "I'll go and help Sergeant Harris. If there is anything else, I shall ask one of the servants. I'll try not to interrupt you again."

"Thank you." She sat quite still and did not even turn to watch as he walked to the door and opened it. He left her motionless, looking neither at the fire nor at the white flowers on the table, but at something he could not see and had never seen.

It did not take them long to find at least one answer. Sergeant Harris had brought the empty bottle found in Mina's bedroom and shown it to the servants. The butler recognized it.

"Did you give one of these to Miss Lagarde before Mrs. Spencer-Brown came here the day she died?" Pitt asked him grimly.

The man was not unintelligent. He saw the importance of the question, and his face was pale, a small muscle ticking in his jaw.

"No, sir. Miss Eloise never cared for it."

"Mr. Bevan—" Pitt began.

"No, sir. I understand what you are saying. We bring half a dozen bottles or so when we come back from the country. But Miss Eloise never had any of it. She disliked it. Neither does she have keys to my pantry. I have one set, and Mr. Tormod had the other, but he left them in Abbots Langley last year at Christmas, and they are still there."

Pitt took a deep breath. There was nothing to be served by shouting at the man.

"Mr. Bevan—" he began again patiently.

"I know what you are going to say, sir," Bevan cut in. "I gave the wine to Mr. Tormod, a bottle at a time, as he asked for it. He had a bottle the night before Mrs. Spencer-Brown came. He used to drink it sometimes, and I thought nothing of it."

Pitt could not blame him. When he and Harris had been there before, they had searched discreetly, but, fearing a guilty or even a protective servant would destroy the bottle, they had not described it or brought the one they had.

"What happened to the bottle, do you know?" he asked. "May I speak to the upstairs maid?"

"That will not be necessary, sir. I've asked her just now, since Mr. Harris came. She doesn't know, sir. She hasn't seen it again."

"Then it could be the one given to Mrs. Spencer-Brown?"

"Yes, sir, I imagine it must be."

"Is every other bottle accounted for?"

"Yes, sir. It is rather strong stuff, so I keep a check on it."

"Why did you not mention it when we asked before, Mr. Bevan?"

"It is not a table wine, sir, so I imagine the other servants had not seen it. Such things are more usually kept in a medicine chest, or by a bedside. Since that was the last bottle, when a search was made no more would have been found."

Pitt was irritated that a butler should explain his job to him so thoroughly. Or perhaps he was still thinking of Eloise, alone and unreachable. This man was not to blame. He could not have known the composition of the wine with which Mina was poisoned.

"So Mr. Tormod had the last bottle?"

"Yes, sir."

"In his bedroom?"

"Yes, sir." The man's face was very solemn.

"Did he complain of missing it?"

"No, sir. And I would have heard of it if he had. We are most strict about intoxicating liquors."

So when had Eloise poisoned it and given it to Mina? Bevan moved from one foot to the other.

"If you'll excuse me, sir, what makes you think Miss Eloise had the wine or gave it to Mrs. Spencer-Brown?"

"Information," Pitt said dryly.

"Not from anyone in this house, sir!"

"No." There was no point in being coy. "Mrs. Denbigh."

Bevan's face changed. "Indeed. Mrs. Denbigh is a very wealthy lady, sir, if you'll pardon me for making so ill-mannered an observation. Very wealthy indeed, and handsome too. She was remarkably fond of Mr. Tormod, and I believe they might well have married. Always providing, of course, Mr. Tormod had no other involvements."

Pitt took his meaning perfectly.

"Are you suggesting, Mr. Bevan, that it was Mr. Tormod, and not Miss Eloise, who murdered Mrs. Spencer-Brown?"

Bevan met his gaze without flinching.

"It would seem so, sir. Why should Miss Eloise kill her?"

"Jealousy over her brother's affection," Pitt replied.

"The relationship with Mrs. Spencer-Brown was over some time ago, sir. If he had married, it could never have been Mrs. Spencer-Brown—but it could well have been Mrs. Denbigh—a rich and handsome lady, free to marry, and, if you'll pardon me, more than willing. And yet Mrs. Denbigh is alive and well."

Pitt turned to Harris. "Have you looked in the conservatory, Harris?"

"Yes, sir. No nightshade. But that's not to say it was never there. I don't imagine our murderer would be foolish enough to leave it."

"No." Pitt's face tightened. "No, probably not."

"Will there be anything else, sir?" Bevan inquired.

"No, thank you. Not now." Pitt was reluctant to say it, but it was the man's due: "Thank you for your help."

Bevan bowed very slightly. "You are welcome, sir."

"Damn!" Pitt swore as soon as he judged the butler to be out of earshot. "Hellfire and damnation!"

"I'll lay any odds you like he's right," Harris said with sincerity. "Makes a lot of sense. Rich and handsome widow, like he says. Old mistress making trouble, threatening to tell all, very embarrassing. Stand in the way of a lot of very nice money. Wouldn't be the first time. Never prove it!"

"I know that!" Pitt said furiously. "Damn it, man, I know that!"

They walked through to the hallway and found Dr. Mulgrew coming down the stairs. He looked bleary-eyed, and his hair stood up in a quiff at the top of his head. He must have been there to treat Eloise.

"Good morning," Pitt said tersely.

"Perfectly bloody," Mulgrew agreed, not with Pitt's words but with his tone of voice. "We've lost Tormod, you know. Injuries proved too much for him—heart finally carried him off." Then he gave a sheepish smile. "I've got a head like a tin bucket. Need a hair of the dog, I think! Much obliged to you, Pitt. You're a good man. Join me in a drink? Call for Bevan. I need something to clear this headache. Shouldn't drink champagne at my age and then get up at dawn. Not natural."

"Champagne?" Pitt glared at him.

"Yes, you know, fizzy stuff? 'There is nothing like the fizz, fizz, fizz,' " he sang very softly in a remarkably pleasant baritone. " 'I'll drink every drop there is, is, is.' "

Pitt was forced to smile, although it hurt.

"Thanks," Mulgrew said, clasping him by the arm. "You're a generous man."

When Pitt arrived home in the evening, Charlotte was waiting for him. As soon as he entered the door, she knew from his face something had happened that had saddened and confused him. The day had been warm, and the parlor faced south. She had had the windows open onto the garden, and the smell of fresh grass was in the air. A few white narcissus sat in a slender jug, their fragrance as sharp and clean as spring rain.

"What is it?" Another time she might have waited, but not tonight. "What happened, Thomas?"

"Tormod is dead." He took his coat off and let it

fall onto the sofa. "He died this morning."

She did not bother to pick it up.

"Oh." She looked at his face, trying to match the news to the pain in him. She knew it was not enough. "What else?"

He smiled, and there was a sudden sweetness in it. He put out his hand and took hers.

She clung onto it hard. "What else?" she repeated.

"Amaryllis Denbigh came to the police station and told me it was Eloise who killed Mina. She said she had guessed it a long while ago but had said nothing, to protect Tormod. Now that he was dead, she didn't care anymore."

"Do you believe her?" she asked carefully. Her own mind wanted to reject the idea, but she knew that murder did not always lie where it was easy to understand, or to hate. Sometimes there is darkness underneath what seems to be light.

"I went to look." He sighed and sat down, pulling her down next to him. "I found evidence. I don't know whether it would stand in court—it might. But it doesn't matter, because all I could say is that it was someone in that house, and the butler swears it must have been Tormod. He'll stick to that—but whether it's the truth or to protect Eloise, I don't know. I probably never will."

"Why should Eloise kill Mina?" she asked.

"Jealousy. She was intensely possessive of Tormod."

"Then she would have killed Amaryllis. Amaryllis was the one he could have married," she argued. "He wouldn't have married Mina—she was no danger. She could never have been anything more than a mistress, and I doubt she was even that!"

"That's what Bevan said—"

"The butler?"

"Yes."

"Amaryllis is the possessive one." Charlotte was thinking, turning ideas over in her mind, memories. "She hates Eloise enough to come to you and tell a lie like that. Even with Tormod dead, she still hates."

"Well, don't worry, I shan't arrest Eloise." He tightened his arm around her. "I haven't any proof."

She pulled away and looked straight at him. "What do you believe?"

He thought about it for a moment, his eyes on her as if he would explore her thoughts also.

"I think it was Tormod," he answered at last. "I think Mina was being troublesome, pestering him, and he wanted to marry Amaryllis—for her money, among other things—and he killed Mina to keep her quiet. Perhaps she was threatening him."

Charlotte sat back slowly, thinking. Poor Amaryllis had been so infatuated with Tormod that it had destroyed the gentleness in her, all the power of friendship, and had left no room for other loves or even decencies. Now she and Eloise could not even comfort each other.

"Strange what obsession can do," she said aloud. "It's very frightening. It seems to devour everything else. All your other values get eaten up." She thought of Caroline and Paul Alaric, but she did not want to say it aloud. Better it was forgotten, even by Pitt, especially now that Edward showed signs of reforming. Last evening he had escorted Caroline to the Savoy Theatre to see the *Mikado* and had presented her with a garnet brooch besides.

Had Paul Alaric ever glimpsed the power he possessed to arouse women's emotions? He had the kind of face that suggested great currents of passion underneath—a suggestion built upon all too easily by romantic women needing mystery, escaping from familiar men they believed they read without effort. Whether he had ever felt such great tides of passion himself, she could not know, but in that last moment when she and Caroline had left him staring at them helplessly, the shock of their passing had been like a wound in his face. For that alone she would always think well of him.

Tormod had awoken an even wilder hunger in Amaryllis. Something about him, some quality of body or mind, had enraptured her till she could think of nothing and no one else. He must have had an overwhelming charm, a magnetism that obliterated all other judgment.

And naturally Eloise had loved him; they had spent all their lives together. No wonder Amaryllis was jealous, excluded from all those years—

Suddenly an appalling thought flashed across her mind, so ugly she could not even name it, and yet the breath of it left her body cold.

"What's the matter?" Pitt asked. "You're shivering!"

The thought had been so hideous she was not prepared to give it words, even to him. Now that it had come to her, she would have to talk to Eloise and see if it was true, but not tonight—and perhaps she would not tell Pitt?

"Just glad it's over," she answered, and moved closer to him. She took his hand again and held it. The lie did not bother her. After all, it was only an idea.

In the morning she dressed in her darkest clothes and caught the omnibus. She got off at the nearest stop to Rutland Place and walked the rest of the way. She did not call on Caroline; in fact, if she was not seen, she did not mean to mention her visit at all.

The footman opened the door.

"Good morning, Mrs. Pitt," he said in a hushed voice, stepping back to allow her in.

"Good morning," she replied gravely. "I have called to express my sympathies. Is Miss Lagarde well enough to receive me?"

"I will inquire, ma'am, if you care to come this way. Mr. Tormod is in the morning room, but you will find it very chill in there."

For a moment she was startled by the mention of Tormod as if he were alive; then she realized that naturally he would be laid out, and there would be those whose last respects included a look at the dead. Perhaps it was expected of her also?

"Thank you." She hesitated, then went to view the dead man.

The room was dark, and as chill as the footman had said, possessed of the peculiar coldness of decay. Black crêpe festooned the walls and the table legs, and there was a black cloth on the sideboard.

Tormod was in a dark, polished coffin on the table in the center, and the gas lamps were unlit. The outside sun, filtered through the blinds, gave a diffuse light, quite clear, and she was compelled against her will to go over and look at him.

The eyes had been closed, and yet she felt as if the expression were unnatural. There was no peace in the face. Death had taken the spirit, but his features held the unmistakable impression that his last emotion had been one of hatred, impotent and corroding hatred.

She looked away, frightened by it, trapped by something cold and all-pervasive that grew in her mind and rooted firmer and firmer.

The door opened silently and Eloise stood still a moment before coming in.

Now that they were face to face with the corpse between them, it was far harder than Charlotte had expected.

"I'm sorry," she said awkwardly. "Eloise, I'm so sorry."

Eloise said nothing, but her eyes stared straight back at Charlotte—direct, almost curious.

"You loved him very much," Charlotte went on.

There was a flicker across Eloise's face, but still she said nothing.

"Did you hate him as well?" Charlotte found the words coming more easily. Pity was stronger than embarrassment or fear. She wanted to reach out and touch Eloise, put her arms around her, hold her close enough to give her warmth, feed her own life into her frozen body.

Eloise breathed in hard and gave a little sigh. "How did you know?"

Charlotte had no answer. It had come from impressions gathered, a look, a word, things remembered from the dark understandings of the mind, hidden from thought because they are forbidden, too ugly to own.

"That was what Mina knew, wasn't it?" Charlotte said.

"That was why he killed her—it had nothing to do with past affaires, or marrying Amaryllis."

"He would have married Amaryllis," Eloise said softly. "I wouldn't have minded that, even his not—loving me anymore."

"But she wouldn't have married him," Charlotte replied. "Not if Mina had told everyone that you and Tormod were lovers, as well as brother and sister." Now that the words were out, they were not so frightening—they could be said, the truth of them faced.

"Perhaps not." Eloise was looking down at the dead face. She did not seem to care, and Charlotte knew suddenly that she had not reached the core of it yet. There was more truth to come, and worse. The self-hatred in Eloise, the despair, was more than a knowledge of incest, and then rejection, deeper than anything she had yet understood.

"How old were you when it began?" Charlotte asked.

Eloise reached out and touched the winding-sheet.

"Thirteen."

Charlotte felt the tears well up inside her, and she experienced an overwhelming hatred of Tormod so profound she could look on his mangled body and his dead face without regret, as coldly as if he were fish on the market slab.

"You didn't kill Mina, did you?"

Eloise shook her head. "No, but it doesn't matter if the police think I did, because I'm guilty anyway."

Charlotte opened her mouth, then closed it again.

"I let Tormod kill my baby." Eloise's voice was no more than a whisper. "I was with child, about four months. I didn't realize for a long time—I didn't know enough. Then when I did realize, I told Tormod. That was when I first met you. We didn't go to the country because of Mina's death. I went to get an abortion. I didn't know till we got there. Tormod said I had to, because I am not married, and what we were doing was wrong. He said the child was not formed, that it would only be like—like a little blood."

She was so ashen Charlotte was afraid she would not be able to stand, but she dared not move to help her. These words came from an agony so deep it must burst.

"He lied to me. It was my child!"

Charlotte felt the tears run down her face and, without thinking, her hands went to the surface that contained her womb and the child in it.

"It was my baby," Eloise said. "They never let me touch it. They just got rid of it."

Silence filled the room, but it seemed nothing could be vast enough to contain the pain.

"That is why I killed him," Eloise said at last. "As soon as I was well enough, he took me out for a drive in the carriage. I pushed him off, and the other carriage and horses drove over him. It didn't kill him. It only crippled him. We brought him back here to lie in that bed upstairs, tormented with pain, knowing he would never walk again. I used to go in and look at him. He was paralyzed, did you know? He couldn't move, couldn't even speak. He would just stare at me with hatred so strong I felt it would burn his body up. My own brother, whom I had loved all my life. I stood at the end of the bed and stared back. I wasn't sorry. I hated myself, and I hated him. I even thought of killing myself. I'm not sure why I didn't do it. But I wasn't sorry for him. I couldn't pity him.

"I can still see my baby's body—in my mind. The doctor said I shall never have another. It was something they did."

Charlotte moved at last. She walked around the coffin and closed the lid; then very gently she took Eloise's hand, holding it in both her own.

"Are you going to tell the police?" Eloise said quietly.

"No." Charlotte put her arms around her and held her hard, the sobs inside her struggling to get out. She must control herself. She took a deep breath. "No. He killed Mina— he would have been hanged for that anyway. It was wrong to kill him, but it's done now. I shall never speak of it again."

Slowly Eloise relaxed and let her head rest on Charlotte's shoulder. At last, for the first time since she had seen the tiny body of her child, she began to weep.

For a long time, beyond counting, they stood together

beside the closed coffin, letting the tears come, sharing the pain.

It was not until Inigo Charrington stood in the doorway, his eyes full of sympathy and affection, that at last Charlotte let go of Eloise.